"HE MOVED THROUGH THE DESERT STILLNESS, THE DAY'S HEAT REDUCED TO A MEMORY. ABOVE HIM, A PAIR OF HAWKS CONTINUED THEIR SLOW, WATCHFUL SPIRALS AGAINST THE DARKENING SKY. NUMBED BY FATIGUE AND A HUNGER OF BODY AND MIND, HE RAN HIS SWOLLEN TONGUE OVER HIS CRACKED AND BLISTERED LIPS. POSSESSED OF WILL HE DIDN'T KNOW HE HAD, HE STUMBLED BUT CAUGHT HIMSELF, HIS EYES STILL SET FIRMLY ON THE FAINT GLOW OF THE CITY ON THE HILL."

THE
PRODIGAL
PROJECT

THE PRODIGAL PROJECT

BOOK 2
EXODUS

KEN ABRAHAM
AND
DANIEL HART

A PLUME BOOK

PLUME
Published by the Penguin Group
Penguin Group (USA) Inc., 375 Hudson Street,
New York, New York 10014, U.S.A.
Penguin Books Ltd, 80 Strand, London WC2R 0RL, England
Penguin Books Australia Ltd, 250 Camberwell Road,
Camberwell, Victoria 3124, Australia
Penguin Books Canada Ltd, 10 Alcorn Avenue,
Toronto, Ontario, Canada M4V 3B2
Penguin Books (N.Z.) Ltd, Cnr Rosedale and Airborne Roads,
Albany, Auckland 1310, New Zealand

Penguin Books Ltd, Registered Offices: 80 Strand,
London WC2R 0RL, England

First published by Plume, a member of Penguin Group (USA) Inc.

First Printing, June 2003
10 9 8 7 6 5 4 3 2 1

Copyright © Penguin Group (USA) Inc., 2003
All rights reserved

℗ REGISTERED TRADEMARK—MARCA REGISTRADA

CIP data is available.
ISBN 0-452-28447-3

Printed in the United States of America
Set in Janson Text

PUBLISHER'S NOTE
This is a work of fiction. Names, characters, places, and incidents either are
the product of the author's imagination or are used fictitiously, and any resem-
blance to actual persons, living or dead, business establishments, events, or lo-
cales is entirely coincidental.

BOOKS ARE AVAILABLE AT QUANTITY DISCOUNTS WHEN USED TO PROMOTE
PRODUCTS OR SERVICES. FOR INFORMATION PLEASE WRITE TO PREMIUM
MARKETING DIVISION, PENGUIN GROUP (USA) INC., 375 HUDSON STREET, NEW
YORK, NEW YORK 10014.

For Catherine Mary McDonald, my mother

—D. H.

ACKNOWLEDGMENTS

Special thanks to Joel Fotinos, Gary Brozek, Brant Janeway, and the tremendous team at Plume for your indefatigable efforts to take this story to the world. I thank God for the creative gifts, talents, and abilities He has given you, and I thank you for the way you allow Him to use you.

—K. A.

I would like to thank Ken Abraham for his guidance and enlightenment, Gary Brozek for his firm hand, and my family for their faith.

—D. H.

"Blessed is he who reads and those who hear the words of the prophecy, and heed the things which are written in it; for the time is near."

—Revelation 1:3

THE
PRODIGAL
PROJECT

CHAPTER ⊕NE

In search of his son, Thomas Church gripped the steering wheel of the battered and dusty Ford Bronco, and tried not to look too far down the road. The distances were unnerving, the far horizon an undulating line running west with the sun, unreachable. A long road of dust and ash, bleak, hot, and unending, headed west into a sheet-metal sky bloodied by a sun hidden in haze. The landscape cut by the road was harsh and unforgiving, sand and rock, low craggy hills hunkered down on the far horizon rippled by waves of heat. Where a tree dared to push its way up out of the hard ground, it stood tough and twisted, ripped by the dry winds, soured by the mean dribble of acid water. Brindle brush lay rusting along the contours of ancient and mocking streambeds, and clusters of tumbleweed gathered like crowns of thorns around angled outcroppings of rock. Here and there the road was bordered by a barbed-wire fence that looked as if it had grown from red dirt sewn with nails, the broken and coiled wire clinging to the weathered posts like iron vines.

Church had seen several bleached and staring long-horn skulls wired to gnarled trees, and twice saw the same empty and haunting look from human skulls, with their silently shrieking grins, jammed onto fence posts. Fewer wrecked or abandoned vehicles sat on the road than he had seen in previous days, and fewer people too, dead *or* alive. Sometimes bodies lay sprawled next to obvious accident scenes, decayed and scattered by carrion birds, but most often the carcasses of trucks and cars sat stripped, broken, and empty.

Thomas Church had driven away from his home on Long Island almost two weeks ago, after his world, and *the* world, had been forever changed in an instant. He was in his mid-forties, solid, a man who kept himself in good shape. He wore a graying beard, which he usually kept neatly trimmed, but in recent days it had gone shaggy, as had his hair. He noticed that the few strands of gray at his temples had multiplied, crept toward the crown of his head. His clothes were not filthy, but he had worn them for a couple of days—blue jeans, hiking boots, and a T-shirt. He had spent his life as a carefully groomed and fastidious man, but these things did not matter now. Nothing that he used to be mattered. His life, which he had accepted as carefully and almost pain-lessly scripted, had gone along as he had supposed it was meant to. He had grown up in a white middle-class neighborhood, had decent, loving parents, finished school, met a nice girl, got married, had kids, raised them, got divorced, and bought a Harley-Davidson. Simple Americana. He was the lead player in a predictable film titled *The Life and Times of a Regular Guy Named Thomas Church*, rated NS, for "Nothing Special."

He slowed his Bronco now as he saw a figure in the road a few hundred feet in front of him. The man was standing out in the middle of nowhere, his ragged clothing the color of the dirt on both sides of the road. Church planned to simply accelerate and drive around the man and keep right on keepin' on—no time for losers, no time for strangers, no time for someone looking for a helping hand. Since his world had been turned inside out, since he had been on the road in a lawless, chaotic land that for a time had become a dangerous and unpredictable place of near-anarchy, Church had learned from experience.

He was an intelligent man, and a quick learner. He had spent his life avoiding conflict if possible, had gone to college, missed the military draft, settled into the age of computers like a true believer, and flourished there. He had built a career as a financial consultant and computer guru, and had reached a level of success that allowed him to avoid his office in Manhattan like the plague, and work from his home. He had built an office in his house that was actually a state-of-the-art multimedia center, with all the supertech toys that allowed him to surf the Web, bathe in a constant stream of information from many sources, and literally feel the pulse of the entire world coursing through his fingertips.

His was a world of comfort, and he had no desire to

test himself by climbing mountains, windsurfing, or playing full-contact football with a bunch of younger guys. He had become interested in the "survivalist" pursuits, and researched them with the same zeal he did everything. He had purchased various weapons, camping gear, foods and clothing designed for someone "roughing it," learned how to use them, and always kept a stash of cash and gold coins for the day something cataclysmic happened, like a nuclear war—not that it ever would. He turned that prospect, that fear, into something lucrative by developing gaming software in his spare time. He'd licensed a fantasy adventure game called "Good Samaritan" that gave the player a chance to start from ground zero—a chance to see how he or she would do in a postapocalyptic version of survival. Then something *did* happen, and it had hurled him out of his carefully structured multimedia world, and onto this long road to nowhere in search of his son, Tommy.

He was in Texas, west of Abilene, west of Sweetwater, west of Big Spring, Midland, and Odessa. He was headed for a place called Pyote, or around there. Someplace near Pecos, to a ranch where his daughter said Tommy had last called her from. He felt the fear in the pit of his stomach again, the fear that Tommy had been taken. He looked through the dirty and starred windshield of the Bronco at the man in the road. The man was waving his arms at him now, leaving small clouds of dust above his head. At one point in his life Thomas Church would have stopped to help the man without hesitation, but that Thomas Church lived in the old world, where stopping to help was still a viable practice. He'd learned some valuable lessons in plotting out the logarithms of his game's various scenarios that served him well in this present reality. In *this* world being a Good Samaritan was a dangerous and frightening thing.

When he first left his home on Long Island he kept the guns he carried unloaded and under the backseat of the truck. Before he got to his daughter's campus apartment at the University of Virginia he had the occasion to brandish one of his handguns to dissuade a man who was aggressively begging for a ride one minute, and clawing at the passenger-door handle the next. On the outskirts of Johnson City, Tennessee, he had shot a man in the leg after buying fuel off the back of a truck on the side of the road. The man had pulled a hunting knife from his belt at the sight of Church's gold coins, and chased the Bronco limping and screaming curses as Church sped off.

Two nights ago he had been attacked by three men while sleeping in the Bronco parked in a Wal-Mart lot. He had shot one in the hand while the man had tried to smash the driver's window open, blasted a shot over the head of the second man with his shotgun, and knocked the last one down with the Bronco as he made his escape. He had driven away shaken, and now he kept all of his weapons loaded, and close.

The new, hardened Thomas Church drove closer to the dusty man in the road. He angled onto the right shoulder to keep distance, and let his window down halfway. The man had wild eyes and a drawn face, his jaw stubbled and bloody. His open mouth was stretched and pink as he lurched toward Church and screamed, "You're going to *hell*, mister! Don't you know you're going to *hell*?" Church didn't answer, almost hit the gas to get out of there, then hesitated. He reached into a bag next to his seat, grabbed a small bottle of water and a bag of cookies, and threw them out the window onto the road. Then he drove off, still westbound, and may or may not have heard the dusty man yell, "Thanks, mister! You're still goin' to hell . . . but thanks."

Thomas Church drove on, and watched the fire in the sky go out as the silver evening turned to soot. He wanted to find his son.

He spent the night in an abandoned truck stop, his Bronco backed in between two empty Texas Highway Patrol cars. He had placed small electronic sensors in a perimeter around the vehicles before he went to sleep in the backseat, with the loaded shotgun by his side. The sensors would beep softly if anyone triggered them. The night had been cold, and quiet, and his dreams were made of snapshots of his children when they were young. His wife, Iris, seemed to be smiling as she held the birthday cake, or the basket of Easter eggs, or the Christmas stocking, and the kids jumped up and down like a noisy two-cylinder engine, full of life, full of love. But Iris had disappeared after their divorce, and his dreams, like the snapshots, were faded, left in a drawer, only to be discovered when in search of something else.

He awoke stiff and cold. He looked all around carefully before getting out of the Bronco. He walked around a bit, stretched, and performed his basic morning ablutions. The sky was still hazy with dust and smoke, and the sun came angrily red from the east. From far off he heard three gunshots, then two more, and decided it was time to get moving. He collected his sensors, grabbed a pouch of sun-dried fruit and a large carton of juice from a cooler in the back of the truck, and drove back onto the roadway, headed west. His gas gauge showed a little over half, and he carried two five-gallon jerry cans for emergencies. He was okay for now, but would keep an eye out for anyplace selling fuel. Given all the recent developments in the Middle East and beyond, he didn't hold out much of hope of finding any gas with the ease he once took so for granted.

Two hours later he stopped the truck and sat staring at a small sign beside the road. It indicated he had come to Pyote, Texas. The town consisted of a few buildings with broken windows, a short stretch of cracked sidewalk, some windblown piles of trash, and nothing else. The place was so weathered and forlorn, Church could not determine if it had been this way long *before* the disappearances had happened. On one corner, a squat cinder-block building with a fiberglass roof sat with a pair of rusty gas pumps looking like slot machines. He craned his neck, did a 360 sweep, and saw not one living thing. His daughter had told him what Tommy had last told her, almost two months before. He was on a ranch near Pecos, near Pyote, in West Texas. Well, he thought, maybe it's in between the two. He drove on.

After a few miles he realized he was gripping the

steering wheel so hard his fingers were cramping. His chest felt constricted, and he took thin breaths between clenched teeth. He really wanted to find Tommy. He wanted his son, wanted to look at him, hold him, hear him talk. The anger that had propelled him from his house on Long Island washed over him. What had happened to the world? So many people—millions, literally millions, if the media were to be believed—just taken, gone, disappeared. The president of the United States, and his wife, a few of Church's neighbors, people from all walks of life, colors, nationalities, gone. The children, gone. But not the Muslims, he thought. Oh no, not the Muslims. Whatever took those people seemed to have cut a great swath through the Christian world, although *they* weren't all taken either. He shook his head. Why lump them into religions, anyway? It couldn't be a religious thing, no way. Church labeled himself an "elastic agnostic." He was comfortable with the hypothesis that most organized religions were feel-good faiths created to help take the sting out of everyday life. But this, this *completely* unjustified taking of human life on such a monstrous scale—it just wasn't right. He couldn't make it fit into any satisfactory scheme. If it *was* done to the world by the Muslims in some macabre attempt to force their culture and beliefs on everyone, then total war—which appeared to be coming soon—was necessary. In all the postapocalyptic scenarios he'd created for his game, a holy war had been discounted as too unrealistic.

But if it was some Biblical thing, which he had heard seriously discussed by scholars and theologians, then it was simply wrong in his opinion. That thought is what angered him most, that the disappearances were caused by God. That there was a controlling, omnipotent God, a God who had created Earth and mankind, who could then cause so much grief, sorrow, and pain, was beyond his comprehension and acceptance. No programmer would ever create a routine that would result in the destruction of his creation. The whole thing just stunk to high heaven. He ached for his son . . . ached. He clenched the steering wheel even tighter, and screamed out the driver's window, "It's *wrong*! It's all *wrong*!"

A while later he came to the outskirts of what had to be Pecos. There he saw a gathering of eighteen-wheelers, two or three Texas police cars, county and state officers, and small groups of people. The trucks carried water, fuel, and food, apparently, and people were lined up to get what they needed. Those gathered were orderly, subdued. They stood staring off into the distance or dragging a toe in the dirt. He parked across the road from the police vehicles, and watched as an older man staggered under the weight of a large box as he carried it across the road. The man wore faded jeans and scuffed work boots. Dark half-moons of sweat stained his checkered shirt.

"Excuse me," Thomas Church called as the man dropped the box into the bed of a battered gray pickup truck.

The man ignored him.

"Excuse me, sir? Sir?" tried Church again. This time the man stopped beside the cab of his truck and turned his wary gaze. The man stared at Church a moment, then spit, and said firmly, "I got nothin', mister. Barely enough for me an' my wife, nothin' for you."

Church gave the man a nod and a tentative grin, and said, "A question, that's all."

"Like, is this the end of the world?" replied the man. "Like, why weren't *you* taken after you was bein' a good Christian and all? That kinda question?" He grinned back. "I *still* got nothin' for you, mister."

"No.—No," said Church hesitantly. "I'm looking for my son. I believe he was working on a ranch near here called the River Cross Ranch. Do you know of it, or where it is?"

The old man slowly closed the door on his truck, and his pale eyes were washed with sadness. He rubbed his nose with one knuckly hand, scuffed his right boot in the dirt, shrugged, and replied, "Yeah."

"Yeah? You know of the River Cross?"

"Yeah." The man hesitated, watched Church's eyes a moment, then went from suspicious to talkative. "They was decent folk, that had that place. It lays back down the road a piece." He pointed in the direction Church had come from. "It was of a size, for these parts, and well run, cattle mostly, raised 'em, sold 'em. Had a fair number of cowhands on the payroll most of the time. Decent folk. I was out there coupla times every year, doin' small engine repairs, pumps, tractor parts, that kinda thing. They'd pay right up, no fuss, and the wife, she'd bring out lemonade and cookies and stuff while I was workin'." His face darkened. "Had some young guys, too. Mostly good boys, I guess, but . . . you know. They'd be there for a while, then drift off. The wife told me there would be things missing—small pieces of equipment or gear, you know." He shrugged.

"Can you give me directions to it?" asked Church, unsettled by the man's demeanor.

"I can, I surely can, mister, but you don't want to drive out there now." He shook his head sadly.

"Why not?"

"You know how a while back people sort of went missing? Disappeared and all?" asked the man.

"Yes," Church answered, knowing that people forevermore would base their time line on "before" or "after" the disappearances, and once broached, some wanted desperately to talk about it.

"Well, I guess the couple—their name was River— they were some that were taken. Went to bed that night, next morning there's nothin' but a handful of dust on the sheets. The way I heard it, there had been some kind of celebration or somethin' the night before in the bunk- house where the hired hands slept, drinkin' and carryin' on, and then the morning came and people had disap- peared, and some of those newer guys, just went crazy, I guess. Started beating the foreman, then shot him, had their way with a couple of the young girls that worked in the big house, set the place on fire. Crazy. Then a small group of the hired guys, I heard it was cowhands that ac- tually rode the spread, worked the cattle—anyway, this group tried to stop all the looting and burning, and an honest-to-Pete gunfight broke out. Couple boys dead.

Then the cowhands went crazy and hung three of the troublemakers from the front of the barn, and everybody scattered. Man I know went out with a Texas Ranger and some of those National Guard kids, said it was a horrible thing to see, bodies, dead cattle, burned stalls. Just ruination." He stopped, licked his lips, and added, "Shoot, mister, if your boy was workin' the River Cross, if he ain't been killed, then he's probably taken off outta here anyway. Nobody stuck around after that. He's probably long gone by now."

Church stared at the man, silent. Then he said quietly, "Uh, thanks."

The old man shrugged, opened the truck door, and said, "Welcome. Now I got a question for you, mister."

Church already had the Bronco in gear, his mind on the road, on his son. "What?" he asked.

"*Is* this the end of the world?"

Church drove away from the man, angry, and frightened.

The trucks on the side of the road were still in the Bronco's rearview mirror when Church was flagged down by a deputy sheriff backed up by two National Guardsmen. Church slowed, and pulled to the side of the road. The deputy walked up, looked at Church, walked all around the Bronco peering in the windows, then back to the driver's side.

"Everything all right, Officer?" asked Church.

"Saw your New York tags, sir," replied the deputy, a

big woman with black hair dusted with gray. She had dark skin, and Native American features. Under her uniform collar hung a delicate turquoise necklace, and around her left wrist was a watch mounted on a silver-and-turquoise band. On her name tag was printed "Gonzalez." "Just wanted to take a look at you, sir." She took off her sunglasses, exposing pale skin around tired eyes. "You're free to go. Just so you know, there's some fuel here, and some food and water. Back in Pecos there's some little things, not much. East of here will be easier to find the basic essentials. Up toward Abilene, right?"

"Thank you," said Church. Then he asked, "Do you know where the River Cross Ranch is, and have you heard anything about it? My son was working there, I think, and I'm trying to find him."

The deputy sighed, covered her eyes again with the sunglasses, and said, "Bad thing happened there after the disappearances. Shoot, you've probably come across bad scenes out on the road, bodies and wreckage we still haven't gotten to." She scratched her nose absently, then went on. "At the River Cross it was bad, arson, murder, lynchings. Unbelievable. I was there, I saw it. Because of the way things are, our guys used a backhoe that was on the property, dug a trench, and they, all the bodies, were all buried together. Don't know if any words were said over 'em. Could be your son was one of those killed. What was his name?"

"Church. Tommy Church."

"I'll see what I can find out for you, Mr. Church."

He sat, numb, while the deputy stepped a few feet away and murmured into her radio. Church saw how his windshield had turned sepia from the dust. He saw a large hawk circling high in the hard metal sky. He saw the fingers of his own left hand, naked without a wedding band. He stopped breathing.

"No, sir. No luck," said the deputy briskly as she moved closer to the side of the Bronco. "We don't have a Tommy Church identified as one of the dead Caucasians out there. Dispatcher said as far as she knows, there were none found that couldn't be ID'd, so it should be accurate. He probably just took off like most of 'em did after the, uh, incident."

Thomas Church felt the air return to his lungs, felt his tongue find moisture again as he said, "Thank you, Officer."

"Of course," added the deputy with a troubled look, "he might have been one of those *taken* that morning." She hesitated. "Like my husband." She looked into Church's eyes and said softly, "Maybe he was a good Christian, like my Sergio, and now he's gone to heaven while we're stuck here like a bunch of dopes who didn't get the Word."

Church saw the pain in her eyes, and understood how anxious many people were about what had happened, lonely without partners who had been taken, eager to share their personal story with strangers once the thin boundary of suspicion was broken. "Would that be a good thing or a bad thing, Deputy?" asked Church, more determined than ever to find Tommy.

The deputy shook her head, turned away, and said without looking back, "God only knows."

Church headed east again, fighting the nearly over-powering feeling of dread that seemed to blanket his heart. He had come so far, had actually found people who knew of the ranch, but he still hadn't found his son. His fears, he realized, were selfish. If Tommy had been one of those taken, or if he had been killed in the insane carnage that followed, he would be sleeping the big sleep, gone from this world of pain and sorrow, gone to a place of eternal unawareness, or a place of peace. Thomas Church never could come to terms with the concept of "heaven," but did accept, intellectually at least, the hypothesis that if there was a controlling deity, and life after death, then that life would probably be better than this one. But he didn't want Tommy to be at peace. He wanted Tommy *here*, where he could hold him, hug him . . . be with him.

He slowed the Bronco as he came around a long curve and saw a group of buzzards low in the sky to his left, wheeling and circling as if they had found something good to eat. Good and dead, he thought. He drove by a winding dirt road, little more than a rutted path, that snaked off into the low rocks and brush. He slowed, then stopped. Buzzards eat dead things, he told himself, and Tommy is alive, out here somewhere, but alive. But he couldn't drive on. He had to check. This is stupid, he told himself as he backed up, then turned onto the track and began following it as it meandered through the battered landscape.

The road was very rough, and he had to drive slowly, bottoming out with a sickening thud a couple of times. Finally he came around a bend and found what the carrion birds had gathered for. An emaciated cow, ribs showing, hind legs twisted, head up, mouth gray with dirty dried froth, eyes wild and staring, was tangled in a barbed-wire fence. The animal had managed to pull fifteen or twenty feet of the fence down in its crazed efforts to break free, and its flanks were torn and bloody. It wasn't until Church shut the Bronco's engine off that he heard the pitifully labored breathing of the beast. He shielded his eyes from the afternoon sun, which blazed down on the sad tableau with an unforgiving ferocity. He opened the door, swung one leg out, and stopped. There was nothing he could do for the animal, why get out? He pulled his leg inside again but stopped.

He got out. This time he had his pistol in his hand. The cow's pitiful bleating got stronger as Church slowly approached it, and its hind legs jerked in painful spasms, the barbed wire stretching and singing as they did. Church hesitated. The cow was a living thing, with its own destiny. Church felt the unrelenting sun on his shoulders, saw the froth around the gaping mouth of the beast, heard the cries. He knows of the fall of each sparrow, thought Church. He shielded his eyes with one hand and watched the buzzards circling above the trapped cow.

Life he thought, death in the wild, all part of nature. One of the great black birds swooped low enough for him to hear the wind rushing across the feathers on its outstretched wings, and he shuddered. He looked once more at the maddened eyes of the cow, took two steps closer, pointed the pistol at the head of the beast, and squeezed the trigger. He did not hear the blast of the gun, but sensed it buck in his hand, then felt the heat. The cow wrenched its entire body in the wire for a brief second, then stiffened, and collapsed into the dust and gravel.

Church approached the animal. It was the immediate and absolute stillness that held his gaze. Death came, the cessation of life. What was a moment ago a living thing was now simply inanimate flesh. Even the painracked and sun-maddened thrashing in the wire, the confusion, the fear, were part of life, warm blood pumping through the heart, spit falling from the tongue, the role of the carrion eaters in anticipatory attendance, all a part of this earthly life.

Church turned in a slow circle and surveyed the bleak and harsh landscape that surrounded him. Sun-parched and arid, dust, gravel, sand, rock, punctuated here and there by sparse gray-green bushes, gnarled dwarf trees, brooding rocks, it was a desolate place domed by a forever sheet-metal sky. He looked at the dead thing lying still in the wire, the flesh already corrupt. He watched the circling birds, black and watchful, and was overwhelmed with a sense of seeing the entire world, the entire *now*, displayed for him. His mind reeled. You put the animal out of its misery, he thought, and maybe God is putting us out of *our* misery. It *is* the end of the world, baby. Long live the arrogant and inconsequential human race.

He hurried to the Bronco, climbed in, threw the gun onto the passenger seat, and slammed the truck into gear. He wanted to get away from there, to get back to the main road and resume the search for his son, Tommy. He turned the wheel and hit the gas to steer a three-point turn on the rutted track. He was almost all the way around when the Bronco lurched to the right and fell at enough of an angle to make him lean over, pulling on his seat belt. He clenched his teeth, tried reverse, then drive and reverse again, hoping to rock it free. No way. He left the engine running and got out.

Church knelt down near the right rear wheel. It had fallen into a large cut in the ditch beside the track, deeply enough for the wheel to hang awkwardly on its axle, and for the frame of the Bronco to rest in the dirt. Muttering, he stalked back to the driver's seat, pulled the handle for four-wheel drive, revved the engine, and amid the roar and rattle and huge cloud of dust observed he was going nowhere. He checked to make sure he was in low, and tried easing back and forth. The truck rocked and bucked but remained canted to the right, trapped. For a fleeting angry instant he thought of taking his pistol and putting a bullet in the *Bronco's* head, but settled for a hard punch on the dash.

Massaging his right hand with his left, he got out and glared at the scene. He sighed, opened the back of the Bronco, and pulled out a shovel. He went to work, and let his mind drift. He thought of his son. Like a lot of fathers, he supposed, he wished he had spent more time with Tommy as he grew up. Their family life was fairly normal, Church believed. His wife, Iris, stayed home while he went to work. She ran the house, he brought home the bacon, and the kids grew up comfortable and loved. He had worked very hard to make enough money to keep them up and running. What he didn't have for them, of course, was time.

They went from being children to stomping around as teenagers while he was at work one day. He had started a small computer and investment business with a partner, it took off, and his partner shoehorned him out without looking him in the eye. He had struggled for a couple of years, and managed to climb back up with his own company. During that time his son and daughter left high school and found colleges, and his wife played lots of tennis. With the kids both in college, he and Iris looked at each other, shrugged, and divorced. His daughter, Lynn—they called her "Sissy" because she resembled Iris's sister—cried and turned her back on him, and Tommy called him a loser, and worse. Their reaction had stung him. That pain stayed with him because they did not want to hear his explanations or rationalizations. Why the blame had fallen squarely on his shoulders he couldn't be certain, except maybe that Iris had complained to the kids about him all those years.

He finished digging around the rear tire and frame of the Bronco. He stood, rubbed his back, and wiped the sweat off his brow with the back of one hand. He had tried to make the trench in front of the tire longer, a more gentle grade. Looked good. He stuck the shovel into the dirt, hurried to the driver's seat, turned the truck on, and hit the gas. More dust, more rocking, more muttering through clenched teeth. He did manage to slew the truck a few feet forward, but it actually leaned at a greater angle than before and was still stuck. He gulped some water, got out, and went back to work and his thoughts.

Sissy seemed to adjust fairly quickly to her parents' splitting. She had met a young man named Mitch during her first semester at the University of Virginia, married, and continued taking classes. She maintained her relationship with her mother, and communicated with her dad regularly. Church knew she did so grudgingly, with a sense of duty. Sissy apparently still felt she and her mother were trying harder than he was, and he sensed some jealousy when he asked her for information about Tommy. Church's wife, Iris, had "flowered" after the divorce. She began to study New Age disciplines, became a vegan, let her hair grow, and read books by "channelers" and "spirit guides" billed as "new revelations." The last Thomas had heard of Iris, she was searching for "inner truth and peace" with some cult out in Utah, Idaho, or someplace. Her search bothered him, for some reason. He was the first to admit he had only gone through the motions regarding their Methodist membership, but he found himself defensive about it when Sissy told him about the "latest things Mom learned."

The blade of the shovel pranged off a rock hidden in

the dirt, and Church dropped it. "New Age," he said. "Bah!"

He grabbed the shovel and went back to his thoughts. Tommy, despite Church's efforts, drifted away from him. He made it through one term at college, then just walked away. Hitchhiked away, looking for "something real," was the explanation he'd gotten well after the fact from Sissy. Church followed Tommy's progress through reports from his dutiful daughter, and he constantly badgered her for more. He knew Sissy had come to resent his questions about Tommy. To her it seemed Tommy was all her father cared about. Hearing things she *didn't* say—perhaps enhanced by his own guilt—told him she thought he had not spent that much time with either of them as they grew up, so why should he be so focused on Tommy now? And why Tommy more than her? She was the one who kept up their relationship, she was the one who communicated with all of them. Church had no answer for her. He couldn't explain to her the mystery of a father's relationship to a son any better than he could explain to her the origins of the universe. Some things just were, he supposed.

He leaned forward to lever a large clump of dirt away from the frame of the truck, and the shovel handle snapped in two. He slipped as it did, and fell hard against the right rear fender with his shoulder and cheek. He wound up on his hands and knees, bruised and exhausted. He got up slowly, drank some more water, and rested a moment, frustrated.

He ran his tongue around the inside of his mouth, felt

it snag momentarily on a broken tooth. He rinsed his mouth, and felt an electric jolt as the cool water made contact with an exposed nerve. He spat out the water, saw its pinkish hue disappear into the parched soil. Not too much blood. The pain was manageable, he'd just have to be careful how he chewed. The likelihood of finding a dentist out here was remote. Any man or woman who could have made a living tending to the dental concerns of ranchers would have to been a Christian martyr and was surely taken. He laughed at his little joke.

He looked around, saw that the shadows were lengthening and the sun was low on the horizon. Man, he thought, I don't want to spend the night out here. He got behind the wheel again, spun the wheels, shut the truck down, and climbed out. He struggled for another hour or so. He moved rocks, dug the trench, and pulled twisted tree branches into the ditch for traction, all for naught. He slumped to the ground, rested his head between raised knees, and thought that digging a grave for the beast would have been easier.

The Bronco was stuck, he was worn out, and night had fallen without his noticing. He washed up using water from a large jerry can he carried, set out his perimeter sensors, ate some cheese and bread, careful to chew on the left side only, and locked himself into the Bronco for another night. While he waited for sleep, he thought of his son, not the slow-mo misty-eyed memories of Tommy the child, or Tommy the awkward teenager, but Tommy the young man. The last real conversation they had was the first time he had *really* heard the man in his son.

"You don't have the fire," Tommy had said through clenched teeth. "You've never had the fire in your belly."

They had been arguing over his decision to leave college, and it had gone from there to the divorce to why Tommy felt he no longer had to bow to his father's wishes or advice. Church couldn't believe that he was hearing an echo of what his own father had said to him. Now, to hear it from his son was almost too much for him to bear.

"Dad," Tommy continued, "look at your life, how you lived it. That's not the life I want."

"I've lived a good life," replied Church defensively, "and I've been a responsible person, a contributor. A husband and father and provider." He paused, and shrugged. "I got married and had kids, Tommy, like a lot of people. But I had a college education, and the smarts to start my own business, and because of its success you and Sissy had everything you needed. Now I'm paying for your college education, is that so bad? I want you to be ready for the world."

"I want to go *see* that world, Dad. The one you watch on the TV, or read about on the Internet. Yeah, you've been a success, but what have you *experienced* of it?"

Tommy could not know it, but that was a bad question to ask Thomas Church at that point in his life, a question his father had asked himself. He said nothing.

"Dad," said Tommy, less angry now, more beseech-ing, "I can't just sit here. I'm all about doing things, going places."

"Do them after you've got your degree, Tommy," tried Church again. He knew that it was hopeless. And in a way, he admired his son, saw some of his youthful self in the tall, lanky young man with the shock of unruly brown hair that he tried to corral with an ever-present stocking cap.

"Why do you think Mom left?" responded his son, on the offensive once more. "She told me herself you guys were just going through the motions. Said you were a good and decent man and she didn't regret the years with you, but she knew there was more. . . . There was more, Dad . . . and she's out there now, looking."

"She's out there, all right," Church had replied, stung by his wife's words to their son. He had heard the pain and anger in his son's voice, and knew the boy was more hurt by the divorce than he thought. Sissy had been angry too, but Church attributed that to her siding with her mother. Those two had always been a team.

"Dad. Look. I'm not dropping out or disappearing, and I'm not going to become some loser out there beg-ging on the streets. I'm leaving college, that's all. Do some traveling. That's how I want to learn. By doing things."

"You don't think I've shown you the way?" asked Church. "I haven't been a good example of how to live, how to succeed?"

"Dad," said Tommy quietly, "I'm hitting the road. I'll

keep in touch when I can . . . through Sissy. You are a good person, and you've lived your life the way you wanted. I love you for being my dad, but I don't want to be like you."

I don't want to be like you. His son's words still stung him. Church thought about Tommy's travels. His daughter would call him now and then with news. Tommy was in Florida, working on a shrimp boat. Then he was a deckhand on a barge somewhere on the Mississippi. He was headed west, into Texas. Tommy discovered horses. Tommy got a job on some cattle ranch. Tommy loved it. Tommy did not share any of this with his father, but with his sister . . . and probably his mom, too. Fine. Church lived his life after divorce. He got a Harley-Davidson motorcycle, he bought all the electronic toys there were and set up his own personal multimedia center in his home, a place where he had the world at his fingertips. But from there he could not talk to his ex-wife, or his son. He heard from Sissy, yes, but the resentment in her voice almost drowned out whatever news she shared. He liked her e-mails better, but every now and then the bitterness crept through those digitized bytes.

It had been from his media center that he learned of the cataclysmic worldwide disappearances. Something wondrous and terrible had occurred in the blink of an eye on a global scale, and Church sat there watching it all unfold. After seeing a world thrown into chaos and turmoil as a result, he had decided to find Tommy. Some said it was the end of the world. Fine. He would find his son. While he lay in the Bronco thinking of it all, he realized he had to admit something to himself. It wasn't only Tommy he wanted to find. He wanted to show his son who he really was, of course, but he also wanted to find each of them, Tommy, Sissy, and Iris, and put his family back together.

It took a long time for Church to fall asleep, and when he did he dreamed of sacred cows and flesh-eating birds.

The cool of morning fled with the sun, and Church was up and once again attacking his immediate problem. After stowing his perimeter sensors, he walked away from the Bronco and examined it for a few minutes. Then he gathered more tree branches, more rocks, and filled in the trench as much as he could. With his shovel reduced to a short-handled backbreaker, he had to come up with an alternative plan. Freshened by a night's sleep, he remembered reading something somewhere about worst-case scenarios and getting a vehicle unstuck.

He decided to try it. He used the Bronco's jack on the right side, forcing the frame up as high as he dared. Then he gingerly climbed behind the wheel, made sure it was in four-low, and hit the gas. The three wheels that had a purchase spun, then grabbed, and the Bronco lurched forward, falling off the jack as it did. With enough momentum to get the right rear wheel onto solid ground, he lurched back onto the rutted road. Church straightened the vehicle, stopped in the middle of the road, jumped out, raised his fists into the air, and yelled, "Yeah!" He gathered his tools, stored them, had a celebratory breakfast of granola bars and water, and headed back to the main road. "No more buzzards," he said to himself in the rearview mirror.

+ + +

Later that day he came to a place where a gravel road met the pavement on his right, then wandered off through the scrub brush toward a distant rise. On the west side of the intersection stood a small copse of rugged trees, and the gravel road was protected by a cattle break and barbed-wire fencing in good repair. On the east side, next to a post with a rural route mailbox, stood a small sign. Surrounded by tall, dry sage grass, the sign would have been difficult to see if he'd been coming from the opposite direction. The sign was cut in an oval shape, tan in color, and across it ran a wavy blue line over which lay a white cross.

He hit the brakes, skidded, and backed up. Then he pulled off onto the gravel road, bumped across the cattle guard, and stopped. His hands gripped the wheel tightly again, and he felt his chest swelling. He chewed his lower lip, unsure of himself, both angry about what had happened here and afraid of what he might discover now. He looked down the gravel road and thought, Okay. You've found the River Cross Ranch. This is where Tommy was on the morning of the disappearances. Let's go find him. Still he sat there, the truck's engine idling. He was so close now, he knew, but so afraid of what he'd find. Sure, the deputy had told him none of the bodies had been identified as Tommy's, but could the cops, or he, be certain? What could he do now? Go there, look around, stand over the common grave the cops had buried the dead in and say a prayer for his son? Watch the circling buzzards?

He stalled, afraid he would find pain no matter what decision he made. He opened his door, climbed out of the Bronco, stretched, and walked to the back of the truck to get a bottled water out of the cooler. He sensed movement behind him from the small copse of trees, and froze when he heard the unmistakable sound of the hammer being pulled back on a pistol.

"Hey, buddy, I'm holding a dead man's forty-five. A big old-time Wild West gun with real bullets, and I'm pointing it at the small of your back. Understand?" The voice was strained, labored, with a hard edge.

Church licked his lips. No, he thought. Not now, not this close. He managed to say, "Take it easy. . . ."

"You take it easy," said the man behind him, "and you won't get shot. I'll leave you food and water, but I got to take the truck."

"Listen . . . ," tried Church.

"I don't have time," interrupted the man. "I'm sorry, but that's the way it is. You are completely wrong if you don't think I'll shoot you right here on this road." There was a pause. Church could hear his assailant moving closer, his breathing shallow. "Turn around, slow."

Church turned around, his hands loose at his sides. Standing five feet away was a ragged and angular cowboy, with worn boots, frayed jeans, and a long-sleeved shirt that had once been blue but was now the color of the hills around them. The man even had a worn Stetson hat slouched over his head as if it had been there forever, darkened with sweat around the band. He wore a wide leather belt with a big silver belt buckle, and he did indeed hold a large black revolver in his right hand. The cowboy stood just over six feet, young, lean, and hard, his face gritty with rust-colored beard, his lips compressed, his eyes narrowed and intense. His left arm was tucked across his chest, with a crimson puddle of blood caked and dried above the elbow. The man stood with his feet braced, swaying slightly, pain clouding his strong features. Thomas Church looked into the young cowboy's eyes, and smiled.

"Hello, Tommy," he said quietly. "It's me . . . Dad."

The man's eyes widened, but the barrel of the gun did not move. He swayed again, licked his lips, and said, "Don't do that. Don't play games with me, man. . . ."

"Tommy," said Church gently, "no games. It's me. I've come looking for you."

Church could see that his son was in a great deal of pain—likely he was close to delirium from thirst or hunger and the madness of what he must have experienced. It was no wonder that he didn't recognize his father's voice.

The wounded cowboy became perfectly still, his eyes locked on Church's face, his tongue ran across cracked and swollen lips. Slowly, wobbling slightly, the gun in his right hand was lowered until it hung for a moment on his fingertips before dropping to the ground with a soft thud. Church watched as the man's eyes searched his face, softened, and warmed with recognition.

"Dad?" he said tentatively. "Dad? I'm . . . I'm . . ." He took a step, began to fall, and fell into his father's arms.

+   +   +

Thomas Church watched his son sleep for most of two days and two nights. He had managed to heft and tumble Tommy into the backseat of the Bronco, had picked up and made safe the old .45-caliber revolver lying in the dirt, and had driven slowly toward the River Cross Ranch on the gravel road. He did not want to go to the site, but sought a place where he could set up a secure camp away from the main road. He found a good spot halfway between, on a rise with good visibility all around, and a small stream cut into the rocks below. If he stood on the roof of his truck he could just make out the ruins of the ranch house in the far distance. He set his sensors out in a perimeter, pulled camping gear and sleeping bags out of the truck, and dragged Tommy over onto one of the bags.

Using the first aid kit that was part of his gear, he cut away the left sleeve of Tommy's shirt, and examined the wound. It was a two-inch gouge in the skin and muscle on the outer arm above the elbow. He didn't know combat medicine or wounds, but to him it looked like the arm had been either grazed by a bullet or cut with a dull knife. It looked infected, and the area around the wound was warmer than the rest of him, but it didn't look as though the limb was in any real jeopardy. He cleaned and disinfected the area carefully three times while Tommy slept, and only when he pushed the swab deep into the wound did the young man jerk or twitch. After the wound was clean and dry, Church applied antibiotic salve and wrapped it securely with a clean bandage. Then he checked his son's body for other wounds.

A walnut-sized bump rose on the left side of Tommy's head, its center split by a small cut. Tommy's lower lip was split, bloodied, but already healing, and he had two deep scratches over his right knee under his torn jeans. The knuckles of his right hand were bruised and swollen. Whenever the boy woke for even a few minutes, Church forced him to drink water; Tommy refused any food before he fell back to sleep.

Church talked to his son under his breath as he worked, cleaning each area, applying whatever first aid he thought was necessary. He got a bucket of water from the stream, some clean rags, and sat with his back against a large rock. He pulled his sleeping boy onto his legs and gently washed his face, neck, and hands with the fresh water. Then he wrapped him in a sleeping bag, rolled up some towels for a pillow, tended a small fire, and watched Tommy sleep.

The first night, while Church dozed, he was startled awake by his son crying out.

"No!" cried Tommy. The rest was an incoherent mix of moans and grunts. Then he tossed and turned for a few minutes before settling down again. A few hours later, as the eastern sky began to brighten, he sat up, looked at his father sitting cross-legged a few feet away, and said, "Dad? Dad . . . what are you doing here? It's bad here . . . *bad*." Then he fidgeted around until he was comfortable, pulled the edges of the sleeping bag up around his face, and fell off to sleep once more.

During those many hours while his son slept, Thomas Church drifted in thought. He found it was easier to be grateful—and he was absolutely, genuinely grateful—for his son's life if he directed his gratitude at some *thing*, some *force*, some *one*. Attributing the fact that he had somehow found Tommy, found him in time—the fact that Tommy was here, *alive*—to fate, synchronicity, blind luck, or some other impersonal happenstance just didn't cut it. Too many things had to go right for him to wind up at the exact place his son was wandering. Perhaps a divine deity, he argued . . . perhaps *God*.

That thought drew him once more to the conundrum he had been wrestling with since the disappearances those weeks back. How could an all-powerful, supposedly merciful God cause so much pain, sorrow, and chaos with one global and horrific act? And if He had, why then save Tommy to be rescued by his father? Life, and death, had been a capricious and seemingly arbitrary process before the disappearances, and apparently still were. He wrestled with it for hours, took aspirin for the headache formed by frustration, then slept.

While Tommy slept and as a way to get away from so many personal concerns, Church listened to his radio, to learn the news of the world. Perhaps he could put all this into perspective somehow. He laughed quietly to himself, thinking about the old cliché of misery loving company. It's going to be awful crowded in the Bronco tonight, he thought.

Somehow that cynicism didn't feel right to him any-more—after all, his son had come back. He thought about how we marked our days, the beginnings and the endings, that gave shape to our time spent alive. The history of man was now apparently split in two sections: before the disappearances, and after. Before was well documented. The exact number of years man stumbled around on the planet were argued over; creationists who adhered strictly to Scriptural interpretation disagreed with evolutionists, who attempted to validate their hypothesis with science. Either way, most of what the human race was, what it had accomplished, what it had warred over, built, destroyed, written, discovered, was known. The societies, religions, cultures, and governments, and the acceptance or de-struction of one by another, were dutifully recorded and studied, and helped man form strategies for future growth and enlightenment.

The greatest civilizations of the human race, and their accomplishments, including the never-ending wars, were documented in countless volumes. What the human race was, how it had gone about the business of life here on planet Earth, was stored in those volumes, which pro-vided a comforting base. Man and woman had been around for quite a while now, stated man's own history, and they apparently had a *reason* for being. The world's religions, of course, strove mightily to explain this in far-reaching terms. Any person who wanted to look beyond the life of flesh and blood, beyond the average mortal life span, and be emboldened with the idea of even *more* reason, could turn to religion. There, within the faith and mystery, could be found hope. What more could any man or woman desire?

Then came the disappearances.

"Maria!" said Tommy Church softly, "Oh . . . Maria . . ."

Thomas Church saw the smile that made his son's face young again, and felt saddened. Tommy was still asleep, but moving around a bit, and it was not the first time he had spoken the girl's name. Church guessed Maria had been one of the young women employed at the River Cross Ranch. The sheriff's deputy over near Pecos had told Church two young women were killed at the ranch in the aftermath of the disappearances, and a gunfight had erupted when the working cowhands had returned to the ranch house.

Church looked at the wounds on Tommy, and could guess from the emotion in his son's voice when he said the girl's name how it had affected him. He was startled at that moment with the acceptance of a truth: It would be less painful to realize you had lost a loved one to the disappearance than to some crazy and hateful act of a fellow man. He wasn't sure of the significance of that truth, and stored it for future consideration.

He took a walk around the perimeter he had set up in

the rocks, checking the sensors he had placed. He checked his Bronco, washed his face, and opened a can of pineapples. He leaned against a round boulder, swept the horizon all around, saw no movement, and slowly ate the fruit. He watched his son for a moment, then carried the small radio back to his rock and played with the dial until it picked up a station out of Dallas. The station had apparently decided to make every effort to sound like the world was still okay and on track. Things are normal, blared the commercials for new cars and electronic equipment. Things are normal, joked the DJs with their patter about happy hour and call-in contests. "Be the ninth caller! Win a brand-new bass boat!" Only the news told it like it was, and it wasn't pretty.

War ravaged the world once more, in the form of Muslim armies called the mujahideen. There had been conflict in the Mideast, North Africa, and Indonesia for years, of course. But after the disappearances, things broke wide open, with the Muslim hordes convinced of their invincibility and eager to claim their rightful mantle of world dominance. They had even found a leader, a dark man who had emerged from the bloody and charred battlefields with a voice and power that drew them to him even as they recognized his cruelty and ferocious love of war.

His name was Izbek Noir, and he was shadowed in the black patina of mystery. The mujahideen deemed him invulnerable. According to their propaganda machine, he could not be killed. They backed up their audacious claim with little evidence other than that they believed this because they had seen it with their own eyes on more than one occasion. He lived when death devoured all around him, and he let them wreak lawless havoc anywhere war took them. He even partook of the spoils of war when it pleased him . . . and it pleased him often. Women were considered by the hordes as spoils of war, and these Izbek Noir shared with his Muslim brothers.

War between Noir's mujahideen and various hodge-podge armies had begun in parts of central South America and the African continent. Already much of North Africa had been overrun, and advance elements of the mujahideen fought through Yemen and Saudi Arabia, curiously bypassing Israel for the moment. The mujahideen had become the new scourge, and those who were considered "infidel" feared for what was left of man's puny civilizations.

Another emerging personality was looked upon as a possible savior. His name was Azul Dante, and he had come, like his nemesis Noir, out of the landscape of war. Azul Dante spoke as a man of reason, however, a man of hope. He preached cooperation, and faith, and managed in a short time to build a coalition of free nations perhaps strong enough to withstand the mujahideen onslaught. He had reluctantly taken the reins of leadership, and had already had an impact, addressing the United Nations, meeting with the new American president, and even forming a "covenant" between Israel and his European Coalition. Many people, from all around the globe, looked to Azul Dante as the answer. He would defeat the mujahideen and Izbek Noir, protect freedom, and bring peace, stability, and prosperity back to a world reeling from the effects of cataclysmic and cancerous injustice.

"Dad?" said Tommy Church as he slowly sat up and rubbed his face. "Dad?"

"I'm here, Tommy," said Thomas Church as he turned the radio off and smiled at his son.

Tommy stared at his father, rubbed his face again, stood, stretched, winced, looked quickly at the clean dressing on his arm, and said, "How long have I been sleeping?"

"Two nights, most of two days."

"I dreamed about a lot of things." Tommy hesitated, licked his cracked lips, and added, "I knew I was dreaming, you know? But when I dreamed *you* were with me, I was upset because I knew you *couldn't* be. But here you are."

"Here I am, Tommy," said Church. "Your sister is okay, by the way. I stayed with her one night on my way out here, and she gave me the information on your whereabouts."

"Mom?"

"We don't know, Tommy. . . ."

Tommy looked all around, stretched again, and looked at his father as he said, "They killed Maria, Dad. She wasn't taken like the others, but it seemed like everybody turned crazy, and before I could get back to the ranch house she was dead. Killed while she fought them off, I guess. Killed." He shook his head, his eyes black. "Seems so senseless. All of it."

"But we're together now, Tommy," said Church

briskly, "and we'll go to your sister's place, and we'll figure out what to do next."

"Was it God, Dad?"

Thomas Church watched his son's face, saw the pain,
confusion, and sadness in those black eyes, and said gently, "Let me fix us something to eat. I know you must be
starving, and while I do you tell me about Maria."

"Maria," repeated Tommy, knowing there would be a
place of hunger in his heart for the rest of his life.

CHAPTER TWO ✛

Ivy Sloan-Underwood sat at a battered wooden table in a small quiet room in the back of the New Christian Cathedral. She found the stillness in the room pleasing, and she did not break it. A golden shaft of morning sunlight swept down from a high window above her left shoulder, holding motionless points of dust-light within. On the table in front of her was a still-life bowl of fruit, autumn colors subtle and dusty. A heavy ceramic mug with a chipped handle, over which hung a twist of steam, sat at her left elbow; beside it lay an old Bible in repose.

Embraced by the warm morning, she allowed herself to bask in the memory of that one small word spoken by her six-year-old son, Ronnie. He had spoken it but once, as clear as a bell, priceless and heartbreaking. She had waited for so long to hear him say it, to hear him say anything she could recognize, but he couldn't. He had been a "special needs" child, denied the gifts of normal abilities, condemned to live trapped within a stunted and twisted body incapable of communication or expression. She had prayed for him, prayed that he be allowed to change, to grow. Her prayers were answered with silence, hard days endless and inexorable, and she stopped praying, allowing the anger and bitterness to shove aside acceptance and hope. The stillness of the room was broken by an almost imperceptible shake of her head. No. This golden morning she would not let her memory go anywhere but to that impossible moment, the moment her son spoke the word.

It had been during the pause of evening, shadows reaching away from the fading light. She had been sitting at the window in Ronnie's small bedroom, staring out as the day whispered its farewells. Her son sat behind her, silent in his wheelchair, mute and relaxed, his sweet face turned toward her. She had sensed a ripple, a momentary shrug in time, and watched as the shadows seemed to stretch and breathe, and the light softened, then crystallized in brilliance before dimming to normal. Then, from so close behind her, unmistakable, undeniable, even if she had never heard it before, came the word from her son's lips.

"Mommy," he said.

Then he was gone.

But he had spoken that one word universal in its identity, value, and meaning, arguably the most powerful of all the world's words. It was the word that was immediately understood by those who received it no matter in what tongue. If the human race, pitiful creatures of flesh and intelligence, could spiritually ascend to any limited state of divine awareness, to a state of Love, it would be through mother and child. Through the child's eyes, voice, tears, gentle breath, was manifested life, the continuation of man and woman, the children of God.

To hear the word spoken by a child is a gift, a unique and precious moment of intangible worth and beauty. Such a simple utterance, yet it carries with it the triumphs and struggles of the ages, a symbol of a clearly identifiable miracle, a sign of a covenant at once pure and powerful, of a bond between the souls of living beings. It is a word spoken by God, through the mouth of the Son of Man. God's own Son. His child's face pressed warm against his mother's, the small curl of skin in the middle of his tummy proof of the loving cord between them. It is a small word at once sublime, simple, and complex as the meaning of life itself.

Now Ivy Sloan-Underwood sat in this small room near the back of the large and beautiful church in Alabama, thinking about it. She was a sharply attractive woman, comfortable and adventurous in her female body, a woman who enjoyed the attention of men. She had always dressed as if on the hunt, and was flirtatious and teasing when she had a chance. That had been her problem, of course—getting a chance to be any of those things. She and Ron had a good marriage in the early years, and he was tolerant of her edgy behavior around other men, in part because of their comfortable and pleasing physical relationship. But then she became pregnant with Ronnie, and he was born "damaged."

After that her life had spiraled inward, as she saw it, smaller and smaller it became, choking and cloistered. Ronnie took all of their time, forced her to stay home and mostly with him, and she had resented it. Her husband, though not sold himself, had even attempted to get her involved with a church group so she could find peace, to no avail. She had no time for a God who would let Ronnie be born the way he was, who would let her life turn out as it had.

Before she or her husband had resolved any of it, Ronnie was taken. Her child had not been the only one, of course. All of the world's children were gone, taken, during what many called the disappearance. So many broken hearts, so many tears. Teens and adults had been taken also—literally millions of them—in some unfathomable blink of a universal eye. Gone, leaving the rest to struggle with life after such an event, to struggle to identify what had happened. The fate of humankind on the planet Earth was precarious, and the dark forces seemed intent on seizing power while righteousness, justice, light, hope, and reason seemed to live in the memory of only a few.

That there were dark forces, Ivy Sloan-Underwood had no doubt. She had traveled from her home in California—her husband, Ron, refused to leave Ronnie's room, and was probably there still—to this New Christian Cathedral, emboldened with the knowledge that the very prince of darkness was alive and real, walking among the men and women fighting to retain the tatters of order and spirituality. She had made a deal with the devil, and the beating of her heart had become a bitter metronome. She had been pulled there, to the cathedral, by the voice of its pastor, the Reverend Henderson Smith. She wasn't sure what her mission was, but she knew that if the devil lived, there had to be a God, and if God lived, perhaps someday, somehow, she might stand before Him.

The only reason she was still alive, the only reason she cared about anything, was the one word she had heard her son speak. Now all she wanted was an answer.

+ + +

That same morning, in another part of the New Christian Cathedral, Shannon Carpenter and Reverend Henderson Smith leaned close across a cluttered table in a noisy and bustling dining room. Other church members and volunteers came and went; breakfast was almost over, and the dishes were being cleaned. Coffee was still hot, and strong. Many church leaders, of varied faiths, found their congregations suddenly filled after the disappearances. People who had not been taken, whether they had lost loved ones or not, sought answers, guidance, some comforting words that might explain things, past, present, and future.

The Reverend Henderson Smith was a whiplike African American man, a hard worker, a serious student of Scripture. He had responded to the calling while young, and had labored to become a real preacher most of his life. Now he was pastor of a large church housed in a new and beautiful cathedral, with all of the support systems, communications, and large projection screens, a bookstore, and just as important, more devoted volunteers than he could ever have dreamed of. He had lost his beloved wife and children—they had been taken—and this made him a sympathetic brother in the eyes of his flock.

He was also regarded to be a good Christian—a man who prayed, studied the Scriptures, and lived life as Christ taught men and women to live. But he was not taken, was not suddenly lifted up as had been the children and so many others. He was left here on Earth, the flock told one another, to teach us, to comfort us, to show us how we can still survive and find salvation. His sermons had become stronger, even more certain and eloquent, and only he knew they were a carefully crafted and subtle lie.

Shannon Carpenter was a woman in her late twenties, plainly attractive and groomed, with a young girl's complexion and expressive eyes. The Reverend Henderson Smith looked at her sitting across from him, and said with a smile, "You know, Shannon, you don't look like a girl who would be drivin' a pickup truck."

"It was Billy's"—Shannon paused, her face warm with regret—"my husband's truck. It carried him to work every day, and he worked so hard to make a life for us, for me and our three kids."

Smith knew she had lost them all.

"I don't know," she continued. "After I found they

had been taken and I knew I had to come here to hear you . . ."

"Tell me again how you knew that."

"Oh, Reverend," said Shannon. "It seems so simple to me now, but at the time? I mean, Billy and the kids just loved their little church, and they were always trying to get me to go with them. When I did go I found it all to be so simplistic, like it was a nice story and we were all hoping it was true and in the meantime we're going to act like good Christians." She looked at him, and added, "My children were beautiful. Not saints, but good kids. And Billy was for real. He tried so hard to make me understand about Christ as our Savior, and I just didn't want to hear it. But I was a big deal, a career woman— legal secretary to a big firm that handled a lot of church business up there in Cleveland—and I was too busy. I used to actually get angry with Billy sometimes when he told me he was praying for me every day." She shook her head. "Can you imagine?"

Smith made a mental note, and said, "But?"

"I'm sorry, Reverend Smith," said Shannon. "You wanted to know how I knew to come here. After they were gone and I was alone in the house, I picked up Billy's Bible. This one."

He nodded.

"I began looking through it." She stopped and looked into his eyes. "I know you understand, Reverend. My heart was just broken, totally broken, and I didn't know whether to be angry or frightened, kill myself or what? I was looking for something to grab on to. Billy's Bible always gave him so much comfort, and peace. I flipped through it, saw where he had made notes for me and saw your name and this church written inside the back cover. 'Go there,' he had written, and I didn't know if it was for me, or him, or us."

Reverend Smith waited.

"So," she said, "I closed up my house, took the Bible he loved, took the truck he loved, and headed out onto those crazy roadways to find you."

"And find me you did," said Smith with a smile. Then he said, "And you found Jesus along the way, you told me."

"Yes."

"Tell me again," he said with sudden intensity. "Tell me how it . . . what you . . . felt."

"I was driving, Reverend. You know how wild and upset everything was right after it happened. I was trying to be careful, stayed behind those convoys of National Guard soldiers, or the state troopers I came across. While I drove, and when I stopped to rest, I read a lot of the passages that Billy had highlighted over the years. I would read it, and hear Billy's voice, reading it with me, hear him explain it to me, how it connected with real life . . . my life. I was tired, sad, frightened. I don't know. But it was like that Bible was a map for me. Leading me someplace, guiding me." She stopped, then said, "Are you sure you want to hear this? You know all about this, and I don't know if I can say it right."

"I do want to hear it, Shannon, from you," said Smith. "I enjoy hearing how our Lord comes to us."

"Well," she replied with a small laugh, "He came to me right there in Billy's pickup truck." She paused again, reflective. "I felt myself just letting go, Reverend, just letting go of the physical, the me, all that was happening around me. I let my anger go, tried to put my sadness aside, and then just . . . opened up. I had been holding my heart in a fist . . . maybe my whole life, I don't know. But I began letting it go, asking Him to help me, telling Him I was ready, I was giving myself over to Him."

"Yes? Yes?"

"It was like a soft shower of emotion, Reverend, like a golden cloak of light and feeling at the same time. I experienced a feeling of completeness, somehow. In one moment I knew He was real, and I was held in the palm of His hand. I could stop worrying, stop being frightened, I could just put myself in His hands, and follow my heart. It was funny, in a way, because I wanted to *shout*, you know? I cried, I laughed. I was giddy, really. I felt for the first time like I could really trust someone. I'd never had that before, there were always doubts and concerns and what-ifs, but they all went away. I was simply His from that moment, and I immediately understood what Billy felt and why he was always so excited about having the Word and knowing what He was all about. I knew also that Billy knew, and our children: 'Mom finally got the Word, bless her heart.'"

She saw he was staring at her, a troubled look on his face. "Reverend?" she asked.

He sat up and rubbed his eyes. "Yes, Shannon, it's okay. Please go on."

"Well," she said, "I guess that's it. In a way it's like a near-death experience. I mean, now everything I see and hear seems brighter, clearer. The food tastes good, the coffee, it's all a gift and I'm aware of it. The smells, the people, your sermons, everything is in place. When I read Billy's Bible now the words make sense, and I find so much comfort there—like he used to." She stopped; her vision went out of focus for a moment, then came back clear. "You know, the sadness burned into my heart by the loss of Billy and the kids. It will never go away. But the anger has softened. Now I know there is reason, and a plan, and I know they are with their Lord, and He is Love and I am here to do my best to learn and grow and help. And with His blessing maybe someday soon I'll be with them."

"I'll pray for you, Shannon."

"Thank you, Reverend."

He watched her for a moment, then looked down at his hands on the table and said, "Um, Shannon, you said you worked for a law firm that handled financial matters for your husband's church?"

"Yes"—Shannon shrugged—"the firm specialized in financial matters really, for a group of churches. The firm was made up of civil lawyers and CPAs. They formed and maintained retirement accounts, investments, all the various money matters."

"Do you think they did well by their clients, Shannon?" asked Smith.

Not sure what he meant, or why he would care, Shannon answered, "I guess so. I mean, of course. Even though it was church money, they invested it to make a profit, to make the funds stronger, so the churches could operate."

"And they made profits?"

"Yes, Reverend."

He smiled and patted her hand. "Shannon, I sense your confusion, wondering why I would be so interested. Fact is, any church—like any other organization—needs working capital, and fiscal strength for future work and expansion. This is a big ol' church we got goin' here, with lots of people putting money into the collection baskets to ease the burden of their souls—especially in these troubled times. No matter. The church can remain strong on faith, but it needs cash to keep the lights on, right?" And to keep the good Reverend Smith in these fine threads, with his fine lifestyle here in his fine cathedral, with his powerful voice over the radio so he can reach out to his adoring flock, he thought to himself.

She watched his face closely, troubled by some undefined thing in his eyes. She was glad that she hadn't told him about her boss's suicide, the odd meetings that had preceded it, his fearful and angry rant just before he pulled the trigger. Something inside her told her that these incidents were best left in the past, not to be spoken of.

"Right," she said.

"Well, sister," continued Smith, taking Shannon's hands in his, "perhaps you could help me, um . . . us . . .

here in this cathedral. We have Barry and Marge in the office now, but the money that we're bringing in—that's given up by joyful hearts—it's just sitting there. Sure, the stock market is just now coming back on-line, and our new president is telling us our economy is still strong if we give it a chance. But Barry and Marge, they just don't know how to make our money stronger. We're with Selma Eastside National Bank, and they're giving us like some paltry percentage while the money lies there. It could do better, we could do better. Then our money— the New Christian Cathedral's money—could do more to spread the new gospel." He squeezed her hands. "Won't you help me with this? We could use your experience."

"Of course, Reverend Smith," answered Shannon. "Anything I can do to help."

"Thank you, sister. And thank you for sharing your story of finding our Lord."

The dining room began to quiet as the breakfast was done. Church members and volunteers left for their places of work or worship, and the kitchen staff gathered at a back table for a Bible study session. Reverend Smith usually sat with them for a few minutes, genuinely enjoy-ing their discussions. Now, however, he searched deep inside the eyes of Shannon Carpenter, who gazed back without fear. She did not know what he sought, but her heart was open and confident. He sought confirmation, but he did not tell her that. In this woman's eyes, her heart, he knew, was the light of the real Savior. In spite of his dominating worldly self, he wanted, somewhere deep in the spine of his soul, to bask in that light.

Of the two people sitting at that table, only one really knew Christ.

+ + +

John Jameson welcomed the tang of salt sea air as he climbed out of the deck hatch on the USS *Finback*. He didn't particularly care for submarine insertions, but agreed that this was the way to go on this one. He clambered into the small black inflatable boat manned by four heavily armed sailors, turned and gave a quick salute to Captain Campbell Sims, the boat commander, and they shoved off. The quiet motor on the inflatable moved them over the calm waters off the coast of Tunisia rapidly, and before long the sinister black hull of the sub dipped from view.

Now comes the dicey part, thought Jameson as they searched the dark waters in front of them for the small fishing vessel that must be there. Satellite technology had already confirmed a day ago that the vessel was in the port of Tunis, but it wasn't the boat he worried about. One of the sailors in front hissed and pointed, and the young officer at the helm of the inflatable, his eyes wide and white against his naturally brown skin, headed the craft toward where he pointed. They heard the diesel engine on the fishing boat; then it stopped, and the boat slowed and turned broadside to the approaching inflatable. It was a tired and battered sister of its breed, with stringy nets, old tires for fenders, and rust streaks on the multicolored hull. Scrawled with improbable romanticism on the bow was the vessel's name, *Dulcinea*.

"Alors!" hailed Jameson. French was the agreed upon language for this rendezvous.

"Stand away there!" came the reply, faint because of their distance. The sailors had their weapons trained on the man at the helm of the fishing boat. They watched as he leaned out and shouted, "Unless you carry the blessings of Allah!"

"May the blessings of Allah fill your nets with fresh fish, and not the poor souls of men!" responded Jameson, adhering to the code.

"And may the fleas of a thousand wretched camels fill the undergarments of your first three brides!" floated back to them, and the sound of laughter.

It wasn't the code, Jameson knew, but it had to be Omar. He gave the young officer a nod, saw his grin, and readied himself as the inflatable was placed alongside the fishing boat long enough for Jameson to grab the salt-crusted gunwales of the vessel and swing aboard. Behind him he thought he heard "Godspeed," and when he glanced back the small rubber boat had disappeared into the night.

Omar looked just as he should, a hefty man with swarthy skin, a full beard, and the shiny black eyes of a thief. His enormous teeth gleamed within his conspiratorial grin. He slapped Jameson hard on the shoulder, then turned and pushed the throttles forward. The boat slewed around and headed for the shore. Jameson pulled his backpack off, took a quick look around the deck and the small cabin below to make sure they were alone. He looked Omar over. Jameson had worked with him on several operations through the years, from the Urals to South Africa. Omar was an independent; he swore allegiance to no particular agency or country. He was a Turkish Muslim, Jameson knew, but didn't let religion get in the way of adventure or profit. Omar worked for money, so it was understood that he was as trustworthy as the last deal he made. The man was a survivor, though, Jameson gave him that, and he had always done just what he said he would on past ops.

This time his job was to get Jameson ashore, then to where any unit of the mujahideen might be, and "introduce" him to the Muslim fighters. The mujahideen were a loose bunch when it came to recruiting, interested in good fighters for Allah who didn't let ethics or morals get in the way. It was known there were non-Arab Muslims, Westerners, within the ranks, and Jameson was first to get into a unit, then move forward with his mission.

"I don't know, James," said Omar with a shake of his head. He had only known Jameson as "James" through the years, no matter what work name Jameson used for the mission. "This job of yours"—he waved one big hand at the far shoreline—"it's a little bit crazy, no? Yes?"

"Yes," replied Jameson. He knew Omar did not know what his mission was, and understood basic human, compounded with any agent's, curiosity. Omar fished for information. In his world it could bring a profit, or save his skin.

"Look at you," continued Omar as he piloted the old boat. "Your mixed bits of different uniforms, Eastern Bloc backpack and webgear, Swiss boots. You could be from anywhere. You come as a soldier for Allah, yes? And you want to fight alongside the mujahideen? Crazy. There must be more to it, yes? No?"

"I'm on a mission from God," responded Jameson with a grin of his own.

"Ah!" laughed Omar. "*The Blues Brothers!* You think Omar doesn't know great Western films? I know." His face lost its grin, and he added, "These are serious people, these mujahideen."

"It's a serious world, Omar."

An hour later Omar slowed the fishing boat as they approached a ramshackle dock on the outskirts of a small town on the coast. A few lights shone here and there in the gloom. Omar and Jameson stepped lightly off the boat as another, older man stepped on. The older man, dressed in dirty clothes and wearing a thin turban on his head, quickly went to the helm, pushed the throttles forward, and piloted the boat away from the dock and back out to sea. No words were spoken. Jameson followed Omar as his guide hurried to a battered jeep parked in the shadows of a warehouse, and they climbed in. Omar drove. Though his adrenaline surge was long since over, Jameson still remained alert, watchful. There'd be time for rest somewhere down the line.

The sun was rising when they began to come across signs of recent battle. A broken Russian helicopter lay on its side a few yards from the gravel road they headed south on, and here and there in the distance they saw burned-out trucks and tanks. All the bodies they saw appeared to have been stripped, and the carrion birds circled lazily above, waiting for the jeep to pass. Columns of billowing black smoke broke the horizon like large exclamation points, and the smell of burning gasoline, and other things, filled their nostrils. Over the rush of wind and the rattle of the jeep on the rough road, Omar shouted, "You know Bernard Fall? His book *Hell in a Very Small Place*?" He swept the area with his left hand. "This is hell without end."

A few minutes later they were stopped by a three-quarter-ton truck that was parked across the road. Jameson could see about thirty armed soldiers, on the sides of the rutted and pockmarked blacktop, backed up by two sandbagged machine-gun bunkers. Many more similar mounds receded into the distance.

"Mujahideen," said Omar as he slowed the jeep and put a big open smile on his face. Then he added softly, "If you keep tilting at windmills, James, one might fall on you someday." Then he said loudly as he threw Jameson's backpack out of the jeep, "May Allah have mercy on you, peasant!"

"And you, goatherd!" responded Jameson gruffly as he jumped out of the jeep.

"Only one this time, Turk-man?" asked one of the mujahideen as he approached them with his AK-47 leveled at Jameson. These mujahideen troops were a trailing part of the rear guard, many kilometers from the main army, farther still from the headquarters units, where Jameson needed to join somehow. He spoke in Farsi, but Jameson knew the mujahideen were such a hodgepodge that French and English were also commonly used among them.

"Yes . . . but he's a big one, okay?" replied Omar with a shrug.

"He's old," said the mujahideen.

Before Omar could respond, Jameson said in French, "Older than you, yes, which means I have fought many battles on the side of Allah all over the world." He picked up his backpack, looked at the man steadily, and added, "I came to fight with you, the mujahideen. The word is out, all over. Even in Amsterdam, where I was before talking to this thief." He jerked one thumb over his shoulder at Omar. "You need fighters. I have come to fight with you."

"You have only the side arm, and K-bar knife?"

"Only to travel with," replied Jameson. "But I know many weapons, and will pick one up out here."

"We have weapons," said the mujahideen soldier. "You can have the M-sixteen, or the Uzi perhaps?"

"Pieces of junk," said Jameson with a shrug. "Give me an AK anytime."

"For Allah?" asked the soldier.

"For Allah and his needs in paradise, and for my needs here in this poor world," answered Jameson. Then he added, "Test me, if you want."

"We will, soldier," said the man. "We will."

That had been almost two weeks ago, and during that time Jameson had traveled with the company-sized unit of mujahideen. They had moved inland, skirted one large battle, and had participated in two small skirmishes with a mixed force of Jordanian and Egyptian soldiers. They had ridden a convoy of trucks through Libya, and were practically escorted by the cheering mobs, who didn't seem to notice how their young men were conscripted at gunpoint. They saw some action along the northern border of Sudan, then drove toward Eritrea and Ethiopia.

They rode trucks or tracked vehicles when they could, mile after long and desolate mile, and dismounted for battle. Jameson knew he was being closely watched. He had shown he could carry his weight, he could keep up, he knew weapons and tactics, he took his turn on night watches with no complaint. Now, in a small action again, he watched, and waited. He sighted along the barrel of his AK-47 assault rifle, focused on the burned-out hulk of a large tank a few meters in front of him. He watched for movement, he waited for change.

An enemy soldier hiding behind the tank had raked the squad Jameson was a part of with a long burst of automatic rifle fire, and punctuated this by flinging a hand grenade, which exploded in their faces. The ambush killed one and wounded another, who writhed and twisted in the sand a few feet from where Jameson lay partially protected by the tattered carcass of a goat. The wounded man made a small keening sound from between clenched teeth.

The squad of soldiers lay on the hard ground under the searing glare of an unforgiving sun, covered with dirt and dust, their mouths parched craters in the lunar surface of their faces. Through wide eyes made angry and aged by war, they scanned the wreckage of an old Egyptian armored convoy that lay before them, a twisted and charred desert sculpture of steel.

Behind the shattered bones of trucks, tanks, and armored personnel carriers crouched the enemy. The squad had already begun to act in the face of the ambush, a few soldiers laying down a base of fire while their comrades attempted to close the distance to the enemy. The soldiers were mortal men, and knew fear. With the initial burst of fire blasted at them as they approached the destroyed convoy they had thrown themselves to the ground, flattening themselves behind any cover they could find, the air from their nostrils forming tiny dust storms around their bearded faces. But they were soldiers, and knew war.

To stay in the kill zone of any ambush was to die, so within seconds they began to return fire, the basic fire-and-maneuver practiced by infantrymen for centuries. They were mortal, these soldiers, they knew fear, but they were the mujahideen, fanatical Muslims hardened by war, deprivation, and desire. They were driven by at least two powerful emotions: They believed that to die for Allah in battle was a promised blessing, and they feared their leaders more than their enemies.

Now Jameson watched as a hard edge of blackened steel that formed the ruptured cupola of the tank to his front became slightly blurred, softened. It was the change he had waited for, the moment the enemy soldier behind the tank was forced to edge out a bit to check for movement among the mujahideen. John Jameson, Special Agent, American, hesitated.

He had been accepted by the mujahideen as simply another mercenary-type soldier, a wayward follower of Muhammad, European perhaps, or South African. A reinforcement was always welcome. Before his arrival, the mujahideen had been involved in fast-moving attacks along northern Africa for weeks; many in their ranks had perished, and had been replaced along the way.

The areas of battle were scenes of total waste and despair, a part of the world where drought, famine, and war had ravaged the people for years, until one wondered why one man would still take the time to kill another over it. Jameson, tall and dark, not a young man, but trim and hard, experienced with many weapons and tactics, who followed Allah and was not an infidel, was assimilated into their ranks with barely a second glance. He had shown his willingness to suffer the soldier's hardships during the campaign, and had displayed his toughness and savvy once when a foolish man had attempted to make off with his pack. He had cut the cheek of the thief very quickly with his knife, and had sent him sprawling into a rocky ravine with a kick. The squad made a place for him in their ranks, and called him by the name he had given, "Rommel."

Jameson aligned the sights of his weapon on the temple and left eye of the enemy soldier behind the cupola of the tank, and increased pressure on the trigger. With a gentle squeeze, he knew, he could send a bullet into that left eye, and kill the soldier. But John Jameson, "Rommel" to the mujahideen in his squad, apparent mercenary soldier intent on making war for Allah and grabbing any spoils that came his way, was a Christian, recently saved in a world that seemed lost. He was there, with that squad, with the company, battalion, and army of the mujahideen led by the dark and apparently unstoppable Izbek Noir, for one reason: to kill.

But he hesitated, an extended and excruciatingly brief moment, hesitated and pondered the voices arguing in his heart. He had killed men in his lifetime, as a soldier in combat, and later as an agent on missions for his government. Through the years he had engaged in deep moral introspection about killing on a few occasions, mostly after some intense and dangerous mission that left him emotionally drained. Each time, he concluded that he killed only as part of his job, he took no enjoyment from it, did not take it lightly, but felt very strongly that he fought for what was right. And if he had to kill in the process, so be it.

Those feelings were further validated by the sure knowledge that in most cases it had come down to a "kill or be killed" situation, and he had acted with professional certainty. He was aware of the clear lines in his arguments becoming blurred as he aged, almost a softening of his views. A short time ago an informant embedded in a terrorist cell had been executed because he had failed to get her out, and her death had hit him hard. He had begun to look at things differently.

That was before the disappearances, of course.

Everything had changed since that moment, his wife and children gone in the blink of an eye, his deep, searing sorrow and desperate feeling of loss exacerbated by anger, hopelessness, and helplessness. The world was changed, forever. He was different in another way. Words his wife had spoken to him through the years had clung silently to the walls of his heart, but were revealed to him again after she and their children disappeared. He began to hear her voice when he picked up her Bible, and as he read it he felt as though she sat beside him, her heart beating with his, her lips brushing his ear as they read the Scripture together. John Jameson, draped in the dark and dusty clothing of the warrior mujahideen, known to his new squad-mates as Rommel, inserted among them for the express purpose of finding one man and killing him, had accepted Jesus Christ into his heart as his Lord and Savior.

He had opened himself to Jesus, learned that of course He had been there all the time. What he read in the passages of Revelation fairly convinced him about the nature of the disappearances, about what was happening to the world. He accepted that, too, and did not worry about his fate.

But he was there to do a job, and if he *was* successful in killing his target it would have an immediate effect on the state of peace or war in the world now. With one simple act he could change so much, by taking a life he might save many others. All he had to do was kill a man.

He focused on his sight picture, tightening the trigger as he slowly let out a long, steady breath. He was in battle now, and still a long way from his intended mission target. First things first. Then, as he watched, before he could pull the trigger, the enemy soldier behind the tank was hit by flanking fire from soldiers to his right. The enemy, a young man with smooth skin and the face of a boy, stood, staggered to the edge of the tank, and collapsed into the sand, a large stain of blood darkening the back of his uniform shirt. Jameson took it in at a glance, then lunged forward as his squad rushed toward the now retreating enemy. He paused and turned to the wounded man in his squad to offer a sip of water and check his wounds.

The man was curled into the fetal position, the high-pitched keening coming from his parched and cracked lips softer now, a song of beseeching supplication. He was in agony. Perhaps he could be saved, if given good medical attention immediately. But the mujahideen did not encumber themselves with such niceties.

Jameson, his face a mask, looked a few yards away to see one of the company sergeants standing there, his assault rifle aimed at the wounded man—one of their own. The sergeant grimaced and shrugged, and nodded toward the action as it moved away from them. He watched Jameson, and waited. Jameson hated what he knew he must do. I can't do this, he said to himself. Bad enough to kill in battle, surely a sin to do it in cold blood. He glanced at the sergeant, who motioned with the barrel of his AK toward the wounded man. He will die either way, and you have a bigger mission, Jameson told himself.

Many will live, many will live. He grimaced also, muttered, "Allahu Akbar, God is great," and fired one round into the wounded soldier's head. There was no more keening. The sergeant nodded and turned away, and Jameson stepped over the dead man and lunged forward to catch up with his squad. God forgive me, he thought.

CHAPTER THREE

The Reverend Henderson Smith stepped up into the grand pulpit overlooking the interior of the fine and spacious New Christian Cathedral. He wore a purple robe of exquisite quality, and as his hands caressed the smooth railing of the pulpit he marveled at how majestic it all was. He gazed down upon his flock: black and white, young and old, wealthy and poor; they filled the seats, faces upturned to him, eyes reaching out to him, ears waiting expectantly for him to give them the Word. And the Word he would give them. That it was the *new* word should have bothered him more than it did, but he looked all around at the opulence, reverence, and power that surrounded him, and mentally shrugged. They hunger for the Word, he thought, and the Most Reverend Henderson Smith is goin' to give it to them.

"My brothers and sisters," he began, bowing his head slightly, "good evening."

He heard the comforting murmuring in response.

"And it is a good evening, is it not, for us who live here in Selma, Alabama, which is still part of the United States of America? Yes. It *is* a good evening for us, because we still live, we breathe, we walk with one another." He looked out at the faces. "And we *pray*, don't we? We pray to our God in heaven, asking Him again and again: Why, Lord, why? Why have you forsaken us, your own little children, Lord? And we ask Him . . . we ask Him to watch over us, don't we? To watch over us and keep us safe in this new world of turmoil, of *lawlessness*, of rage, rabble, and rampaging hordes bent on destroying us all, do we *not*?"

"Amen," he heard floating back to him. "Tell it, Reverend."

"Since the sudden and unfathomable *taking* of so many of our loved ones we have been prayin' so hard to make some sense of it, prayin' for the Lord to help us understand, help us regain hope in this bloodred darkness." He stopped, the large church completely silent. He nodded, as if in secret confirmation, then went on: "He has responded, brothers and sisters, oh yes. Our Lord has responded by *giving* us hope, and you represent it simply by being here, being here in this New Christian Cathedral to listen to this puny, unworthy voice pass on His beautiful message. God doesn't want you to lay down and die now, lay down wailing and gnashing your teeth and praying for death so you no longer have to wander in darkness and fear. *Yes!*" he thundered, "yes, you were not taken while others were, others you loved, and even some others you may have felt were not quite the Christian soul *you* are."

He paused again, and surveyed his audience, listening to the echo of his words fall among them like the steady patter of raindrops from soft leaves. Quietly, he began again.

"Yes. You were not taken. But are you lost? Are you lost?" He shook his head, and said, "No. No. You are *not* lost, we are not lost. There is still a whisper of hope. He whispers to us. And if we are to find salvation, we must listen carefully, and look around in this new world. Look. Listen. Seek. Open our ears, open our hearts, and find the *new truth*."

He put a surprised look on his hard black face, his eyes wide as he said, "Whoa now, Reverend Smith! Did you say *new truth*? Uh-uh, noooo. No sir, there ain't no new truth, Reverend. There is only and always has been only the *truth*, baby, that truth that we all learned from the sweet Scripture. Been the truth since you were nothin' but a diaper-wearin' baby, Reverend Smith, and you know it. Don't *even* try to talk about no new truth . . . no . . . no."

He rubbed the long fingers of his right hand across his face, and with his left he brought up his Bible, which he rested against his left cheek for a moment. He smiled, then continued. "Believe me, brothers and sisters, I love this ol' Book as much as you, was raised with it, and believe in it, and know the truth lies in it. I am not gonna throw this Book away while I'm talkin' about a new truth for a new world . . . and this *is* a new world. No, I'm wanderin' through this new world just like you, keepin' my sweet Bible right by my side. But you know what?"

He held his Bible up high with his left hand, and stared up at it. "You know what? When I read these God-given words now, *I read them in search of a new truth, a truth for this new world . . . for this world where the old prophecies have already come true.* Did you hear what I just said? I said where the old prophecies have already come true."

He put his Bible down and took a sip of water from a heavy crystal glass. The water was sweet and cold. His hand shook slightly, and he sought out the red light of the television camera that was capturing his image and sending it out to millions more. "Let me give you an example of what I'm ramblin' on about here," he said as he scratched his head and made a funny face. "You remember the old story of the Exodus?" He returned their nods. "Of course you do, we all do. Well, brothers and sisters, I'm here to tell you there is a *new* exodus. An exodus of today, not some ancient act involving people long dead, people who have become dust and ash but right now, while we speak and pray, there is an exodus. 'Well, Reverend Smith,' you say—'what is this new exodus? Is it the exodus of all of us who were not taken? Is it our traveling across the desert of fear and uncertainty in search of the promised land of hope and explanation? Is it the exodus of our heart, leaving behind all we held dear and precious and real. Leaving all of that behind while we put one tiny spiritual foot in front of the other as we traverse the darkness in search of the light?' *Yes*, my brothers and sisters, *yes*."

He looked out across the pews filled with those who hungered, and said, "There is, as you have probably seen, a physical exodus also. All you have to do is look out the window, all across town, and you'll see signs of it. The new exodus, in part, brings people here—to this cathedral—from all over. In fact, you can look to your right or left where you sit, and chances are your neighbor has come here from somewhere else, drawn here by the promise of hope." He grinned. "C'mon now, you who have traveled here since the disappearances, raise up your hands."

Tentatively at first, then boldly, many hands were thrust up among the congregation. There was some shy laughter, and then the crowd broke into spontaneous applause, pleased with the fellowship and reality of the reverend's words.

Beaming like a proud father, Henderson Smith watched it happen. He waited for them to settle down again, then continued. "You know what? People have made the journey—an exodus—to this cathedral, and not just this one. There are others scattered across America, Canada, and Mexico, and people like you . . . and me . . . are journeying to them to hear the new truth. The truth that will sustain them in a new world." He held up his Bible once more, and looked at it lovingly as he said, "Brothers and sisters, I think we might say this new world, and this new truth, sort of *begin where this sweet Book leaves off* . . . do you understand? Has the end of the world come to us even as it was prophesied in these pages? If so, is that it? No . . . no." He laid the Bible down on the rail and went on. "What about this exodus, then? Did you know it is happening across the sea also? Millions—did you hear me say that number, brothers and sisters?—millions of souls hungry for the new truth, the new sustenance . . . they are on the move. They travel in their heart, as we do, and they travel, physically travel, from their place in the ruins of their old world, to a place in the new world where a shining beacon has emerged from the lies." He stopped, made another face, and said, "Even in France, of all places . . . as if the darned French weren't insufferable enough already." There was a smattering of laughter.

"You know of the mujahideen, so we don't have to speak now of that misguided rabble. They are misguided and *dangerous*, and now they make war on a world brought to its knees by spiritual uncertainty. They are totally bent on destroying what remains of us, believe it. They bring darkness. They bring darkness." He paused. "But there is light . . . light in the form of reason, strength, and promise. There is a man given the name Azul Dante—you've heard me speak of him before—and he is that light, that beacon. He has formed his European Coalition, and he speaks of hope and salvation for us so forcefully and eloquently that the spiritually hungry and frightened are beginning their exodus toward him . . . toward his truth . . . from all over the world."

He gazed upon them, exuding confidence, enjoying his own power, his own words, as he said, "Now we are all familiar with Exodus in Scripture. The Israelites were growing in number, prospering, and the kings of Egypt were concerned about them, and enslaved them. Basically, they used them as forced labor, and tried to work them to death. But the Israelites could not *be* worked to death, even when the slave drivers were ordered to deny them the straw needed to strengthen mud bricks. Then Moses gets the Word, brings down plagues of blood, frogs, gnats, flies . . . what else? Oh . . . hail. Boils, the firstborns, Passover, God put a serious hurtin' on the Egyptians until they let His people go. They made their Exodus out of Egypt, into the desert, seeking their promised land. I say to you today, an exodus denotes movement. The Exodus of old had a purpose, as does this exodus of today. We—I've heard us described as 'Christians Not Taken'—are on the move. We are moving across miles of dangerous roads, across countries torn by war, across the very oceans of our planet, moving toward the beacon. And at the same time we join the spiritual exodus taking place in our hearts, our poor hearts, in our desire to find peace, hope, and salvation. We too seek the promised land. But it won't be a place to set up our tents, no. It is the promised land in our hearts, a promised place for our souls. We join the exodus away from the old and toward, oh, *thank you God*, toward . . . the . . . new."

He felt his own heart beating strong, the beats almost loud enough to drown out the searing whispers of guilt, doubt, and remorse that blew within his soul. He looked upon his faithful flock, smiled, and said quietly, "And now, brothers and sisters, let us pray. . . ."

+   +   +

Thirty minutes later, the Reverend Henderson Smith finished shaking hands with those who had attended his sermon and were leaving the church. He found it to be fatiguing, the facade of strength, confidence, and good-will he wore for them. Their hands grasped his, their eyes bore into his, their hearts hungered for solace, and reason. He tried to give them all of those things with his posture, his grip, his clear unwavering gaze, his mes-sage—but it could make a man *tired*. He was impatient to be done, to be left alone for an hour or so. He wanted to have a cup of coffee, a doughnut or something, and stare out the window at nothing for a while. It was not to be.

"Reverend Smith?" said a carefully coiffed middle-aged black woman wearing the deep blue satin gown of the choir.

"Yes, Sister Folks?" responded Smith.

"If you're done here on the front steps, Reverend, we're ready for you back in the dining room."

The dining room? thought Smith. "Uh," he said.

"Remember, Reverend?" added the woman with a shy smile. "You said you'd talk to some of us about *that ques-tion*. . . ."

"Uh . . ."

"About those of us—you know—um, how some of us who felt we were good Christians and all, um, why we were not taken."

As if I knew, thought the Reverend Henderson Smith. "Of course," he said with a smile.

+   +   +

There were perhaps a dozen, and this number included Shannon Carpenter and Ivy Sloan-Underwood. They sat around several dining-room tables. Coffee and sweets had been served along with conversation about the day's sermon, church business, and a smattering of gossip. Finally, Nateesha Folks smiled tentatively and said, "Reverend Smith? I guess I'll be the one to embarrass myself in front of everybody, and ask you right out—why wasn't I taken along with my sweet babies, and my sisters? I'm goin' around calling myself a Christian Not Taken . . . have you seen those T-shirts some people are wearin' that just have the letters CNT on the back? I mean, Christian Not Taken? If I'm a Christian—and I thought I *was* a Christian—why wasn't I taken?"

Before Smith could begin to answer, a small old man, his pink skin flaked and dry, said, "You've said a few words here and there in some of your sermons, Reverend Smith, but never really explained it. To be honest, in my view if there are Christians among those still here, then it gives credence to the possibility that the disappearances are *not* a Biblical or God-generated event."

Several others tried to comment then, and Henderson Smith smiled, held up his hands, and shushed them.

"My brothers and sisters," he said, still smiling, "perhaps it is a question I cannot answer. Perhaps in our discussions and sermons we'll travel toward an answer together." He turned to Nateesha Folks and said, "Sister Folks, don't you think I asked myself that very same question? Why, here I am—a reverend—standin' up on the pulpit, teaching the Scripture, prayin' hard all my life to be of value . . . studyin'. . . . I've carried my Bible with me since I was a young boy. Then came the disappearances—they are most assuredly an act of God as outlined in Revelation—and not only am I not taken, some crazy fool comes along and burns my little church down."

He rubbed his face with both hands, well aware of the *why* in his particular case, and added for those who did not know his personal history, "I was pastor of a small, old neighborhood church and had been called to work here, at this new cathedral. On the day of the disappearances a man walked into my old church with a can of gasoline, and burned it and himself to ashes."

Some gathered at the tables gasped; others were silent.

"So," continued Smith, "why would some Christians not be taken, if these are the end times according to Scripture? I would guess—it's an educated guess, seasoned with many years of study, observation, and prayer—that there are two parallel factors involved." He stopped and grinned, and years fell away from his face as he did. "Of course, we must remember first that God and His works are for the most part beyond our mortal comprehension, and not all things will be revealed to us, and God doesn't *have* to tell us everything. Okay, that said, let me suggest that although many of us were—are—Christians, believing in the Bible and its truths . . . perhaps there was some teeny bit of our heart that we held back, something inside we did not completely give over to our Lord. He would know of our reservation. I believe some of us, maybe when we're put into a position of responsibility, trust, or authority, might feel somehow *vulnerable* if we absolutely and completely let go, completely open our hearts and souls to the Lord. He would know." He let his gaze sweep them, one by one; many met his eyes, while some stared at their hands in their lap. "We would be what to all appearances would be a complete Christian, but deep within, *perhaps so deep it is unknown even to us*, there lies a crumb of doubt, or a misguided bit of mortal self-preservation. We would not be ready, *really* ready, to sit with our sweet Lord."

No one spoke. For a moment a soft patter could be heard as heavy, glistening teardrops slid off Nateesha Folks's round cheeks and fell onto the tablecloth, until one of the other women handed her a tissue.

"Another possibility," said Smith quietly, "would be what I might call your basic 'flawed' Christian. You know these people," he said to the group, smiling again to lighten the mood. "They can be found in every church. Nice folks who read the Bible, sing the hymns, listen intently to the sermons, wear a little cross on their lapel, and *almost*, but not quite, get the message. They will be pious and righteous at a church event, then go out into the world during the week and act like marauding pagans on the prowl. They wear the cloak, but they don't really *practice* the teachings of the faith. They're not bad people, and they really believe in Jesus Christ, pray to Him, and seek His forgiveness after they do what they choose to do. They just don't *get it*. They can fool themselves and many of us, but they can't fool God. So they would not be ready either."

Smith shifted in his seat uncomfortably, took a sip of

strong coffee, longed to be left alone for a while, and continued. "Lastly," he said, "and remember, we're just kicking this around here, there may be more to it. Lastly, and I kind of like this possibility, is that *our work here on this poor world as Christians simply isn't finished.* Yes, it is the end of the world. All of Revelation is coming to reality now. . . . These are the end times. But God—loving and merciful—God knows there are still those among us who can be saved, and those of us who *need* to be saved. He could have simply lifted up the chosen saints and turned His back on the remains of humanity, could have turned His back on the millions still floundering around. But He didn't. He kept some of us *Christians* to keep the flame, to keep the message alive and share it, to get the Word one more time out to those who might thirst for it, and baby, if they're not thirsting for it now they are *fools.*" He stopped, sipped his coffee again, and shrugged. "Maybe it's all three of those reasons and maybe more we haven't thought of. Know this, *God knows.*"

The group sat perfectly still, silent, until the old man cleared his throat, scratched his head, and said, "I think there's truth in everything you said, Reverend Smith, and I thank God for you." A few of the others nodded, including Shannon Carpenter. Ivy Sloan-Underwood sat next to Shannon, staring at something far away, quiet. On the other side of Shannon sat a man who she knew was a new arrival at the Cathedral, and named Ted, she seemed to recall from a hasty introduction. "And you know," continued the old man, "you have such a simple way of explaining things. The more I listen to you, the less I have doubts."

I wish I could say the same for me, thought Henderson Smith.

He shook a few hands, received some hugs, and wished them all a good night.

The group began to break up, most going their own way, deep in thought. Ivy said nothing, but squeezed Shannon's hand as she walked away. Ivy looked so sad Shannon wanted to reach out to her, but before she could, the man who had been sitting beside her cleared his throat and said, "Excuse me."

Shannon turned and looked at him. She had seen him in the church during the week, and knew he was a recent arrival. He was a big man, bigger than her Billy, with thick black hair worn in a neat style he had probably kept since high school. She guessed he was a few years older than her Billy was, too, early forties maybe. He was fit, though, with just a bit of a tummy pushing at his wide leather belt around his jeans. He had wide shoulders, long arms, and big hands, and Shannon knew by looking at his hands he was a man who worked with them—just like her Billy. The man wore a light blue checked shirt with short sleeves and a collar, and black boots. He had nice dark eyes and an easy, sort of timid, smile.

"Yes?" she responded.

"I, uh . . . I just wanted to introduce myself," said the man with a shrug. "You're Shannon, right? Shannon Carpenter?"

She nodded. "I know. We met earlier."

He ducked his head in embarrassment. "I'm sorry. So many new people."

He stuck out his right hand, and she took it tentatively. The skin of his palm and fingers was dry and warm, and she could feel his strength. "I came here from Ohio. You know that woman, Nateesha Folks? She was one of the first people to welcome me here, to the Cathedral. She's been real nice and sort of telling me who is who and what is what around here and she told me you were from Ohio too, from up around the lake and all. I'm from down in Columbus but I lost my family. I mean, my wife and our one daughter was taken on that day and Nateesha told me you had lost your family too. And I—" he stopped, gave her a sheepish grin, and added quietly, "I've never been considered a talker, but here I am ramblin' on like a fool."

Shannon squeezed his hand, let it go, smiled, and said, "I'm pleased to meet you, Ted."

He smiled back, hesitated, and she saw the familiar cloud of sadness, pain, and loss pass over his broad face as he said, "My wife, Rhonda, she always called me 'TG.'"

"My husband, Billy, always called me Shan," she replied. "You can call me Shannon, and I'll call you Ted. How's that?"

"Perfect," he answered, then added, "Can I join you for dinner?"

I'm not ready to be joined for dinner, thought Shannon, but she replied, "Sure. I have to go to my room, and they're not quite set up yet, so I'll meet you back here in a few minutes, okay?"

"That would be great," he said.

+   +   +

As Shannon headed back for her room she was intercepted in the hallway by Nateesha Folks. The imposing black woman with the beautiful voice and powerful smile leaned close and asked, "He's a nice guy, isn't he?"

"Who, he?" asked Shannon with a grin. She thought she knew what Nateesha was doing, but couldn't help feeling a bit like a schoolgirl.

"Who, he? *Ted Glenn*, girl," said Nateesha as she shook her head. "I think he asked me about you the second day he was here."

"Well is he just nosy," asked Shannon, "or too obtuse to realize we're witnessing the end of the world here?"

"Oh," replied Nateesha as she stopped in front of Shannon, blocking her way, her hands on her hips, "so it's the end of the world, but a man can't see a pretty girl and not want to talk to her, not want to spend sometime with her? *Obtuse*. What kinda word is that? You the one who's obtuse if you think men are gonna stop acting like *men* just because it's the end times, girl." She leaned closer, "I think he likes you . . ."

Shannon looked into Nateesha's bright eyes, liking her, knowing she was a good woman, and a new friend. "He likes me?"

The black woman winked, and said, "I think he *likes* you likes you . . . know what I mean?"

"I know what you mean," responded Shannon as she gently pushed past Nateesha, "but I'm a woman, like you, and *we* are able to think of the big picture, the important things during challenging times, without being distracted by the little things . . ."

"Sometimes it *is* the little things that make up the *important* things that make up the big *picture*, scaredy-cat," said Nateesha as Shannon walked away.

"Ain't scared," she said without looking back.

"Are too. . . ."

"Ain't. . . ."

"Are. . . ."

+   +   +

Catherine "Cat" Early, bounced and jostled in her seat on an ancient and dilapidated bus, dozed in the midday heat despite the noise, smells, and fear that surrounded her. She was bone tired, physically and emotionally, and dreamed of a long hot bath and clean clothes. She wore khakis, the long pants tucked into the tops of heavy socks and hiking boots. On her left wrist was a simple watch a soldier had given her, and around her waist was a light green web belt.

She was in her mid-twenties, with a lean body, dark brown hair cut short in a fashionable and practical shag, and a face that might have been even prettier if it were relaxed and open. She had dark brown eyes, intense, and with them she inspected and challenged all things around her. Even through the dust, fatigue, and wariness, it could be seen she was an attractive woman, but her general manner of no-nonsense professionalism and defensive standoffishness kept most men from taking a romantic interest.

The bus traveled with ponderous and precarious solemnity through the border region of Armenia and Turkey. She was trying to make her way out of Iran, east to Ankara and a functioning airport, and eventually to Paris. She was an international print reporter, only on the world beat for a couple of months, but already a veteran. She had been a big-city reporter for the *Herald*, back in Miami, for a number of years, and felt she had found her place. Then her sister, Carolyn, who covered stories across the globe for Reuters, was killed while following war on the African continent. Cat had received a few letters from Carolyn in the weeks before her death, and her sister's observations about the brutality of war and the emergence of a sinister leader named Izbek Noir had intrigued and unsettled her. She had left Miami and begun to trace Carolyn's footsteps.

From a combat photographer named Slim, an awkward and gangly young man who had worked with Carolyn, she was given her sister's old leather backpack and Bible. She carried both everywhere she went. She spent most of her days immersed in the cruel firelight of man in the act of destroying man. She traveled from one conflict to another, reporting in a factual, comprehensive manner, while always attempting to humanize those affected by the actions. Each step she took through the charred landscapes, each soft footfall beside the huddled remains of innocents killed in the conscienceless and random acts of war, resonated against her soul, and the winds of fear and despair chilled her to the marrow.

She had begun to feel very lonely, or alone—even more so after she lost the companionship of Slim. The disappearances had occurred by then, of course. She was a journalist, with a world-weary eye and skeptical outlook, but she could not dismiss the gentle but persistent voice that spoke of a truth she knew could be found only in her sister's Bible. She could not explain it, but she knew her heart was somehow softening, bit by bit, day by day, and she understood that no one had ever been saved with a closed and hardened heart. She had Carolyn's Bible, and no matter what horrors her day took her to, she could now open that Book and find refuge in its waiting pages.

The bus made a lurching turn, and a man's voice was raised in anger. Cat looked across the aisle at a woman holding a baby to her breast, leaning down to gaze into the child's face, cooing to it. Next to her a man half stood in his seat and yelled something guttural in a language that might have been Russian. He yelled at a heavyset woman wearing a flower-patterned dress and an old military-style coat. The woman's pinched face was dark with anger, and she reached again for the mother with the baby.

Baby?

Cat saw that the man, apparently the husband of the woman with the baby, was attempting to protect her from the questions of the other woman. He batted the woman's hands aside and leaned in front of his wife, his face sad and angry at the same time. The woman in the military coat scowled, looked again at the baby, and hissed, "I should have known." Then she turned in her seat, sobbing quietly.

Cat cautiously leaned across the aisle a bit to get a better look at the child. She knew all the world's children had been taken during the disappearances—had, in fact, recently confirmed that even Muslim children and children of other non-Christian faiths were gone—so she understood the curiosity a suckling infant would bring—curiosity, yes, but even more so envy, anger. The young woman, dressed in a burka without the veil, the long robes faded purple, dirty, with tattered hems, gazed down at her child, and tears left uneven tracks on her dust-covered cheeks. She continued to coo, and hug the child, which was wrapped in an old blanket. When she lifted the bundle briefly to place the child against her shoulder as if to burp it, Cat got a good look. The child had a beautiful little face, with light brown skin, puckered red lips, and eyes that opened and closed with the movement of the bus. The skin was plastic, of course, the eyes glass, and the sweet lips colored by paint. The woman had lost her child to the disappearances, like so many mothers had, and her grief transcended her ability to accept an unacceptable reality. The child was a doll, and the doll for her had become a child.

Cat straightened in her seat and sighed. So much pain, she thought, so much sadness, loss, and pain. To keep from sinking into a morass of bleak thoughts, she forced herself to think about her new assignment, Azul Dante. The new leader of the European Coalition was in Paris, and Cat was ordered to go there, listen to any of his talks or briefings, and attempt to snag him for an interview. She felt a lightening of spirit as she thought of Dante. A light in the dark wilderness was how she had already heard Dante described. He was such a force, such an energy, that even a skeptical newsie like Cat had to admit he could not be ignored.

In preparation for the interview she hoped to be granted, she had read extensively about him and his programs. His was positive energy, apparently, his efforts to bring together varied cultures and countries to unite them in peace and survival, well documented. His European Coalition was gaining in strength every day. He had almost stabilized the economy, managed to get international trade working again, most important with the United States, and represented a chance for the world to get back on its feet after the one-two punch of the disappearances and the uprising of Izbek Noir and the rampaging mujahideen.

More interesting to Cat than his politics, Azul Dante seemed to be growing as some kind of spiritual leader. He was not shy about referring to the Bible, the Talmud, or even—in arguments designed to show how the mujahideen were the true infidels—the Koran. He spoke of a great misunderstanding among the peoples of the world throughout history, man's inability to correctly interpret the revelations from God sent to them through the ages. This inability to *know* the message, he stated, had led to all the trouble. He was careful not to dispute the sanctity of man's religions, careful not to insult the character of various churches and their leaders, but at the same time he pointed to the present condition of the world, and argued that clearly our spiritual leaders missed *something*.

Cat knew from reading recent news stories about him that many Christians were looking toward Dante as the best new guide on the planet. She had heard about a "new Christianity," which emphasized that the teachings of Scripture were still valid, but now the passages must be examined in the light of a new dawn, a new world. Clearly the world had changed with the disappearances, argued Dante, and many were the experts and leaders who would try to take control of the survivors.

People hungered for answers, thirsted for truth, longed for a new hope and promise; and because these desires were so intense, people were vulnerable to charlatans and false prophets. He would offer no false hope, he said, no false promise. He would only try—like his fellow struggling human beings—try to make sense out of what had happened, and to believe in a merciful and loving God who would not abandon His children.

If chosen, he had humbly admitted, he would do his best as teacher, as new interpreter, to lead what remained of mankind out of darkness, out of a world racked with pain and confusion, and toward a path of new understanding. To help him in this task, Dante had formed what was called the Prodigal Project. This was dedicated to bringing about what Dante called the "restoration of a one-world family," the "welcoming back" of those who had strayed, the "rejuvenation" of governments who would work in harmony toward one apparent goal. Peace would come with the fading of borders, and the concurrent forming of a one-world government. The Prodigal Project, with its own logo and flag, and headed by Azul Dante, was already established as a positive entity on the world stage.

Cat glanced again across the aisle at the woman cradling her "child," saw how the woman's husband held them both in his arms, saw his clenched jaw and sadly defiant eyes, and was swept with a momentary disorientation, like an onslaught of seasickness. She bunched her hands into tight fists, and told herself, No. You can't. You must not lose it simply because you are surrounded by people who are completely and forever destroyed and just don't know it yet . . . and that includes *you*, Catherine Early. C'mon, girl, grit your teeth, listen to your heart, remember your sister Carolyn, think about Slim out there somewhere, and hold on to hope. Hope!

She took a deep breath, pulled a water bottle out of her sister's old leather knapsack, and took a long drink. She used a bit of the water to wipe her eyes and the back of her neck, then put it away and thought about Paris, Azul Dante, and hope.

CHAPTER FOUR

S ophia Ghent looked across the Seine at the gray and imposing structure of the Cathedral at Notre Dame. She sipped from a cup of thick and delicious café au lait, and nibbled on a tiny sweet pastry. The small hotel provided a simple breakfast every morning, and Sophia allowed herself to enjoy it, and a few moments of quiet reflection, before launching into the day. The French, of course, had collectively shrugged their shoulders after the disappearances. So what if it was the end of the world, as many were suggesting? We still have to eat, we still must have wine. But bad wine, *bad* food? Never. In this, the City of Light, we will carry on! Millions across the globe faced starvation, war, the collapse of order and the intrusion of anarchy, but here, in Paris? *Non, non.*

She was dressed for work already, in a fine-quality tailored business suit with low-heeled shoes. Her hair was pulled into a tight chignon, and her glasses sat on her briefcase. She carried herself with a quiet, professional bearing, was an expert at time management, travel and dining reservations, and public relations, and could be forceful and determined in the face of recalcitrance.

Rarely was she seen with her hair down, literally or figuratively, but then she showed a distinctly feminine side, with a soft, full figure, fine skin, and a lovely face. From her teenage days to now, over ten years later, she had rarely taken much of an interest in men. Her parents had divorced when she was only two, so she'd really not known her father at all. By all appearances this was what her mother seemed to prefer. Though she'd never spoken poorly about the man, it was almost as if her silence on the matter was a more effective condemnation.

Sophia grew up living a life that was dominated by the presence of women. First, while her mother established a career in international finance for a London brokerage house, she was cared for by a series of nannies. Many of the them were of West Indian descent, fiercely loyal to her and as proud as peacocks. Sophia smiled as she remembered how Louisa's lilting voice could take on a knife-sharp edge.

Once when they were in Harrods to pick up a party dress that Mrs. Ghent had bought but that needed alterations, an unwary and dismissive clerk had ignored Louisa and assisted other customers. Each of them was white and clearly not the hired help, but Louisa stiffened her back and demanded to see a manager. Even by the time the situation was resolved and apologies were extended, the fire was still burning in Louisa's eyes. She told six-year-old Sophia, "So girl, don't ever let them think that they can push you where you don't want to."

The same message was made clear at the succession of boarding schools and the all-women college she attended while her mother was living abroad—in Belgium, Luxembourg, and finally Paris. You didn't need anyone to look out for your own best interests. That was your primary job. Men were not a means to an end; they were simply another obstacle to overcome in your drive toward success and fulfillment. They were competitors for the same jobs, the same grants, academic appointments, and influential mentors and advisers that were so necessary for a career in academia. So when Azul Dante came along and plucked her out of the university graduate school program, Sophia was glad to have been saved from the prospect of developing hawklike talons to hold on to whatever share of the academic world she could grab hold of. She was also truly frightened. She had no idea what this man expected of her, nor did she know if she possessed the necessary skills to succeed in the rarefied atmosphere he existed in.

She had felt equally unprepared last night when at a state dinner with the French premier, Henri Gardaine, a young envoy who was a part of the U.S. delegation began exerting considerable effort to charm her. His name was James Devane, and he was an undersecretary of something or another. Sophia was so taken by his amazingly beautiful hair and dazzling smile that she couldn't remember exactly what his title was. Maybe it was the French penchant for wine with every course and a nice champagne to help the dessert be even more of a temptation that had her feeling such a rush of pleasure. She had been so busy in her first few months with Dante that she'd had little time for a social life. She and her mother had grown distant—her mother wasn't thrilled with her choice to pursue a career as an academic—and the only young man she'd ever dated had dissolved in a pool of self-pitying tears when she told him that she would be taking the position with Azul Dante.

So if she let herself be carried away by James's attentions, it seemed harmless enough. The evening went by quickly in his company, and the usual blathering chitchat—even with the world in crisis, diplomats could still manage to carry on with the equivalent of nonstop weather talk—receded into the background, like the sound of crickets on a summer evening. When James took her by the arm and led her to a balcony, she felt like what she really was—a twenty-five-year-old woman in the world's most romantic city. The lights from the Eiffel Tower, the traffic around the Champs-Elysées, all seemed to pulse in time with her own heartbeat. They talked and laughed, exchanged a few sweet kisses that were as discreet as they were thrilling.

James was the son of wealthy Connecticut senator, a man who had been one of those taken, and though there were some in his family who wished it otherwise, voters in his district seemed to be leaning toward electing James's older brother Benjamin to fill his father's vacant seat. James didn't seem to care too much—he wasn't fond of politics. What his mother and other family members might have worried about in Ben—his sometimes overbearing sense of entitlement and greed—would probably serve him well in that new role.

James had apologized for sounding so cynical, and when he did, he dropped his head in a way that reminded Sophia of a repentant puppy. She was about to fold him in her arms again when she heard her name being called. She turned around quickly and saw Azul Dante standing in the doorway. Though his face was hidden in the shadows cast from the lights behind him, Sophia could tell by the harsh tone of his voice that he was angry.

She quickly excused herself and rushed to her employer's side. When they turned to go back into the reception, she was amazed at how quickly his expression seemed to change. He still, however, kept his arm firmly around her shoulder and guided her to a table, where he introduced her to another in a long line of dignitaries that she couldn't imagine ever needing to know. She was puzzled by Dante's reaction—after all, he had told her to enjoy herself and that she was essentially off duty that night. The people she met at the table—members of some economic-sustainability legation from Uruguay, she thought—paid her little attention. After a few moments, she drifted away again, hoping to meet up with James.

When she finally managed to track him down, she saw him at the far end of a corridor a considerable distance from the reception, engaged in an animated conversation with Azul Dante. By far the taller man, Dante loomed over him, his eyes fierce, the cords in his neck taut. The paneled woodwork and stone floor did nothing to muffle the sound of Dante's angry accusations and James's equally angry replies.

Sophia hurried toward them. It was only when James caught sight of her that he stepped away from Dante.

"The guy's out of his mind," James said, and swept past her. After a few paces, he turned and said, "I'll be in touch, Sophia. We need to talk."

Torn between her sense of duty and her emotions, Sophia stood looking from one man to the other.

"I'm sorry. I suppose I get a bit carried away." Dante blotted his forehead carefully with his handkerchief, folded it neatly, and returned it to his pocket. "I was just telling your friend Mr. Devane about how important the U.S.'s efforts are to our success."

Sophia looked at him, saw him drop his head in a pose that reminded her of James's earlier apology.

"I suppose that's to be expected when one is so passionate." She smiled to herself and looked back down the hallway to where James had disappeared. When she returned her gaze to Azul Dante she thought she saw something flicker across his expression, something she couldn't quite make out. For a moment, she thought it was something feral, like the expression she saw on the faces of the countless dogs and cats that had suddenly to fend for themselves with their owners gone. He appeared wounded and aggressive at the same time.

By morning, she had dismissed that interpretation entirely. She hugged herself and thought of last night, of her departure from decorum. While it wasn't likely to make headlines, her flirtation with James hadn't been the wisest course of action. She'd let her heart rule her head, and that wasn't the right thing to do. After all, she wasn't a schoolgirl at a social; she was a staff member of one of the world's great leaders. Dante had never had to remind her that how she behaved reflected not only on her, but on him as well. Any hint of scandal was all the media would need to deflect attention from what really mattered: Azul Dante's accomplishing his mission.

As she finished the last of her drink, she heard a knock at the door.

"Un moment."

When she opened the door and saw Azul Dante standing there, her heart skipped a beat. Though she'd already decided that she was responsible for last night's unpleasantness, to have him show up at her door like this was unsettling. He'd never come to her before; instead, he'd always used Drazic as his envoy.

"Mr. Dante. I'm sorry. Was there something that you needed?" She cast a quick look toward the phone on the secretary just inside the room. Her heart sank when she saw the dim glow of the incoming-messages light.

"No, Sophia, I left you no messages. May I come in?"

"Certainly, sir. I'm sorry. Forgive me. I'm slightly out of sorts this morning."

Dante crossed the room and sat on a wide-striped chaise. He looked somewhat odd sitting there so formally on a piece that called for lounging.

"As am I, Sophia." Dante folded his hands in front of his face and balanced his chin on them. "I'm afraid that I might have been a bit too overzealous in my desires."

Sophia kept her expression calm, though at his use of the word "desires" a hundred images popped into her mind.

"You see," Dante hesitated, then laughed. "I suppose that I'm not very good at saying these kinds of things. But I want you to know that I hold you in very high regard, Sophia. Last night I told you to enjoy yourself, and that is what I intended for you to do. When I couldn't extract myself from the clutches of those confounded Uruguayans, I thought of using you as my out. I'm sorry for that, but I considered this Uruguayan crisis one of the most serious of my career."

Sophia laughed and thought again of the three stout members of the Uruguayan group, who if they'd gone on a collective diet could have done a lot to sustain agriculture in their native land.

"I suppose also that I'm spoiled. You've done so much for me and added immeasurably to my life in ways that I can't even number. And when you weren't there at my side to immediately assist me, I got a bit, well, shall we say, peevish?"

"I quite understand, Mr. Dante."

"I think that perhaps in the interest of opening up a more productive dialogue"—Dante's eyes sparkled at his intentionally formal diction—"when in private you should refer to me as Azul. In public, of course, we shall retain the same policy as before. 'Your Greatness' or 'My Lord and Liege,' depending—"

"I will make every effort, Azul," Sophia was surprised by how easy it felt to say his first name and how much pleasure doing so gave her, "to remember the sometimes subtle distinctions between public and private."

Sophia was glad that she had managed, with Dante's capable assistance, to negotiate a kind of truce. She didn't have to formally apologize for her innocent indiscretions with James, but she'd made it clear that she understood the subtext of Dante's concerns about using his name—there was a clear line of demarcation between the public and the private spheres they moved in. More and more she was realizing just how much they moved in them together.

"And I will do my best to honor this agreement as well." Azul Dante pushed himself to his feet and adjusted the crease in his trousers. "I understand that a young woman like yourself should lead her own life. She doesn't need an old man like me around to cause her trouble. Please pass along my regrets to your young American friend."

It wasn't until Dante had shut the door and Sophia retrieved her cup that the man's odd choice of words struck her. Normally so precise in his language, he had said "regrets." Sophia didn't have time to dwell on it too long— her coffee had gone as cold as the chill wind that blew in off the Seine. She shivered. For the first time in weeks, she felt a sadness come over her that she couldn't explain, and she fought the urge to call her mother. Perhaps James would make some sense out of all of this for her.

Azul Dante watched from the suite's windows as Drazic left the hotel lobby. His aide was tall, thin, with big hands, stooped shoulders, lifeless eyes, thinning black hair brushed back over his long skull. He was dressed in his habitual black suit, white shirt, black tie. His demeanor was solemn and quiet; Dante had heard him described as "funereal," and appreciated the word's accuracy. Drazic was a disquieting presence to many, and his mysterious, almost sinister air was deepened by his few communications with Dante, which were conducted in a rubbery Slavic language. If they only knew, he thought as Drazic went out to signal the limousine driver.

+   +   +

Slim Piedmont, freelance photojournalist on temporary assignment with the supreme headquarters group of the mujahideen army, sat on his haunches outside a small tent somewhere in north Yemen. He was surrounded by several hundred Muslim soldiers, most partaking of their evening meal. No one bothered him in any way, as he was there at the behest of the general. The heat of the day was losing its intensity, the prayers had been dutifully intoned, and the soldiers of Islam gratefully prepared for a night of rest. Slim chewed on a piece of gristle that had come from his bowl of soupy rice mixed with a greenish brown mystery meat, determined to get every bit of sustenance from the meager dinner. Logistical support was not one of the mujahideen's strong points, he had discovered. They relied more on what they could forage from their surroundings, but this was Yemen, a place that did not have much to begin with. The Muslim hordes, welcomed as brothers by the local leaders when they first

crossed the border, soon ravaged the land by their sheer
number. So Slim, like the soldiers around him, made do
with what was doled out, and dreamed of better days.

Slim knew he was in an odd situation, but acknowl-
edged that if he had wanted normal or predictable he
could have stayed behind the counter at his dad's hard-
ware store back in Tulsa, Oklahoma, and the U.S. of A.
He had stumbled through high school, managed two
years of journalism in college, then bolted. He had always been a loner, a rough-and-tumble young man comfortable with gadgetry and adventure.

The capturing of an image had fascinated him since
his very first Pentax 35-mm camera, and eventually he
found himself with one wherever he went. When the
digital cameras came along he didn't miss a beat, although he still appreciated the *process* of basic film devel-
opment. While in college he began selling a few shots of
athletic events to newspapers and sports magazines, and
applied for full-time positions, with no luck. Not enough
experience, he was told. How do I *get* the experience? he
asked. Finally he took his savings, his cameras, and his resolve, and went off to find a war.

That had been seven years ago, and since then he had
seen a lot of things through the lens. He found he was
actually more comfortable looking at life on planet Earth
through a camera lens. Life was harsh, unforgiving, un-
just, brutal, and deadly, and if he saw the results of man's
inhumanity to man within the frame, finite, contained,
they were, he told himself, manageable. When he pulled
his eye away from the viewfinder and gazed openly on

the same scene, it sometimes overwhelmed him. There were no limits. What war spoiled, and the spoils of war, knew no boundaries. A wailing mother, cradling the broken form of a child in her lap, swept all around her with her grief, including him. But if he focused on her within the lens, she became *the shot*, and he could safely capture her without damage to his heart. This he also told himself, anyway.

On this evening, as he slowly and methodically chewed the gristle, he thought about his present state of being. He was a freelance photojournalist, but he was not free. He had been given the opportunity of a professional lifetime, but it came in that old and disquieting offer you just can't refuse. He had been in Egypt with an international print reporter named Cat Early, sister of another reporter he had worked with, Carolyn Early. He had loved Carolyn, and felt his whole world turn into one never-ending undeveloped negative when she was killed. He had never told her of his feelings for her, the depth of them, and they had never really been a couple. Carolyn had been a pro, intense and focused while she went from one place of struggle to another, always searching for the truth, and not afraid to write what she learned and let the chips fall. They had traveled together, complimented each other's work, and supported each other when a friend was the best thing you could be. After Carolyn's death, Cat came along. Slim learned that she had been a beat reporter in Miami before going worldwide in her sister's footsteps. Cat had guts, integrity, passion, and a nose for finding the pivotal point of any story. He had liked her immediately, and within a short time of working with her found that a bit of color seemed to be seeping back into his world.

They covered war, of course, a never-ending story, and sometimes he would watch Cat as she slept, wrapped in a meager blanket on the hard ground, and fear for her soul, afraid she was too vulnerable under her brash exterior. The things they witnessed burned him deep, and he did not want her scarred the same way. Then the disappearances had swept the earth, the greatest and most devastating single event in man's history, and despair hung over the land like a hot and clingy fog. He had never been a religious man, was not well versed in any theology, but he didn't buy for one second any theory about aliens from outer space, or some wicked disease, or the diabolical Muslims and their death-ray weapon. Whatever had taken those millions of people—Christians and children, he had heard—it was not within man's paltry level of understanding. No, there was more to this whole *life* thing than intelligent beings walking around on Earth making babies and killing each other, of that he was convinced. Cat had chided him once about his cameras and his undefined beliefs, and he told her he would love to photograph God someday, because "the light would always be perfect."

Now Cat was gone, off somewhere covering the war between the mujahideen and whatever forces stood between them and the total destruction of non-Islamic civilizations, and he had an exclusive assignment some journalists would kill for. First Carolyn, then Cat, had an interest in a singular but obscure soldier-leader among the Muslims. It was Izbek Noir, a frightening and cruel spawn of war who seemed at first to go by several names, all of which meant "night" in various languages. Slim suspected, though he had never mentioned it to Cat, that Izbek Noir had made sure Carolyn Early died in a hail of machine-gun fire after she wrote a news piece specifically identifying him and describing the atrocities he encouraged and participated in.

Then Cat had come along, forewarned about Noir by a letter from her sister, and together they had seen him on the Pakistan-India front line. It was said he could not be killed, and his rise to power was as disturbing as it was rapid. Something about Cat seemed to bother Izbek Noir somehow, Slim had observed, and he was sure Cat was in danger because of him. With a sense of dread he had accompanied Cat to an interview with Izbek Noir, *General* Izbek Noir by then, and when the meeting was over, Noir had murdered one of his own men in front of them, then "invited" Slim to remain in his camp as official photographer. He needed the world to see evidence of his victories, he told them, proof of his invincibility, a photographic record which would help the infidel peoples of the world understand the folly of resisting his mujahideen. Cat had refused to leave Slim, of course, but Noir had made it simple. Slim would stay, Cat would leave, or Noir would kill Slim and give Cat to his troops for diversion from their hardships. Slim stayed.

And it has been one heck of a ride so far, he mused. Defeated, he finally spit the tasteless piece of gristle into the dust, and washed his mouth out with hot tea. He began to check his gear, item by item, as he did each night before bedding down. His cameras were clean, loaded, and in their cases. His batteries were charged because he bribed one of the truck drivers to let him use a converter while the truck sat at idle. He carried an old revolver in a worn leather holster on his hip, though he had never fired it in anger, and he kept a hunting knife tucked into his belt, handy.

Within the inner circle of men where he sat were several headquarters vehicles, including antiaircraft and antimissile rigs, radar, communications, and command and staff lorries. In one of them, Slim knew, was General Izbek Noir, planning his next moves, his next horror. Slim glanced around, unsettled. For days now he had not been able to shake the feeling that Noir somehow *knew* or *sensed* when someone thought about him. Slim could not explain it, wished Cat were there to discuss it with him, and tried to let it go, but it clung to the walls of his heart like a dead bat.

Besides, he mused as he glanced around the darkening landscape again, now I know a secret about General Izbek Noir even *weirder* than his apparent invulnerability.

+ + +

General Izbek Noir found eating to be tedious, necessary, and not altogether unpleasant. He sat in his command vehicle, which was set up like a fully appointed camper in the front half. He watched as the young woman who had been sent to him a few days ago prepared a simple meal. She was lithe and supple, with a pale oval face, green eyes, pouty lips, and shiny black hair. One of his officers had found her hiding in the wreckage of an old United Nations helicopter on the outskirts of a border village, and brought her in as a gift. His staff officers and noncoms knew of his voracious appetite for female prisoners, and were constantly on the hunt for new ones for him.

The way he treated prisoners—the elderly left to their fate, males killed outright or occasionally given the choice of immediately accepting Islam or being shot, women and girls used by the troops for their entertainment—set the example for his army. He usually did not keep any female prisoner for more than a few days. When he was done with them, they would be handed over to one of his staff officers, or even the men of a particular unit if it had distinguished itself in battle. By then the young woman would be cowed and compliant, almost pathologically eager to please. Many committed suicide at the first opportunity, and they were often given that opportunity when their captors were satiated.

Izbek Noir leaned back in his chair, admired the girl's unadorned beauty, and felt the warmth of anticipation fill his chest. He paused, aware of something else in the night air, and psychically sniffed at it. Someone was examining him in his thoughts, close. No, there were two—distinct but unrelated. He determined no immediate threat—what could anyone out *there* do anyway?—and let it pass. He thought about the upcoming movements and battles that faced his army in the weeks ahead. There would be more death, more destruction, pain, loss . . . all the bounty of war. Good, he thought. Let it come, let the blood of innocents bathe me in crimson light, let the melodic cries of the vanquished soothe the never-ending ache deep within, let war, this one act of man he manages with success, provide me with the shrieking and pain-maddened harvest that is rightfully mine.

He knew there was a plan. That he did not know it in its entirety, that the long-range goals had not been shared with him, bothered him not. He was there to *war*, to use the most virulent of incendiary fuels—religion— to turn the world's civilizations inside out. Christianity, man's greatest faith, not *his*, against the upstart followers of Islam, with the hated Hebrews in the middle. What could be better? He was there to *war*, and what better thing? The full-throated roar of battle, the fire, smoke, dust, the tearing explosions, ripping machine-gun fire, mines, grenades, missiles, bombs, gas, was a rich and sweet nectar for his always parched soul, and he drank of it until reeling, drunk and replete. The screams of the maimed, the grotesque postures and expressions of the killed, the helplessness of the vanquished, the horror of the prisoners as they witnessed their own executions, these were coveted treasures, and he was grateful for being granted the license to make them real. He grinned at the young woman as she placed his meal before him and knelt at his feet, her head bowed. Eventually I'll stand beside my master, he thought as he ran his dirty fingers through her hair, and reap what we have sown. It will never be enough.

+   +   +

John Jameson, "Rommel" to the mujahideen soldiers he traveled and fought with, kept his face inches from the face of the man he was killing. Their eyes locked, and Jameson felt his opponent's grip loosening on his throat. Jameson's K-bar knife was buried to the hilt in the man's chest, and he held it there with the weight of his body as they lay tangled together in the dust and gravel of a dry streambed. He saw the man's eyes begin to widen and fade, and he said softly, "Forgive me." He felt revulsion over this act of deadly close-quarter combat, and fervently wished it could have been avoided. In a perfect world, maybe, he thought as he felt the man's body relax under him, the blood warm against his knife hand. I am a Christian, he argued with himself, I have accepted Christ, even if too late; I have accepted Jesus Christ into my heart and I cannot kill another human being, I cannot. The body beneath his became forever still, and he wondered how many more there would be.

Weary of mind, spirit, and body, Jameson pulled away from the death he had caused, and looked around cautiously. Over a dozen bodies lay sprawled and twisted around him, all already dead but for one who gagged, cried out for his mother in Farsi, then ceased all movement. The squad of mujahideen Jameson traveled with had entered the streambed on the way to a small rise of high ground, where they planned to set up a night observation position.

The day had been rapidly coming to a close, and the light was already overcome by looming shadow. The first three soldiers in his squad had reached the far side of the streambed when they had been ambushed by a reinforced squad of soldiers who had lain in hiding as they approached. Jameson's squad was in the kill zone, and they died, but not without coming to grips with their enemy, who made the mistake of leaving their positions of cover with the first scything burst of fire. Jameson had emptied a magazine into the charging figures, then had been knocked down by an enemy soldier who tried to smash his skull with the butt of his assault rifle. Jameson had pulled his K-bar, plunged it into the man's chest, and hugged him close while they fell to the dirt together. The action lasted less than thirty seconds, then was done.

Jameson looked again at the face of the man he had killed, then away, then back. It could not be, but he was sure he recognized the man. He crawled quickly to another, rolled him off one of the mujahideen, and closely examined that face. He sat up, looked at two more, and knew. Impossibly, these soldiers were members of a terrorist cell Jameson had tracked and attempted to infiltrate over a year ago. They had loose ties to the old Al-Qaeda factions, a Saudi-Syrian mix of vicious radical killers. Muslims. He wondered what they were doing in Yemen—he was pretty sure they were still in Yemen— and wondered why they would ambush a squad of mujahideen, their fellow Muslims. He looked at the bodies, and knew he would not get the chance to ask. He mentally shrugged. Who knew from radical fringe?

He heard a hissing noise behind him, turned, and saw another squad of mujahideen, led by an old and scarred Islamic warrior whom Jameson had seen before. They were part of a larger unit, and knew Jameson's squad had gone out to set up the night position. They had heard the sound of the ambush, and came to see what was left.

"Rommel," whispered the old Muslim, and he beckoned with one hand. Jameson low-crawled to where the man crouched beside a radioman. "Bad place," said the Muslim. He knew Rommel spoke French and English.

Jameson pointed at one of the crumpled dead mujahideen and said with a grimace, "I told Ahmet this way was no good—a perfect setup—but he was in a hurry."

The old Muslim shrugged. "I will put these men here for the night."

"Good," replied Jameson. "I will join them—"

"No," said the Muslim as he waved the squad toward the slight rise. They collected the weapons of the dead as they passed through the ambush zone, and Jameson saw a mujahid kick one of the dead ambushers in the head as he stepped over him. "You have good skills, soldier of Islam," said the Muslim. "You have some languages. I have other work for you."

Jameson waited.

"Our supreme general," continued the Muslim, "likes to have around him a special group of believers. Some of the toughest or most experienced of our soldiers. They travel with him in the field, make their camp around his, and act on his personal orders. He has sent word out for us to watch for ones he could use, and I believe you can serve him. You are not young, Rommel, but you fight for Allah, you fight well."

"I am but a humble servant," said Jameson.

"As are we all," replied the Muslim. "I have heard it said our general wants this special unit around him for protection, like bodyguards. Anyone who has been in battle with General Noir knows this is foolishness. He cannot be killed. But I am only a simple soldier for Islam, and do as I am told without worry, knowing paradise awaits."

"With His blessing," responded Jameson automatically.

"Yes," said the old Muslim. "Stay with my unit tonight, Rommel, then tomorrow I'll give you a pass and orders to join General Noir's headquarters. Depending on how you travel, it will take only a day or so. I believe you will serve him well."

+   +   +

The misshapen, tortured face of a monster stared out from the mirror's reflection. The sickly pallor, drawn cheeks covered with matted black hair, and inflamed, watery eyes that showed no trace of human origin frightened Ron Underwood as he turned his head this way and that, studying himself. With both hands braced on the sink in the enlarged bathroom with special-needs fixtures and railings, Underwood leaned closer. His foul breath fogged the mirror, his encrusted lips parted to show mossy teeth. And so it is, and so it should be, he said to himself. He felt his leg muscles cramp. They hadn't been used in so long. I have become the nonhuman, nonsalvageable creature I deserve to be, the human waste, scum, spoiler, failure. He sobbed, and shook his head. He was a college professor, a respected scholar, a husband, and a father. Father, said the voice in his skull, Father, failure, father, failure . . . failure.

"Ronnie!" he shouted to the empty house. "Ronnie, my boy . . . Ronnie . . . my . . . boy . . ."

He heard the voice, heard it as it intoned, "God is truth, brothers and sisters . . . and we must turn now to the truth, we must turn . . . turn . . . turn . . . turn . . ."

It wasn't that *other* voice, he remembered, the one in his head. No, it was that preacher's voice on the radio, the radio Ivy had left on, the one she listened to before she drove off. Underwood looked at his reflection again, and laughed. Dumb Ivy heard that preacher's condescending and misguided voice on the radio they kept in Ronnie's bedroom and *believed* it, all that stuff about God. God, salvation, truth, finding the way. Ronnie had been taken that one horrible and unforgivable day.

Ron had been at the college, had seen the disappearances around him with his own eyes, heard people screaming that it was the end of the world, and had rushed home full of foreboding. He had gotten there only to find Ronnie gone, *gone*, and Ivy in a state of quiet hysteria. He had searched the house room by room, calling for his son. Finally he had returned to Ronnie's bedroom, eased himself into Ronnie's wheelchair, and sat staring out the window, physically and emotionally immobilized.

He remembered that voice on the radio, and he remembered Ivy telling him she was leaving the house, *their* house, *Ronnie's* house. She was going to where that preacher's voice came from, from the New Christian Cathedral someplace in Alabama, for crying out loud. Total insane foolishness. "To find what?" he shouted to the empty house. "To find Ronnie? Does that slick-voiced preacher have Ronnie in his pocket? Tucked between the pages of his know-it-all Bible? To find what?"

He was the husband of Ivy Sloan-Underwood, and the father of Ronnie, who had suffered through an accident during birth that left him with permanent neurological damage. Ronnie lived for six years in a state of total helplessness, a "special needs" child who could not run, play, speak, feed or clean himself, or dream . . . as far as anyone knew. During those six years the marriage of Ron and Ivy had slowly, like the rotting of a tree from the inside out, disintegrated. Ivy had been consumed with bitterness, hating her life, trapped by being the mother of a child whose very existence demanded the subjugation of all else in their world.

She was a total caregiver to her son, never turned away from any task, but her love for her son was equaled by her consuming hatred of the injustice of their plight. *Their* plight. She secretly felt she suffered more than her child, who couldn't know any better, and hated herself for feeling that way. She thought her husband, Ron, lived in a pathetic state of denial, going about his daily life as if it were *okay*, trying to act as if he were *happy* around little Ronnie hunched in his wheelchair, *talking* and *joking* with Ronnie all the time as if Ronnie actually *understood*.

For Ron, what became of his wife, Ivy, was incomprehensible. To him, Ronnie was love, plain and simple. He was their child, he was beautiful, and they should be totally proud of him and themselves. Sure, Ronnie had perceived limitations. He had been dealt a bad hand, that's all. But Ronnie was theirs, and he was love. Ron Underwood lived six years loving his beautiful son and watching his lovely wife slowly writhe and shrivel into a twisted, hateful shrew.

"Don't be afraid to take another look at the Word, brothers and sisters," spoke the preacher on the radio. "There are new meanings to those old words that have sustained us thus far, new meanings for a new world and a new promise. Listen to me before you jump to defend the sweet Scripture we grew up with and love. I'm not sullying it, I'm not diminishing it . . . no, no. God is in those passages, and believe me—I know it. But the world has had an unprecedented thing happen to it, has it not? Yes, I see you nod your heads, yes. This is a new world, a new test for mankind, and in these new and difficult times we must discipline ourselves to *take another look* at the sweet Scripture for the *new meaning* to be found there. God is there, and we must find Him again, we must find . . ."

Will you listen to that windbag? said the voice in Ron Underwood's head. Will you listen to his talk about the old Scripture, the new Scripture . . . all of it leading to God . . . God . . . God. Did God take Ronnie? Is that what happened? Ron and Ivy were failures as parents . . . Mommy and Daddy didn't make the grade . . . so God took Ronnie? Is that it?

He didn't know how long he had been sitting in Ronnie's wheelchair, hips squeezed tight, stomach knotted. He knew he was weak from dehydration and lack of food, and that his clothing was foul. Ivy had heard that preacher, and said she was going to him. She had already told Ron she had met Satan for lunch—*Satan for lunch*—and had sold her soul to him before all this happened. Ronnie was gone to heaven or Alabama or someplace, and he was left to sit there in Ronnie's room pondering it all. He decided he was mostly angry. He could never be angry at Ivy, never could. He loved her, and that was that. Ronnie was only love to him. Love and love—nothing else—so he was not angry at Ronnie, certainly. No, he decided he was angry with God. Philosophically, he reasoned, it was okay to be angry with God. God the Father, who would forgive His children for being angry when they were hurt and did not understand some act of God. He would be okay with it.

He decided he was angry at that radio-voice preacher. It really bothered him that the preacher, the *Reverend* Henderson Smith, spoke with such authority, as if he actually *knew* what was going on. He spoke with enough authority to make Ivy turn toward him. She actually drove away from their California house right after the craziness that followed the disappearances. She thought Henderson Smith, that know-it-all, would *explain* things.

He picked up a small stuffed animal that lay on the floor and brought it to his face. Ronnie's scent was on it, and he let it wash over him. He stood in the middle of the room, swaying, humming a tune about Christopher Robin, dreaming of Ronnie. He pursed his lips, nodded, and came to a decision. He would chase after Ivy, chase after her all the way to that New Christian Cathedral. There he would find the Reverend Henderson Smith, purveyor of distorted truth. So what if it will not bring Ronnie back? said the voice in his head. You will be doing this sad world a favor. It won't bring Ronnie back, it won't make Ivy happy, but it will say something to God . . . a little sacrifice to get God's attention regarding the distortion of truth. His own dank and putrid smell wafted around him, and he remembered the monster in the mirror. Oops, he thought, I'd better clean up a bit. Can't go off across the country looking like this. He began to strip off his clothes, excited about his trip, and his mission.

He would go to the New Christian Cathedral, find Henderson Smith, and show him what it was like to lose everything that mattered to you.

CHAPTER FIVE

Tommy Church stretched his long legs, looked at his dad, and asked, "So what are we gonna do when we get there?"

"We'll listen," replied his dad, Thomas Church. They were in Church's Bronco, headed east on I-20 out of the Dallas area. They had discovered that some semblance of order was being restored around the larger metropolitan areas, power, water, transportation, hospitals, police forces, roadways. Many of these parts of the civilized infrastructure were coming back on-line. It was still a bit wild and unpredictable between the large cities, so they carefully planned each leg around info they learned about the best places for food, gas, and lodging, and the bad areas where it was not safe to stop. "We'll listen," Church repeated. "Listen, learn, and plan. Then we'll go forward."

"Okay, Dad."

The resignation in Tommy's voice made Church turn

and glance at his son. The boy was hurting, and it made Church hurt too. This isn't the kind of world our children are supposed to inherit, he thought. "Here's the thing, Tommy," he said. "Life . . . apparently . . . goes on. The disappearances have happened, millions have left life here on Earth, and it might very well be the Biblical end times. It might be something else, too, granted. But let's go with the end of the world for discussion's sake, okay?"

"For discussion's sake," said Tommy.

Ignoring his son's derisive snort, Church went on. "So these are the end times, and here we are, living life. Those of us not taken can either lie down and die, or wake up every day and keep going. You and me, Tommy, we're gonna keep going . . . that's how we're built. Biblical or not, this is a whole new world, and I'm not sure it's going to be pretty. It will have to be reformed, reshaped, and a lot of that is going to be dangerous and painful. Are you with me?"

"Still here, Dad."

"We could drive back to the University of Virginia, back to Sissy's place, and move in. You always got along with Mitch, right? Could make a new life. I heard on the radio the other day many of the larger universities are going to try to reopen, for the sake of normalcy and continuity. A step in the warding off of anarchy. With our government clearing the wreckage of the disaster, and life's basic necessities becoming available again, we might actually have time for centers of learning and free thought."

Tommy shrugged. "You sound like some kind of TV ad or something. What's the deal? Why can't you just talk to me?"

Church eyed the speedometer—he was holding steady at seventy. If he could just hold steady against his son's anger, he felt, he'd be okay.

"Yeah, I know," said Church, nodding his head. "Who cares about college during the end of the world? But . . . your sister is there with that great thinker of a husband she's got, and she's family, and it would be a place for us." We could find your mom, he added to himself, find her and convince her to help me put this family together again.

Traffic in front of them began to slow, and Church slowed and pulled into the right lane. They crept forward for a few minutes, until they came to a police roadblock. When they finally pulled up to the officers standing in each lane they were told to stop. Two officers, backed by two more with assault rifles, leaned in and took a look at the two of them, then the interior of the Bronco. Then they were waved on, with no explanation.

After getting up to speed once more, Church said, "I didn't want to ask them what was going on. Did you?"

"No, Dad," agreed Tommy. "Rangers don't exactly have a reputation for having a sense of humor. Even before all this."

"Well, I guess that's the way it's going to be now," replied Church. "Life will get back to 'normal,' but it will be forever different. But"—he held one finger up to make his point—"but we still have to *live it.*"

Realizing that his father had a point, and that at least for now his new reality was that his father was back in his life, Tommy decided to drop the attitude.

"What kind of shape are we in? America, I mean, Dad."

Church paused and collected his thoughts. "The good old USA is not as bad off as other places in the world. We took a hit, no doubt. The government had to begin fuel rationing. The military was getting it all and it is justified because of the war now. I mean, even before, when our relationship with the Arab countries was strained, we were getting less, and now . . . forget it."

"Why are there still so many National Guard troops everywhere?"

"Oh, just to keep order, I suppose." He paused, then added, "At first—remember, you were out of the loop there as far as information input—things were messy. People panicked, there were runs on the banks, grocery stores were looted, mobs tore gun stores apart, bad . . . bad. The vice president, Clara Reese, took over in Washington, and she is apparently a get-it-done lady. We had kind of a limited martial law for a while—troops everywhere, cops, checkpoints. They set up grocery days and fuel days, everything was strictly controlled. It worked pretty good in most metropolitan areas, not always so good in the outlying, smaller places."

"Look out, Dad!" shouted Tommy as he pointed out the windshield.

Church swerved the Bronco violently to avoid a cluster of wooden pallets in the left lane. After a moment he grinned and said, "Must have fallen from a truck. Scared the heck out of me."

"So anyway, Dad," Tommy said, "the state of the country?"

"Well, there were brownouts, blackouts, then rolling blackouts. When it first happened, everyone thought it might be a huge terrorist thing, or the terrorist organizations might be part of it, so they shut down the nuclear reactors. You had your key personnel gone. Power plants, hospitals, you name it. We were running, but not on all cylinders."

"Must have been bad in places around the world where it was *already* bad."

"In some ways that's right, Tommy. We are lucky this country was so strong when it happened, or who knows what this would look like. But I'm sure there were other places that remained pretty much the same. Nothing from nothing leaves nothing. That kind of thing."

After a moment Tommy said, "So we'll go to hear this preacher, then to Virginia, to Sissy's school, and live happily ever after?"

"That's a possibility," said Church. Then, hoping to lighten his son's dark mood, he added, "Hey, Tommy, you know those campuses. Bet you could meet some nice young lady and—"

"And what, Dad? Get married, have babies? Continue on with our sorry human race?"

They drove in silence for a few minutes.

"Dad," said Tommy after he took a deep breath and let it out slowly, "I don't think it matters a diddly what we do. This world, as part of God's plan or not, is spiraling down. The couple that ran the River Cross Ranch that I worked for, they were always trying to talk to me about the Bible, about my relationship with God and all. They were good people, and I liked them and my work there. But I figured I'd get to the Bible in my own time, or not. God was there. I mean, you took us to Grandpa's church where you and Mom were married, we did Sunday school, all that. If this is the end of the world as described in Revelation, then we've just seen the beginning of the hurtin' that's comin'. If it's just man destroying the planet all on his own. Well, that will be more hurtin'. Either way, why should we worry about a future if the future looks like a bad deal all the way around?"

"So you want to simply lie down and die?"

"Dad, I don't know what I want to do, okay?" answered Tommy, his voice strained. "I'm just getting used to being with you. And it would be great to see Sissy again. But don't talk to me about meeting girls."

"Because of Maria?" asked Church, knowing he was pushing it.

Tommy stared out the window. After a moment he said, "Dad, have you ever heard a girl's name in your heart every time your foot hit the ground, every time you took a breath? A girl that was in your head constantly . . . like . . . like some life force herself. I mean . . . when she and I . . . were alone, just talking, I would look at her eyes and hear her voice and nothing else in the world would matter. You're probably gonna think this is pretty lame, Dad, but Maria and I knew we were gonna get married, and you know what? Other than holding her hands or kissing her I never, we never . . . you know." He cracked his knuckles, fidgeted with his seat belt, then went on. "I mean, we planned to wait, till when we were married. Then I'd have a better job maybe, might have managed to buy into part of an outfit or somethin'. Then we'd have kids." He looked out the window again.

Church reached behind him, pulled two sodas out of his cooler, handed one to Tommy, and popped the top on the other. He thought about the first time he danced with Iris, Tommy's mother, about the first few weeks they were together, about being young and in love. He took a long sip from the can, wiped his mouth with the back of his hand, and said tentatively, "Maria sounds special, Tommy."

Tommy held the cold soda can against his forehead, his eyes closed. Then he said, "She was sweet and pure, and she went to church. One in town, said her family went there. She was a *nice* girl, and she really liked me. She thought we could make it work."

They drove in silence, both wrapped in their thoughts.

"So here's my problem," said Tommy after a few minutes. "Maria was good. But she wasn't 'taken' during the disappearances. If this is a spiritual thing, then apparently God didn't think she made the grade, right? Okay, so she's not taken, but then in the total craziness and panic that happened right after . . ." His eyes went out of focus, and his voice softened. "I was on the south range, my horse was shying and neighing, just spooked like I'd never seen. She was in the main house . . . you can imagine what was going on there, how frightened she must have been when those animals—they could not have been men at that point, Dad, they must have been *animals*—came for her."

He paused, licked his lips, then went on. "I found her huddled on the floor in one of the bedrooms, her clothes messed up, blood on her face. She had wedged herself into a corner beside the bed, rested her head on her knees, and died. She *died*, Dad, and I came riding in like the big hero . . . couldn't find her, nobody knew nothin', wild things happening. Then when the foreman explained the . . . the . . . disappearances, I kinda figured right off what it was, and it clobbered me but I thought of course Maria would have been taken too, of course she was in heaven. But no, I found her, saw what they had done to her. . . ."

He stopped again, his hands bunched into fists. "Then . . . then it was hell to pay for a couple of hours. They even shot the horses . . . I hadn't even turned mine out . . . he was a quarter-paint, Dad, smart . . . and they shot him and got behind him for cover. I went into a kind of rage, I guess. I just wanted to *hurt them*, to make them pay for what they did. I knew I was wounded while it was going on, they shot at us, one tried to cut me with a big knife, I did some shootin' . . . it was . . . like a crazy movie with no laws . . . just beasts killing other beasts. Then I was walking, thirsty, lost, didn't know what I should do next, didn't know if it was a week, ten days. Was standing beneath those raggedy trees when you stopped there, thank . . . goodness."

"It couldn't have been raw luck that I found you, Tommy," said Church quietly.

"Was it part of God's *plan*, Dad?" Tommy's tone was equal parts accusation and plea.

Church could see that Tommy was teetering on the brink of some void, a hard fall, and knew he had to be careful with what he said. "I don't know, Tommy. . . . I really don't know."

"So why we goin' to this New Christian Cathedral, then, Dad?" asked Tommy.

"Oh," replied Church, "yeah. That's what you asked me before I started talking about what our various choices might be. And don't forget my house up on Long Island. We could go there, I could salvage what is left of my business. We could live a life there." Again, his heart aching for his son, he said, "You could meet one of those New York girls . . . USDA prime, and all that."

"Will you forget about me meeting girls? I met the girl. I loved the girl. There aren't going to ever be any others."

Church let the silence linger.

"Besides, remember our discussion the other day about whether or not we as humans can still reproduce? All the children were taken, this might be the end of the world, and we may not be able to make babies. So what would be the purpose of finding the right girl . . . procreation, or recreation?"

"I didn't know cowboys knew such big words."

"There ain't no horses in New York worth talkin' about anyway." A sly grin spread across Tommy's face.

"So we don't know right now what our future looks like, right?" said Church. "Okay. I've been listening to this Reverend Henderson Smith with his New Christian Cathedral on the radio when I pick up the station. I don't know. He preaches the Scripture and thumps the Bible, but he says things that make me think. He sounds . . . rational. And he has more than once alluded to a leader who might take the world, reshape it, stand it up on its feet again, and make a go of it."

"A preacher talkin' politics?"

"In a way," responded Church. "He talks about reading the Scripture in the new light of the aftermath of the disappearances. About a one-world organization—and church, I guess—that will help men quit killing each other and live in peace. First the Muslim armies, these mujahideen, have to be dealt with. Then all the governments of the world have to sit down and agree to . . . I don't know . . . erase the borders, embrace some kind of one-world unity. This Reverend Smith, he's got the voice, he's got the message, and I thought it would be interesting since we're on the road anyway to go by there, take in a sermon, and see what it's all about."

"Okay, Dad," said Tommy. Then he asked, "So who is the one who will bring all this together? Not Smith, right?"

"No, Smith is just a preacher. The one he keeps mentioning is a world diplomat named Azul Dante."

"Azul Dante? What kind of name is that?"

"It's the kind of name that has millions of people listening," said Church. "I had read a few things about him before the disappearances. He was an up-and-comer before the craziness, jumped onto the world stage, and was being touted as a mover and shaker."

Traffic began to slow down again. Ahead of them they could see many tanker trucks. The fuel shortage was being eased by the formation, and police escort, of convoys of tanker trucks in and out of major distribution centers. They could not see if there was an accident, another roadblock, or what.

"Dad?" asked Tommy, "are these tanker convoys part of the war with the Muslims, or the disappearances, or both?"

"I would say both," replied Church. "It's still being rationed somewhat, and when they move any of it they do it in convoys because of how vulnerable the pipelines are."

"So, is he here, in the U.S.?"

"Azul Dante? Paris, I think."

"So we'll go to Selma, Alabama, listen to the good preacher, then go to Paris to sit at the feet of this new world leader?"

Church raised his eyebrows. "Paris? What a great idea." He rubbed his chin. "Paris . . . Paris . . . now there's a place a guy could meet a nice . . ."

"Dad," said Tommy, "will you forget it?" He grinned. "Maybe *you* could find a nice French girl . . . in the interest of foreign relations."

"And maybe you could find a horse."

At that moment, as Church slowed with the other traffic, a white van came up on the right shoulder, accelerating rapidly. As the van roared past, Tommy could see two young men inside. One wore a shawl or some kind of loose ski mask over his face. The white van swerved around a police car that cut across the swale to intercept it, then roared forward until it plowed into the bunched-up convoy of tanker trucks.

Church slammed on his brakes, and they saw the entire traffic jam in front of them enveloped in a sheet of exploding flame.

"What the . . ." said Tommy, violently thrown forward as Church jammed the Bronco into reverse and stomped on the accelerator. "Dad! What is . . . ?"

Church felt the Bronco hit the car behind them, wrenched the wheel hard over, and heard the screech of metal as he backed against the other car, then cleared it and rolled onto the grassy shoulder. "Suicide bombers!" he yelled. "Muslim bomber maniacs!"

Like Israel, which had experienced it for years, America had felt the frustrating sting of the Islamic fanatic homicide bombers for several months a few years ago. Though deadly and painful, the bombings had failed in the aim of frightening the United States into submission. In the end, the bombers had hurt their own cause, as America denounced the killers as representatives of their imams, their holy men, and held them up as what Islam was really all about. Muslims in America, most of them moderate, though silent, paid a terrible price as a result. The wave of bombings sputtered to an inconclusive, hurtful end, a wasteful gambit that gained nothing but sorrow and retribution.

"Muslim killer bombers," said Church as he felt another car glance off the left side of the Bronco, "blowing themselves up outside of Shreveport, Louisiana, for crying out loud." The mushrooming fireball in front of them grew at an alarming rate. It filled the entire windshield, sucking the oxygen from their lungs. Punching explosions followed the first, and here and there cars and parts of cars were blown into the air, some like a huge string of metal, burning popcorn, turning and twisting as they fell back onto each other in heaps.

The hood of one car spiraled through the air like a giant flaming Frisbee, and fell into a large motor home that had skidded into the relative safety of a line of trees bordering the highway. People could be seen running back and out onto the grass, some leaving smoke trails. Here and there a blackened figure tried to crawl away from the wreckage, only to be caught and consumed by the billowing red-orange beast.

"Oh no!" cried Tommy. "Oh no!" He yanked his door open and jumped out.

"Tommy!" yelled Church. He watched as his son ran toward the flames, slammed the gear shift into park, gritted his teeth, almost fell as he opened his door and stepped out, and followed him.

+   +   +

It was weird being in someone else's place. It was a *nice* little apartment, well appointed, and the few pieces of art hanging here and there in the three rooms appealed to Cat as she made a quick inspection. It was located on a tree-lined block in the Twelfth Arrondissement of Paris, and if she stood on tiptoe Cat could see the bulk of the Bastille off in the distance. All the rooftops around the apartment building looked like the kind a chimney sweep would visit. She plunked her bag down on the floor, went back to the open door, and smiled at an old woman peering out at her from a doorway down the hall. The woman timidly smiled back, and Cat closed the door. She felt grimy and exhausted, but a little bit excited, too. Paris. She had a sudden thought about Slim, out there somewhere with Izbek Noir and the mujahideen. She would have liked him to be here, now, sharing this.

The apartment belonged to a girl named Tanya, who "did something for one of the big airlines." Cat's bureau chief in the City of Light, a smooth operator with a British accent and Italian suit, had given her the key. Tanya was one of his "nieces," he explained, out of town just then, and she would be perfectly happy to make the apartment available to a visiting journalist in need of a place to rest her weary head. Cat was so tired by the time she finally got to her bureau's offices that she would have settled for anything, but her chief had explained that hotel rooms were at a premium because of all the political meetings going on. Azul Dante being in town was a big draw, he added. Cat got her marching orders: "Be there on time, and don't show up looking like you just came from the front, okay? Lose that whole dirt-encrusted combat-journalist look, will you?" Cat had stuck her tongue out at him as she left.

It was known that Azul Dante accommodated the media, though he liked being covered by the A team. He had provided a few gilt-edged press passes for a cocktail reception to be held in his honor this evening, after his various scheduled events, and Cat was given one. Her bureau chief would be there also, and she guessed he had picked her to attend in hopes of avoiding any appearance of favoritism among his own staff. She figured she wouldn't win any Miss Popularity awards from the local female journalists, but . . . oh, well.

She began to untie her boots. No need to look in her bag for something suitable for the evening. She had time to bathe, then run out and try to find something in a nearby shop, but it would be close. She held each sock at arm's length as she pulled it off, then left the rest of her clothes in a sulking pile on the floor. Feeling funny, but emboldened by her assignment, she checked the closet in the small bedroom. Nice. Tanya-who-did-something-for-the-airline had some pretty outfits, and miracle of miracles, they looked to be Cat's size. Hanging fresh in a dry-cleaner bag she found a nifty little evening kind of thing, saw the shoes, the small glittery handbag . . . oh, yeah. She hurried to run her bath, and hoped she wouldn't fall asleep while soaking.

Two hours later she took a long sip of champagne, enjoyed the taste of it, the feel of the bubbles, the feel of the glass in her hand . . . the *specialness* of it. That was her sip, only one. She had never been a drinker, still wasn't, but she liked champagne because it was . . . champagne.

She had also learned that having a glass in one's hand at an affair like this completed your look. She was an attractive young woman with glossy dark hair cut short and shaggy, with a trim athletic body, a minimum of makeup, wearing a simple black dress with spaghetti straps, tight at the waist. Her black shoes matched her bag, of course, and her bare shoulders were smooth and creamy white. She had a direct gaze and kept her back straight, and her champagne glass never needed refilling. Many men in the ballroom of the hotel, and their women, took a long appreciative or calculating look at her. She was a head turner, but certainly someone else's woman.

It was funny, she mused as she took a look around. The setting, the people, it was like the opening of a major new museum, or the opera, or even a well-to-do charity or political fund-raiser. There were chauffeured limousines out front, doormen standing tall, crowds of onlookers hoping for a glimpse of someone famous or notorious. The hotel was beyond five-star, and the staff proud and aloof as only the French can be, showing by their bearing and expression that all there that night should be grateful the hotel had deigned to host the event.

The ballroom was enormous, tables set, several bars serving drinks in addition to the waiters carrying goodies and bubbly. Everyone there was dressed to the nines, women coiffed and bejeweled, men stalwart in their tuxedos, the jewels they flaunted being the ceremonial medals and ribbons on their chests awarded for some long-ago deed of valor. A fifteen-piece band played waltzes and show tunes, lights shone on fine Baccarat crystal and gleaming plates, and uniformed waiters moved through the crowd, trying to be as unobtrusive as the coterie of security types hanging behind every curtain.

Cat felt dizzy for a moment, disoriented, by the rapid change of place, yesterday to today. At least they don't have those champagne fountains, she thought, a bit uncomfortable with this display of opulence and comfort in a world turned inside out. You are in Paris, Cat, she told herself, at a state dinner for Azul Dante. These people are obviously trying very hard to cover the hard reality of what the world has become with this glittery veneer, a bit like the last hour of the *Titanic*. So? You have an assignment. Go with it . . . and enjoy the moment.

Sophia Ghent saw Cat Early before Azul Dante did, and both were affected, if for different reasons. Hovering in attendance these last few weeks, Sophia had found it entertaining to watch how the media types reacted to being around Azul. Supposedly hard-edged skeptics, most of them were quickly swept away by Dante's intelligent and sincere allure. It was difficult to remain distrustful or antagonistic toward someone who was as confident and gracious as Dante, and most journalists were drawn to his side in support of his message within a few moments of first meeting him.

Perhaps because of his decisiveness, his bearing, his mysterious cloak of power, the female newswriters always seemed, to Sophia, almost flirtatious around him. He was wealthy, urbane, and a widower—single, but a man who had known commitment in the past. On occasion Sophia stood to the side while two or three professional women surrounded Dante, hanging on his every word, almost fawning over him. It was as if he were a rock star or something, she mused. Then she turned her mind to more important concerns.

Since the incident with James Devane, Sophia had tried to read Dante more carefully, to detect any sign of interest on his part. She found none. The two of them had quickly fallen into their routine, and there'd been no flare-ups of what Sophia had to admit was her hope that he'd been acting out of jealousy. Worse still, she'd left several messages for James at the U.S. embassy, but when he'd returned her calls, he'd been evasive and aloof. They'd met once for coffee, and he told he that he'd been warned about being seen with her. That an edict had come down from nowhere that he knew specifically that he and Minister Dante's young staff member were to stay away from one another.

James told her he had no doubt that the origin of the warning was from her boss, but he had no specific proof. Sophia was skeptical, but James assured her that the message was made very clear to him. Until they could figure out a secure channel by which to communicate, they would have to let the silence linger. He would figure something out, but he was worried, not so much about his own career, but about what might happen to her.

She missed his company and realized that until she'd gotten to know him, however briefly, it had been a long time since she'd had anyone to confide in. Cat Early struck her as someone who could relate to her sense of isolation.

She knew a number of other things about Catherine Early as well. One of her duties was to screen interviewers or petitioners requesting time with Azul Dante. He liked to know more about them than they knew about him, and this usually kept him from being blindsided by a question or argument. This one had lost a sister, another journalist, to one of the wars, and she was obviously trying to follow in her sister's footsteps. An only child, Sophia could merely imagine what that must have been like.

Cat Early had become a respected reporter in her own right, Sophia admitted. She drew clear pictures with her words, and managed to humanize events she wrote about. Sophia also knew that Azul Dante always asked that any stories she clipped from the international papers for his early-morning perusal, and copies of those on the Net, include pieces by Cat Early, if posted. She admired the ease that Cat seemed to bring to her interactions with Minister Dante, saw the two of them smiling politely and nodding, bringing their champagne glasses to their lips to prevent anyone from overhearing their off-the-record remarks.

"Tell me, Cat . . . is it too soon to call you Cat? No? Then tell me, does the number seven mean anything to you?" asked Azul Dante as he looked into Cat Early's eyes. He watched her closely as she shrugged.

"Seventh heaven, Minister Dante?" tried Cat. "the seven dwarfs? *The Magnificent Seven*? It's a nice number, Biblical, less than eight, more than six." She had no idea where he was going. She had just been introduced to Dante by her bureau chief, who with a smile left them standing together. When they had first entered the hotel foyer earlier her chief had leaned close to her left ear and whispered, "Try to find out what this guy is *really* all about."

"Sometimes I feel I am surrounded by the seven dwarfs at these dreary functions," said Dante. "But then someone like you shines through, and the evening sparkles."

"It must be the champagne," replied Cat, disquieted by the intensity of his gaze. "I'm usually not this shiny."

An attractive woman with her hair done up and sprayed, porcelain complexion, big eyes, and full, crimson lips came from behind Dante and stood at his left elbow. Cat shifted her shoulders in her dress, felt as though she'd erred by not wearing something as formal as the beautiful ball gown that this stunning young woman wore. She'd seen her just off to the side of the receiving line earlier, and Cat had briefly thought that she was someone's daughter. She could tell that the woman was part of Dante's inner circle by the way she brushed against him and placed one hand lightly on his arm. "Ah, Minister Dante, I see Miss Early worked her way to you before I had the chance to properly introduce her."

"Quite," agreed Dante. "But of course Cat needs no introduction, right, Sophia? Cat Early, Sophia Ghent . . . my girl Friday, and Saturday, and Monday, Tuesday, Wednesday, Thursday . . ."

"This is a pleasure."

"Mine as well."

The two women exchanged warm smiles. Cat immediately thought that another way to get the inside scoop on Minister Dante would be through Miss Ghent.

Dante, pleased at being in the vortex of so much energy, went on, "Simon Blake, your bureau chief here in Paris, speaks highly of your work, Cat. Sophia and I have seen some of it, of course, well crafted, direct, discerning."

"Thank, you, Minister Dante," said Cat. "I feel very lucky to have the opportunity to witness world events and try to capture them with words."

"And capture them you do."

"Miss Early, how you manage to keep your perspective when you witness such awful events is extraordinary. Your focus on the refugees, the helpless victims, it truly serves as a rallying cry."

"I think that all journalists hope that their work will resonate with their readers and spur some action. You're very kind."

"Perhaps," Dante said, "I am revealing a bit of my age by saying this, but that is perhaps a woman's greatest strength—the ability to empathize. It's a quality that was sorely lacking before and since." Minister Dante shrugged his shoulders.

"Careful, Minister. I feel a speech coming on, and me without my tape recorder." Cat took another sip of champagne and realized that the jet lag might be taking more of a toll on her than she'd first thought. She was being a bit more forward than she normally was. But there was something about the minister's warmth that seemed to encourage it.

The moment was broken by a tall African American man with graying hair and military bearing. He was on the American ambassador's staff, Cat knew, something to do with security. "Minister Dante? Sophia? Sorry to interrupt," he said casually. "Just wanted to give you a head's up. Ambassador Davies and Prime Minister Gardaine are hoping you'll say just a few words before the night goes too long."

"Absolutely, Clarence," responded Dante with a nod. "Give me a wink and a wave, will you, and I'll be right there."

"Thank you, sir." The man walked away.

Dante turned to Cat and said, "And you're clairvoyant as well as empathic. My speech will be brief, but I have numerous other engagements this evening. There's never enough time, Cat. I know your boss wants you to throw some questions at me tonight, if for no other reason than to justify his consumption of this fine champagne. Fire away now, and perhaps we can arrange a more in-depth meeting sometime in the next day or so, yes, Sophia?"

"Of course, Minister Dante," answered Sophia.

"Clearly the world is in turmoil, Minister Dante," began Cat, not sure if she would in fact get another shot at it. "We may be witnessing the *end* of the world. People are frightened, thus vulnerable. You have stated you believe you can set the world back on an even keel, heal the divisiveness, stabilize the economy, bring 'peace and prosperity.' My question is this: Since an important component of this equation is getting people to trust you, what can you tell us about how you've suffered in the wake of the disappearances? How can you get people to empathize with you? After all, empathy is the cornerstone of trust."

Dante stood quite still. His eyes seemed to harden for a moment; he used the fingers of his right hand to brush the shock of salt-and-pepper hair that fell over his left eye. It fell back, and he said, "Charlatans, hucksters, false prophets. Of course, they are everywhere when a great need arises. Necessity is the mother of invention, but she's also bred avarice and ambition, no?"

Cat couldn't help but smile as she was pulled from the shore of her convictions to remain impartial.

"Your question is a challenge, of course. But let me first assure you that I suffer from neither avarice nor envy. And from any other of the seven which you failed to mention in your recitation. By the way, I'm very fond of the scene in *Paradise Lost* when the seven deadly sins parade. I was taught by a blind professor who surely had an insight into what the blind poet Milton must have felt, and who was himself alight with a fire that must have burned within Milton."

"But you digress, Minister Dante."

"I certainly do. Perhaps so that I might linger a while longer in your presence. But also because, if you will forgive me, I find a focus on loss to be counterproductive. My humble beginnings are documented, where I came from, my early years, the loss of my loved ones several years ago. Yes, I've suffered additional losses, as we all have, but it is only by looking forward that we can move forward. Am I the best last hope? Perhaps. My basic makeup will not allow me to stand by and do nothing while the world and its peoples literally collapse into dust. I am a leader. Perhaps my best skills have to do with coordinating the leadership and capabilities of others, perhaps my voice for some reason cuts through the din of hysteria and histrionics that howl at foolish man while he crouches, cowed, in all four corners of the earth. Perhaps . . . I am simply the last best hope."

Cat, struck by his words and the immediate force of energy with which they were delivered, tried to speak, but her mouth was suddenly dry. She nodded, as if to say, "Okay . . ." Sophia Ghent stood silent beside her champion, a small smile animating her face.

"Yes," Cat finally managed. She took a breath and charged on. "Why 'Prodigal Project'? Are you the prodigal son? If so . . . how?"

"Are we not *all* the prodigal son, Catherine Early?" Dante answered softly. He began to say more, but was interrupted by Sophia, who squeezed his arm, put her lips close to his left ear, and said, "Azul, Clarence is signaling us now. They need you up on the podium to say a few words."

Dante, his eyes never leaving Cat's, let out a breath, smiled, and answered, "Yes, Sophia. Of course, Sophia. So. Cat Early, I must go do my duty, sell myself to the dubious crowd, yes?"

"Yes," said Cat.

"Breakfast, eight in the morning, my hotel," said Dante as he turned away. "Sophia, you will join us of course."

"Yes, thank you," replied Cat. She watched him walk

toward the waiting crowd, and thought, That man is re-markable.

As Azul Dante turned his back on Cat Early, Sophia beside him, a word vibrated in his mind like the toll of an ancient temple bell: *Seven*.

+   +   +

Tommy Church hurled himself into the inferno on I-20 three times. Each time, he pulled smoking or burning men and women from the twisted and ruptured cars, trucks, and campers. Once he had two, one by the hair, the other by one arm as he dragged them onto the shoulder of the pavement, then down the grass embankment and away from the heat. Thomas Church helped his son stretch the victims out, then grabbed at him to stop him from going for more, but Tommy fought him off and ran headlong again into the fire.

The fourth time, Church followed his son, pulling at him, yelling at him. By now those who would live were away, the rest were lost. But Tommy either couldn't or wouldn't see it. A sedan had been trapped between a large SUV and an eighteen-wheeler. The front and back of the sedan were crunched, which warped the doorposts. Tommy could see three people in the vehicle, two in front, one in back. He saw how they heaved their shoulders at the bent doors, saw their gaping mouths as they struggled for breath and gagged on the thick fumes that surrounded them. He ran through a burning stream of fuel to get close enough to grab the right side door handle, and stared into the eyes of the old woman who sat there hitting the glass of the window with the flat palms of her hands.

The handle was red hot, and he could not hold it. He saw the girl in the backseat try to kick out the glass, and looked around wildly for something he could use to free her. But there was only fire, and he was coughing now, his feet scorched, his eyes squeezed tight against the toxins. He felt his father pulling at him, yelling at him, and he gagged as he let himself be hustled away from the heat. His eyes locked with those of the young woman in the backseat of the sedan. *I don't want to die I don't want to die I don't want to die* begged her eyes.

Then, possessed of a strength that he'd no clear sense of having, he broke from his father and jumped, kicking his heels at the car's back window. The pain seared through his legs, but he broke the glass. In a few moments, he managed to pull the trio free. Arms linked, they wound their way through the wreckage.

Church forced his son to sit on the grass. A heavyset man wearing an Atlanta Falcons football jersey ran over with a large plastic jug of water and began pouring it over Tommy's shoulders, back, and head. "Did you see what he did?" shouted the man as he pointed at Tommy. "Did you see what he did?"

Church nodded. Then he coughed, "Yes, yes . . . thank you. He's okay, he's okay now."

The man poured more water into Tommy's hands, and watched as he splashed it onto his face. "Did you see what he did?" said the man again. Then he walked away, shaking his head. Church saw him calling to a group of people helping others who were stretched out on the grass. The man was pointing at Tommy, apparently telling everyone what he had witnessed. Church could hear sirens in the distance, and saw several police officers and firefighters already on the scene. He heard Tommy sob, and looked down at him. Tommy sat with his elbows on his knees, his face in his hands, and sobbed.

Church watched his son, proud and frightened by what he had just watched him do. He patted Tommy's hair clumsily.

An hour later they were eastbound once more, the scene of the explosion miles behind them. Tommy had insisted they leave without giving their names or asking for treatment. His hands had several small cuts and burns, and he had a three-inch worm of burned tissue just above his wounded elbow and a nickel-sized burn on his left temple. His left eyelashes were gone, as was most of his left eyebrow. His shirt was scorched in several places, and the heel of one boot had melted off on one edge. Church had stopped a mile or so away from the carnage, taken his trusty first-aid kit, and treated Tommy's injuries while Tommy quietly drank from a bottle of water. Once they were moving again, Tommy sat staring out the window, and Church did not try to bother him.

+   +   +

"Dad?" said Tommy, finally. "Dad . . . did you see them?"

"Yeah, Tommy, I did," answered Church, not sure which "them" he meant. "You did good."

"Did you see them, Dad? Those people as they burned, as they died?" Tommy turned in his seat, his hands up, an intense, almost angry expression on his face. "They were fighting so hard, Dad, *fighting*: fighting to stay alive. Fighting to keep . . . on . . . *living*!"

"It's a natural thing, right, Tommy? To try to cling to life?"

"But why, Dad?" asked Tommy, his face confused, sad. "Why do they—do we—fight so hard to cling to our lives, our sorry, tiny, worthless little pathetic lives in this huge cold universe? God does this—put this thing in us—something that makes us want to hang on to life even when it *stinks*. Why?" He rubbed his face with his hands, and winced as he hit the burned area. "Now we think it might be the end of the world, and what are we doing? Not just you and me or those poor people burning in their cars . . . all of us. What are we doing? We're clinging to life, to our lives. We are at war all over the world over *religion*, for cryin' out loud. Those guys in that van that crashed into the tanker trucks and blew themselves and everybody else up think they're out there *killing for Allah*. Then the ones caught up in it fight to their last breath to save themselves and their tiny lives. Why, Dad? Why? Is this all part of God's plan? Dad, I've asked you before—is this all part of God's plan?"

"What about those three people you saved, Tommy? Where'd the strength come from for you to do that? I've never seen a person move like you did, especially one as hurt as you are. And what about you? Why didn't you just give up and let those others die? You could just as easily say that you were clinging to the idea of life and surviving."

"Dad," Tommy continued, "those others we watched burn. Were their sins *expiated* by the flames? Did they go to heaven, Dad? Can anyone still go to heaven if this is the end of the world? Did Maria go to heaven, Dad? Can we still go to heaven?"

"The Bible says over and over again, Tommy," Church ventured, "He is a loving and merciful God. If you believe in God, I guess you'd have to believe He was loving and merciful." Don't ask me about the wrathful part, he added to himself.

"Did those people receive mercy, Dad?"

"Tommy. I . . . I don't know."

"Why did we fight so hard, Dad, to live?"

"Maybe because this life is the only life we *really* know of for sure, Tommy," replied Church quietly, aware of his son's bravery and anguish, filled with pain because of it. "Maybe it's the only life we know of for sure."

Tommy was silent for a long time. Then he pounded one fist on the dashboard and said quietly, "It's because our lives mean something, Dad. Our lives mean something, *we* mean something, this is not all some biological accident, God is real, and there is *reason* . . . and our lives *mean something*."

Thomas Church felt his son's words, his son's wisdom, strike his heart, and he was humbled.

CHAPTER SIX

It was a small hotel, perfectly French, old wood, tall glass windows, comfortable without being stodgy. Cat learned where Azul Dante was staying from her bureau chief, used an old tourist map, her fragmented bits of French, and the help of a couple of patient Parisians, and walked from her borrowed apartment to the hotel. She arrived at two minutes before eight, went to the small desk in the lobby to ask, and spotted Dante sitting alone in a reading room off the lobby. Soft light and muted street sounds poured through open windows above the sidewalk outside.

Dante stood and smiled as she entered, and motioned her to a chair to his right. She sat, and he offered American coffee or café au lait and pastries from a silver tray that sat on a small table in front of them. She gratefully accepted black coffee, having somehow botched the pot she'd attempted back at the apartment. She wore no little black number this time, but neat khakis instead. Shirt tucked into shorts, heavy socks rolled down on top of hiking boots. She wore no makeup, and was scrubbed and fresh. This time she had her recorder, and got it out after taking her first long sip of the hot and rich coffee.

"Good?" asked Dante.

"You may have just saved my life," she answered.

"Yes." He watched her a moment, relaxed. Then he sipped from his own cup, and said, "I didn't see you after my short address last night, Cat. Did you go out for drinks with the rest of the journalists? Simon told me that was the plan."

"Simon always has a plan," replied Cat. Her bureau chief's reputation and appetite for young female newsies had not been diminished by the current state of the world. "But, no," she added, not sure if Dante was simply making small talk or if he was actually interested in her night, "I was tired, and I didn't come here to drink with the boys and have wild nocturnal adventures." She finished the coffee, poured herself another cup, sat back, and said, "I got a good night's sleep so I'd be ready for this morning. And here I am."

"And here you are. Sophia will be down shortly."

"I know you are an important figure now, Minister Dante," said Cat, "and I understand your schedule must be crazy, so I want you to know first that I appreciate this time." She had left the event last evening convinced she had put Dante on edge, which was not an uncommon occurrence in her line of work, but she hadn't been prepared for the intensity of his reaction, and hoped to

negate any acrimony, if there was any. "Second, as a journalist I ask questions that can be perceived to be antagonistic or critical, when actually they are designed to get
the best, or least contrived, response."

"As if any response *I* might give would be contrived,"
he replied with a smile. "Worry not, Cat. I understand
the positive side of adversarial debate. Your questions are
direct. So? That's what you get paid for."

Cat nodded. She wanted to try one of the pastries, but
didn't want to try an interview while chewing.

"Go on," said Dante, waving at the tray, "have some.
This is breakfast."

"Thank you." They were, as expected, delicious.

"Now, Cat," said Dante after a moment, "tell me, do
you know your Bible?"

She shrugged, and gave a small laugh. "Would that
fall under the guise of 'doing your homework before any
interview'? I'm like most people, I guess. I don't know it
chapter and verse, I've never really *studied* it . . . although
I have been reading it more lately."

"You asked about Prodigal Project," continued Dante.
"After challenging my sincerity." He smiled. "Much has
already been written about the project, of course. It has
to do with returning to the fold, I suppose. Man, returning . . . I mean. Of course you are perfectly correct about
man's vulnerability now, and of course we should all be
skeptical of anyone who stands up and says he has the answer. It all comes down to instability. The world is in turmoil, this breeds fear, fear breeds desperate acts, and the
world becomes a more fractured and unstable place."

He sipped from his cup; Cat unobtrusively pulled out a pen and took quick notes.

"You already know all this, of course," he said with a shrug, "so what does man need now? What do *we* need? Not a screeching rabble of misguided and power-hungry voices vying to outdo each other with self-centered methods for curing the earth's ills, no. These, man being man, usually have to do with making war on some pretext or another. War will help the economy, war will get rid of those who are hurting us, war will bring peace. Forever. Sad."

Cat nodded, and asked, "The mujahideen? Not a problem? A religious war . . . aren't they the worst? You know already that most of the Judeo-Christian world, including America, is looking to you as the one who will build on your European Coalition, build an army, and eventually destroy Izbek Noir and his hordes." She hesitated. "Isn't that war to bring about peace, peace and prosperity?"

Azul Dante sighed. "Yes." He brushed a lock of hair away from his eye, tried not to sound as if he were being patient with her as he added, "Peace and prosperity will come at a price, of course. There will be much work among men of differing views, languages, cultures. Most successes will come through leadership and cooperation. Some—Izbek Noir is a perfect example—will not listen to reason, will not see the majority of people before them, will not submit. Yes . . . war, in that case, will bring about peace." He leaned forward in his chair, closer to her. "Cat, listen. The reason I've willingly decided to be a part of this entire enterprise, the reason for the Prodigal Project, if you will, is this," he said, his voice intense. "Man can look at what has happened to his world as the end. All is lost, all will die, all of the reasons for man, this whole experiment, have failed. It is the end, and man can fight with himself in a bitter quagmire, until man is no more. Or"—he took the fingers of his left hand in his right—"or man can see this as an opportunity for victory, for a cleansing, unapologetic, shameless acknowledgment that *what was before did not work*. In addition to an individual, the prodigal son can be described as an attitude, or an awareness, a coming back to the things that make man function as a creature with his own *free will*, his own *pride of self*. Not dependent on some abstract or ephemeral deity, but a creature, a race, *in control of its own destiny*." His eyes went out of focus, and he licked his lips. Then he added quietly, "Now bring the robe, the ring, the sandals. Now bring the fatted calf. What was dead, what was lost, banished, is found, is alive again. Now . . . celebrate."

She watched him, his eyes, and felt a ripple of fear.

He let out a long breath, sat back, laced the long fingers of his hands across one knee, and said, "The project has to do with more than any prodigal son, figurative or literal. It has to do with a free world of man. I am simply trying to help orchestrate that happening by bringing like minds and hearts together. I would rather accomplish this through dialogue, but if war becomes the only answer, I will help make war until there comes peace. Then I will get back to the business of"—he forced a smile—"diplomacy in hope of freedom."

"Minister Dante?" said Sophia Ghant from the entranceway to the small lobby. Cat had not been aware of her presence. The tall, thin, silent assistant in the severe black suit stood behind her. "I'm . . . I'm sorry to interrupt." She had seen his intensity as he leaned toward the journalist, and her voice sounded almost timid as she added, "But Drazic has the car ready." She pushed her left wrist out of her jacket sleeve and pointed at her watch.

Cat, somehow glad for the interruption, and hoping to start anew with Dante's assistant, smiled, stood, made a show of putting her recorder in her bag, and said, "No, Sophia. I've already taken too much time, and you must go crazy trying to keep Minister Dante on track with all the distractions . . . like pesky reporters."

She was rewarded with a smile, and a look on Sophia's face that said, *If you only knew.*

Dante, who had stood as Cat did, took another deep breath, smiled, and said, "Not to worry, Sophia. You probably just saved Miss Early from another one of my dreadful and endless speeches." He turned to Cat, took her hand, gave it a squeeze, and said, "Hope you got a little bit more insight, Cat. Enough to write something Simon won't put on the spike, yes? Perhaps we'll meet again."

"I'll look forward to it," replied Cat automatically. He had used a word that bothered her; something . . . didn't fit. She told herself she'd find a quiet moment, replay it in her head, and find it. "Until then." She walked out of the room, smiled at Sophia, and said, "Thank you," quietly as she passed her in the lobby. Then, turning quickly around she asked the young woman for her card. Sophia handed her one, pulled it back quickly and wrote her cellular number on the back. "We're forever traveling it seems. If I can be of any assistance, please let me know."

"I'm sorry we didn't get to speak at length. I'm sure you've got quite a story to tell as well."

Sophia ducked her head and pushed her hair back, uncomfortable with the thought of being in the spotlight. But if that was the only way for her to gain Cat Early's confidence so she could help her and James figure out what was behind their forced separation, so be it.

Catherine Early left the hotel and went for a long walk through the streets of Paris. It was a glorious day, with a blue sky perfect for daydreamers, artists, poets, and other unbelievers.

Azul Dante watched her go, and again the bell tolled *seven*.

+   +   +

The girl's face filled the viewfinder of Slim's camera, and he brought it into sharp focus before pressing the trigger. He knew he had captured her cold, dreamy beauty, her aloof stillness, her look of peaceful freedom. He fought the urge to pull his face back from the Pentax so his eyes could take in the rest of her and the close surroundings. He moved to other targets. Here the maniacally twisted skeleton of a large truck lying canted into a crater, a tendril of black smoke coming from the ruptured skull of a charred body. There a clump of what only moments before had been men, hurled and tumbled together as they died, their mouths open in silent screams. His camera went back to the girl, but he forced it away.

His ears were still ringing from the blast, or blasts. It had been a hot, sullen afternoon, not long before the call to fourth prayer. They were in the low foothills in northern Yemen, dry, barren. Sweet tea and bitter coffee simmered on small fires, soldiers sweated as they worked on weapons or equipment, officers hurried busily from one command vehicle to another. Warnings had been shouted from the command truck and radar trucks at almost the same time: "Missiles incoming from the north!" Reflexively he had rolled off the hood of the small water truck he was sitting on, hit the ground hard, and curled into a fetal position behind a small mound of rock and dirt. As he went down he heard more shouts, saw two or three shoulder-fired missiles launched from the northern perimeter, and heard the buzzing of several track-mounted miniguns as they exploded into life. That was all before the consuming, elongated roar of powerful warheads igniting firestorms throughout the headquarters area.

He was not sure if he had screamed or not. He felt his chest constrict as the air was taken from his lungs, felt the buffeting of the blast tear at his clothing. He hugged his cameras, and waited for the pain of searing shrapnel as it tore through his body. But it did not come, and after a long moment he lifted his head, shook it vigorously to get the gravel out of his hair, and tried to clear his ears. Then he sat up, checked himself for new holes, and began to look around. He heard someone shout as he trotted past, "Some type of cruise missile! Two at least . . . still no fix on them! Where are our early-warning-system aircraft? *Both* of them?" He had brushed his camera off, and began walking around, documenting the results of the attack.

The first vehicle he looked for was the supreme commander's headquarters truck. He was pretty sure General lzbek Noir was inside when the missiles came in. Maybe they took him out this time, he thought. The general's personal command post was completely wrecked, the cab ripped and burned, the large, ungainly body that housed his briefing and communications sections and his living quarters blown right off the frame. There were gaping holes in the sides, the rear doors hung open on their hinges, the roof had a ragged tear along one side, and from this curled a billow of gray smoke. Two or three bodies could be seen in awkward postures in or near the vehicle, with one or two more blown several feet away. The girl was one of those. Slim had walked closer to see if it was the girl who had been serving the general for the last two days. As he confirmed this and lifted his camera, he saw Izbek Noir, simple uniform blackened and dusty, his eyes bright in his soot-darkened face, come into view inside the blown rear doors. He watched as the general jumped lightly out of the vehicle, glanced inside once quickly, then began looking around for his senior officers. He walked away, shouting at someone, and Slim thought, Unbelieveable.

The mujahideen captain in charge of headquarters security had already given all the belated orders he could give. He saw the general, thanked Allah silently for sparing their leader once again, and prayed Noir would understand that the security unit could not be expected to stop incoming cruise missiles. He left the dark soldier who stood beside him and wide-legged it after his leader. The other soldier too had watched carefully as Noir showed himself to have survived. No emotion registered on his face, although he had risked his life to affix a tiny, powerful transmitter the size of a button to the undercarriage of the command vehicle two nights ago. He began to walk toward the wreckage.

Slim could not stop himself from turning once again to the girl. Her sweet face was the only part of her that had not been broken and torn by the blast. She lay flattened in the dust like a shattered child's toy, arms flung out to her sides, fingers splayed. Death had allowed her to escape Izbek Noir, and whatever humiliation, degradation, and pain that would have followed after he was done with her. Those cruise missiles set you free, innocent child, Slim thought as he captured the girl in the viewfinder again.

Then, hesitantly, he forced himself to slowly drop the camera from his face. He saw her then with his eyes, his heart. He wanted to capture her there, wanted her to find a permanent resting place in his memory, never to fade away. As he stared, he saw movement out of the corner of his eye. It was one of the Muslims, a dark soldier, a big man, dusty like the rest. The soldier carried an AK, and there was a trickle of blood on his left hand and arm.

Slim watched as the soldier glanced at him, then at the girl's body on the ground. The soldier turned slowly, apparently checking to see if anyone else was near, but most of the activity was on the other side of the wrecked truck. Then the soldier, unconcerned about Slim's presence, knelt beside the dead girl, pulled a shawl from a pack he had over one shoulder, and quickly covered her broken body with it. Slim could see the man's lips moving as he held the cloth above the girl's face a moment, then gently cloaked her staring eyes with it. He knelt there another moment, leaning over her and the shawl that became her shroud. Then he stood and began walking away without looking back.

"Hey," called Slim after the man. "Uh . . . hey . . . wait a minute there." He recognized this one now. Sure, this was one of the new Muslims brought in from a frontline unit. One of those who were handpicked by their leaders as replacements for the general's security company. Slim had seen the man when he first came into camp three or four days ago. The guy stood out because of his size, his age—looked like he was in his early forties maybe—and his Western features. Not your run-of-the-mill Arab type.

Slim had done a little checking, mostly out of boredom and curiosity—although he *did* want to know how any Westerner could join these crazies, Muslim or not—and had learned a few things. The mujahideen leaders thought highly of this soldier, who was quiet, obedient, good in battle, and secure in the faith. He spoke a couple of languages, knew his way with weapons and equipment, and handled the hardships of living in the field as well as any younger man. That was all Slim had on him, so far.

"Hey," he called again as he tried to catch up with the Westerner. "Hold on a minute."

John Jameson stopped, but did not turn to face the young photographer. He waited for him, though, and when Slim was beside him, said quietly, "Let's keep walking, okay? We're making a damage assessment, right? We're walking the perimeter, you are taking photos, which is your job, I'm checking to see if I can nail down the incoming direction of the missiles, which is my job, yeah?"

"Yeah," said Slim. After a moment he said, "Dutch, right? I heard you were Dutch . . . South African maybe? Don't they call you Adolf, or Hans, or something like that?"

"I'm Belgian," said Jameson. "I'm called Rommel."

"Rommel? What kind of name is that for a Belgian Muslim?"

Jameson stopped, looked into the photographer's eyes, and said, "And you are Slim . . . when you could just as easily have been called Dusty, Disheveled, Snoopy, or Dumb-as-a-post."

"No, really," replied Slim as he walked behind Jameson, who had stepped off again, "Rommel works for me."

Jameson continued walking toward the perimeter. He

had planned to make casual contact with the photographer anyway, as a possible communications or information source. This was as good a time as any, he reflected, pushing the image of the dead girl deeper into his heart. He knew others might die when he stuck the button-sized transmitter under the command truck, but if it resulted in Noir's death, it would be worth it. Thus would go the argument made by his bosses back in Virginia. Collateral damage, baby. The girl was in the wrong place at the wrong time, hanging out with the primo target of Jameson's career. Besides, it was common knowledge how the young female prisoners were treated by Noir and his gang . . . probably did her a favor. Jameson hated being who he was at that moment, hated what he must do, and wondered who Rommel really was. Please, Jesus, help me, he thought.

He was also disquieted by the fact that, sure enough, when the explosions eviscerated the command truck, making it untenable for any living being, out stepped General Izbek Noir, shaken but not stirred, all working parts still in place. Maybe this guy *can't* be killed, he mused. Or maybe I'll just have to do it up close and personal, if I get the chance. The cruise missiles had not been his idea anyway. The strategy noggins back home thought they were worth a try, and if they failed, Noir would not see them as any different from the other incoming stuff thrown at the mujahideen by various enemies all the time.

The captain in charge of headquarters security hurried up to Jameson then and interrupted his thoughts. "Rommel," said the captain, "as you saw, General Noir was not injured, Allah be praised. But he is not a happy general, no. He gathered the staff officers and told us such pinpoint accuracy could only have resulted from pure blind luck—which he discounted—or the best satellite and computer-enhanced technology. He said it was either the Hebrews or the Americans, or the usual dishonorable and incestuous marriage of the two."

He paused, and chewed at his lips. "This cowardly attack will be answered, of course." He turned to walk away, then said over his shoulder, "Massif is dead. Take his platoon. You report directly to me now, Rommel, then to the general."

Jameson looked at the man, and at the small, still figure of the covered dead girl in the distance. "I am humbled at this chance to serve."

"Good," said the captain as he walked off.

"Some promotional system they've got in this outfit, huh . . . Rommel?" said Slim as he watched the man go.

"Yeah."

"Of course Noir would blame it on the Israelis," continued Slim. "You want to get your Muslim brothers fired up, just point your finger at the Jews. Gets 'em every time."

Jameson, without looking at the young photographer, said quietly, "You don't stay here taking publicity shots of the good General Izbek Noir because you want to, do you, Slim?"

Surprised by the question, Slim hesitated before he answered, "Shucks . . . Noir made me one of those offers, you know." To make sure Cat got away from that beast, he thought, I'd have sold my soul. "It may not be the greatest assignment," he added, "but for a combat photojournalist, in these times, it's not a bad gig."

Jameson turned and made eye contact. "I understand," he said.

Something about the way he said it made Slim take a chance. "Listen, uh, Rommel. I'm gonna go earn my pay and take some hero shots of our fearless and peerless leader over there," he said. "In an hour or so, if you can, come by my palatial foxhole for a cup of tea, and I'll show you something of interest."

"Tea would be good," said Jameson. In the distance he could see Izbek Noir, surrounded by a gaggle of staff officers, staring at him.

Two hours later the sun hung low in the streaked and heat-rippled western sky, huge, and syrupy red, like a drop of blood on the skin of the universe. There was less than an hour of daylight left, and here and there small cooking fires brought momentary comfort before the night. General Izbek Noir's headquarters battalion had regrouped, refitted, and reequipped after the cruise missile attack. The ruined vehicles and dead bodies were left where they lay, and the replacement vehicles were in new positions.

It was learned that the forward electronic warning aircraft had been downed by Spanish fighter aircraft seconds before the cruise missiles had been launched. It was thought the missiles came from ships in the Mediterranean, but this had not been confirmed. No matter. New aircraft were up, the perimeter defenses had been

augmented by outlying antimissile, tracked vehicles—
Russian made, seized from the Egyptians—and the losses
had been negligible. Their leader was invincible, the mujahideen said to one another as they shook off the effects
of the attack. He lives under Allah's smile, they whispered, and we are blessed to serve both.

Jameson, his duties as Rommel complete for the moment, made his way to Slim's small encampment a hundred meters from the center of the armored vehicles'
night position. He saw the young photographer wave at
him as he approached.

"Glad you made it," said Slim with a grin. "The tea is
hot, and there's still enough light for me to show you
something."

Jameson accepted the tin cup of hot brown liquid,
sipped it with appreciation, and said, "Allah is merciful,
and your tea is delicious."

"Allah runs with a bad crowd," responded Slim, trusting his instincts. He sipped his own tea, watched Jameson
a moment over the rim of his cup, then reached into a
knapsack resting on the side of his foxhole and brought
out an envelope. "I found the basic darkroom setup in
one of the supply trucks, if you can believe that," he said,
"and I've made friends with a comm guy in one of the
satellite trucks who lets me print from his computers."

"Photos?" asked Jameson.

"I'm supposed to document General Noir, and the results of his campaigns," continued Slim. "That's why he
had me stay, supposedly. So I tag along, shoot some of

the carnage, and when he gives the approval, I can actually get a feed into one of the international pools so maybe the shot will wind up on the front page of one of the biggies." He shrugged. "I have to trust that somewhere my editor-agent back home is keeping tabs on my successes, so someday maybe I'll see a paycheck for my work."

Jameson waited.

"I know," said Slim. "Who cares. But here's the thing. Often the general will call to me—'Photographer, come here, make photo of me with this burned church'—and I'll zip over there and say cheese and freeze-frame the horror. He especially likes ruined churches, piles of bodies, enemy prisoners begging on their knees before one of his staff officers blows their brains out. That kind of stuff."

"A prince of a guy," said Jameson.

"A real sweetheart," agreed Slim. "So, okay. I take his shot, print it myself or hook it up if its digital, and voilà . . . Noir is immortalized. Good. But every now and then, in the action, the heat of the moment, I'll be shooting like I normally do when working, and Noir will be in the frame."

"And you get into trouble for taking his picture without permission?"

"Nah, not really," replied Slim. "I don't think he really cares. But look at these. Tell me what you see."

Jameson took the sheaf of prints and quickly looked through them. Brutal, hard, stark photographs of war, people, places, and things destroyed. Pain, waste, death.

Then he went back and looked at several more carefully. "What are these smudges or blurred places on these shots? Did you erase an image or something using the computer?"

Slim grinned, laid four of the prints on the sand, and said quietly, "Nope. Those are shots that include General Noir in the frame."

"I don't understand," said Jameson, fearing he did.

"Noir was in the shot," explained Slim, "but not posing for me. Then when I got the negative, or the digitized frame, developed, Noir was . . . not."

Jameson looked at the photos again, but said nothing.

"Those 'smudges,' those 'blurred places,'" continued the photographer, "are all that shows of the good general." He gazed at Jameson, a troubled look on his face. Then he turned toward the falling sun. "Unless he *wants* to be photographed."

"Who have you shared this with?" asked Jameson.

"Only the Rotary Club members."

"I don't know what it means," said Jameson carefully, "but thanks for showing me." He made sure Slim's eyes watched his as he added, "I'm just a simple Muslim soldier fighting for the mujahideen and Allah, here in General Izbek Noir's camp. I'm alone, though, in my mission. I wouldn't mind knowing I had a friend here."

"Ditto," responded Slim, liking the big guy, liking the trust. "This faithful servant would be pleased to share things with you, like tea and info, when circumstances allow."

Jameson made his way back toward the unit he now commanded. He was tired, and longed for sleep. He knew he had to eat something, then make a perimeter check, then confirm his night positions and sensor positions were all tied in. Then he could rest, with one eye open and one hand on his AK.

As he walked across the area between the coiled armor units and the command vehicles, he saw a figure approaching him from a few yards away.

"Good evening, Rommel," said Izbek Noir. He spoke in French.

"General," answered Jameson as he stopped and stood at attention.

"Going about your duties, soldier of Allah?"

"Yes, sir, may he always be just and merciful."

"Yes."

They stood facing each other, silent.

"Rommel?" said Noir after a moment.

"Sir?"

"Why did you cover the girl's body? She was just another empty infidel vessel, a whore of the ignorant and repugnant people who resist us." Noir's voice was almost a sibilant hiss, silvery, slippery. "She was nothing alive, nothing dead. Why take the time, and waste a perfectly good shawl woven by the blessed hands of *faithful* women, to cover her body . . . as if you . . . respected what she was?"

Jameson felt his mouth go dry; then he answered respectfully, "I am a simple man, sir, a soldier of Allah, obedient and well-meaning. I did not intend to offend you, but rather I responded to what I remember of the Prophet's teachings."

"From his Koran?"

"Yes, sir," said Jameson, treading lightly. "Normally I ignore the bodies of those who have fallen, as it is not up to me to sort them out. But I saw the young girl, and a passage from the Prophet made me pause, his words that admonished me to kill enemy soldiers, but leave women, the elderly, and children alone. Perhaps I am simply tired. I have seen a lot of war in my years, sir, and sometimes after an action I feel . . . heart-heavy."

"Emotional."

"Yes, General Noir. I don't know how to answer you, sir. Yes, I saw her, she seemed defenseless in death, so on impulse, I wanted to cover her. And I did." He straightened, and added, "If I have offended you, sir, perhaps it would be fitting to remove me from my security assignment and send me back to a line unit where I can better serve you and Allah without acting on foolish impulses."

Noir watched his eyes for a long moment. Night cloaked his own, but Jameson could see every crease in the man's face. Then Noir nodded, and said, "I'll decide if you stay or go, live or die. Understand?"

"Sir."

"I was simply curious, soldier," Noir added, "and wanted to hear your explanation. Your feelings, though superfluous, are yours, and you are entitled to them as long as they don't get in the way of your service to me. I am told you are a good fighter. Stay with my headquarters, and prove it." He paused, then said almost to himself, "Interesting how varied the interpretation of the Prophet's words. At least *he* wrote his teachings down, or had others record them as he spoke, not like the supposed *Christus*, who wrote nothing in his own hand. The meanings of *His* supposed revelation . . . written years after his death by radicals . . . is still fought over by his foolish followers." He looked around at the night, then added, "We go against the Saudis tomorrow, Rommel. Fellow Muslims, but effeminate, soft, led by a family of effete dilettantes. The pure hatred, and pure unflinching belief and obedience, of the mujahideen will teach them about being Muslim . . . yes?"

"Sir."

"Good night, soldier."

As Jameson walked off, Noir stood watching him. He felt a powerful surge of painful energy pulse in his mind, and then one word was whispered: *Seven*.

CHAPTER SEVEN

Ivy Sloan-Underwood tried to pick up her pace as she rounded the turn for the last half mile of her three-mile jog. She had been running the streets in the quiet residential neighborhood surrounding the New Christian Cathedral on the outskirts of Selma, through a misty ground fog that lay still and cool and wrapped around her legs. She wore running shoes, silky shorts, and an old T-shirt. The sun had been up for less than an hour, and the morning showed the promise of a beautiful day. The fog was a bit strange, Ivy thought as she ran, but she attributed it to last night's gentle rain.

She turned off a side street, jogged across a grassy swale, and hit the tarmac of the huge parking lot behind the cathedral. There were a few cars scattered across it, and six of the school buses used to provide transportation for the faithful who needed rides. Ivy felt slightly winded, but good. Her muscles were warm, her cheeks were flushed, she could feel the blood pumping in her veins. She still spent a couple of hours each day exercising, keeping trim, fit, and attractive. The world could come to an end, she reflected, she could have her heart smashed to bits and her soul flushed down the toilet, but somehow being a good-looking, healthy person remained important to her. She wanted to look good, wanted men to notice her.

The discussions about whether or not people could still make babies, after the children were taken, hurt too much to even think about. No, she wanted to attract a man because it had always been important to her as a person—it helped identify and validate *her*. She was aware that men stared at her, flirted with her, even in the church, even in this convoluted world. They wanted her. Sometimes late at night, in her bed, with all thoughts of her husband, Ron, her son, Ronnie, and her former life buried deep, she fantasized. She thought about being hugged, about looking into a man's eyes as he held her tight, his lips close enough to feel his warm breath on her cheek. Sometimes her fantasies helped her sleep, and she knew she would defend them in argument with the simple statement that she was still a *woman* in this two-sex world.

She caught a whiff of something familiar. It triggered a jolting physical awareness, a rushing of warmth around her body, a sudden dryness in her mouth. She looked to her left, in front of her, and saw a man leaning against a large black Lincoln Town Car. She stopped, and stared wide-eyed, her hands on her hips, her chest rising and falling from the run, and from a clash of intense emotion.

"Thad Night," she managed to say.

"Ivy," said the man. He was tall, with a rugged face, full sensual lips, thick, glossy black hair brushed back from his forehead. His body was lean, and he had big hands. He wore a beautifully tailored pearl suit in a light-weight material, a gray shirt, and a gray tie in the same shade. He had what looked like a Rolex watch on his left wrist, and a knowing smile on those lips. He gave off the scent of the same cologne that lingered in Ivy's memories.

Ivy did not know what to do, which way to jump. Instantly her mind told her to simply lean forward, pick up speed, and keep right on running. Past Thad Night, across the parking lot, and into the sanctuary of the cathedral, the place to which she sensed Thad Night would not follow. At the same time her mind told her to lean forward, pick up speed, ball her fists, bring her knees up, and run right into him—pump her knees into his groin, smash him with her fists, run the top of her skull into his smiling mouth, beat him, hurt him, put him down and kick him until he screamed and begged for mercy . . . mercy. But she was transfixed, frozen, immobile.

"Oh," she said as she gulped several large breaths. She gagged, and fought the urge to vomit. "Oh, God, please help me."

"Nope," responded Night with a small laugh. "Just little ol' me."

Ivy pointed one finger at him, licked her lips, and said, "Get away from here, Thad Night, or whatever your name really is . . . get away from me. Leave me alone, you . . . you . . ."

"Now, Ivy, don't use bad language on such a fine morning as this," said Night. "I had to see you again, I *wanted* to see you again. I understand, believe me, I understand why you might be angry and bitter about what happened. We had a deal, and you feel you were shortchanged."

Ivy, not believing she was actually having this conversation, said, "Shortchanged? You sorry, lousy. Lied to and *cheated*, baby, that's how I feel."

Night stepped away from the car, closer to Ivy. He had his hands up, palms out. "No," he said sincerely, his smile gone, his eyes focused on hers. "We—me and my boss—we managed to do what we could before *it* happened. I know how much you loved Ronnie, how angry you were through his pitiful six years of almost meaningless existence. I know how hard you worked, how you sacrificed whatever life you might have had caring for him even though you could never know for sure if he even knew who you *were*."

"You said you'd make him whole."

"And we did, Ivy, we did. But at that exact moment, it happened—the *taking*—that perverted self-serving world-searing act by one who should know better. All that immediate pain, fear, and grief. I didn't do that, you know it, Ivy. I was in the process of doing what I promised, and then Ronnie was *taken*."

Ivy knew she and Thad Night stood in the parking lot behind the New Christian Cathedral, in Selma, Alabama, stood in the shredded fog a few feet apart, surrounded by the morning, by reality. But there was a muted roaring in her ears, and a total awareness of *him*, giving her the sensation that they stood in some kind of invisible bubble. "You are a liar," she said through a clenched jaw. "You are a liar!"

"Did Ronnie speak to you, Ivy?" asked Night, stepping even closer. "Did your six-year-old boy who had never said a word in his sad life sit in his wheelchair a few feet from you as you sat at the window in his room and speak to you? Did he say that word, that one word? 'Mommy' . . . 'Mommy' . . . isn't that what he said, Ivy?"

"Yes," answered Ivy, defenseless against what happened in her heart when Ronnie was mentioned, when Ronnie saying "Mommy" to her was mentioned. She felt weak, strangely free at the same time, but weak, malleable.

"Is it not better to hear your child call you Mommy once during his life, than never at all?"

She hesitated, weakened but still able to think, But at what price?

"Is it not better?"

"Yes."

"Did we have a deal?" asked Night.

"Yes," she replied.

"Did you willingly agree, did you accept the deal?"

"Yes."

"Did Ronnie say 'Mommy' to you before he was taken . . . taken *not by us*?"

"Yes."

Thad Night took another step, close enough for him

to gently, carefully, reach out and place his big hands on her upper arms. He gave her a slight squeeze, and said as he held her eyes with his, "It's okay, Ivy. It's okay. I know what you want, what you *need* now. Your physical self, a lovely, feminine, hungry physical self tells you every night, every morning, doesn't it? I'm here, and I can be what you need."

She felt his hands on her, felt his strength, his warmth, and a hot rush of desire plunged through her like a coursing river of lava through her soul. But it was as he said, *physical*, and she was assailed by a sudden and overpowering yearning, a longing, a stinging hunger. She felt dizzy at his nearness, his maleness, his presence the clear and immediate answer to her needs. She was hot from the run and gleamed with a sheen of fine sweat, her heart beat solidly in her chest, her skin tingled with tactile awareness of her own clothes, and his hands. A light filled her mind, a light that singed her soul and washed out any thoughts of the cathedral, her lost child, her husband, any other part of her that was not *right there*, right then.

"Yes," she said.

"You have your own room here, don't you, Ivy?"

"No, uh . . . no," she managed. "I . . . I stay with another girl, a girl who lost . . ."

"Is she there now?"

"Yes. No. I . . . I don't know, she may be there, or at . . ."

He let go of her arms and stepped back, and she was swept with a cold wave of air that slapped her, startled her, and immediately released her from the impossible yearning of a moment ago.

"Oh," she said. "Oh."

He smiled. "Now is not a good time, I guess, Ivy," he said in a comforting, knowing voice. "But now you know I'm here, here for you, here to be what you need . . . what you want . . . any time you want it."

"Yes," she said, suddenly very tired. Then she looked into his eyes and asked, "What do you want from me? What can you possibly want from me, Thad—you, or your 'boss'? You can take me as a man takes a woman when you want, and you know it. Is that what you came for? Take it then, and don't torment me. But if there is more, if you want more. What *is* it?"

"Ah, Ivy," he answered. "You are such a beautiful woman, a gift, really." He stepped away and opened the driver's door of the Lincoln. "Just relax, and know I'll be around. Don't worry about things you can't possibly fathom. All things will be revealed, as they say, in their own time." He paused, his face clouded a moment, and he asked, "*Seven* mean anything to you, Ivy?" He saw the blank look on her face, and her shrug. "No matter," he said.

"Can't you just leave me alone?" she asked, her arms down by her sides, her heart aching.

"A fine girl like you, Ivy?" he replied with a grin as he got behind the wheel.

He watched her in the rearview mirror as he drove slowly out of the parking lot. Yes, he thought, that woman is ready, for sure. He chuckled at her helplessness. Man, these threads, this fine ride. This is one great gig. He was momentarily startled when a word was whispered in his mind, and it sobered him. *Seven.*

He drove away.

Ivy Sloan-Underwood watched the big black car as it left the parking lot, moving like a great and malevolent beast through the tatters of fog, and felt her legs shaking. She licked her lips, wondering at how depleted, satiated, her body felt. But the tingling was replaced by cold cramps, and any desire was taken over by a wave of loathing. She walked slowly toward the dormitory rooms, wanting only a long hot shower, and peace.

+   +   +

"What do you think of the whole 'devil' thing, Shannon?" asked Ivy as she walked beside Shannon Carpenter from the dining area of the cathedral. "The whole 'Satan' concept?" She had taken a long hot shower, had not found peace, and had accepted Shannon's invitation to join her for a cup of coffee before Shannon went to do some work in the church offices.

"Satan is real," stated Shannon matter-of-factly.

"You. *know* this," said Ivy.

Shannon stopped, turned, and looked at Ivy's face as she answered, "It's in Scripture, Ivy. I mean, a year ago I would have said a *lot* of things are in Scripture but so what? I felt then that a person could read almost anything she wanted to in the Bible. All you had to do was look at the different Christian denominations and it was demonstrated how people took different meaning from the words." She shrugged. "Now it's all—I'm—different. The words are clear, they make sense. More important, the *meaning* or *intention* of the words is clear."

"Because you have found Christ. You've been 'born again,'" Ivy couldn't keep the skeptical tone from creeping into her voice. She regretted the tone immediately because she had grown to like and respect Shannon, and she wished she didn't have to see herself always competing with other females. But Shannon did not seem offended in the least.

"Exactly," she said. She smiled and added, "I used to think born-again Christians I met had this holier-than-thou attitude—and perhaps some do. But since my acceptance of Jesus, I've come to understand that their perceived aloof or condescending bearing might actually be the result of suddenly being able to 'see' things so clearly, while it is very difficult for a person who has not been born again to see them. It is also hard to explain without acting like you are smarter than the other person, or better than them, which is not necessarily true."

They had sat together in the dining room for coffee, sharing small talk, and bits about their personal lives before the disappearances. Ivy found Shannon to be a good listener, and found her to be a woman settled in her own identity. She was groomed and attractive, but not on the hunt, which Ivy had assumed all females to be. They even managed to laugh a couple of times, and Ivy shared more with Shannon than she had expected to. When they finished their coffee, Ivy agreed to go to the church office with Shannon and continue the visit. Then she had decided to test the waters with the Carpenter woman, to take the conversation up a notch or two.

"What would you think if I said I know God must be real, because I know the devil exists," asked Ivy tentatively.

"Makes perfect sense," answered Shannon. "Nothing in the world, the universes, can be, can exist, nothing *is*, unless it is of God, or from God. He is the 'I Am,' not the 'I am, sort of,' or the 'I am to some degree,' He is, always has been, and always will be . . . and nothing is real without Him. The devil, Satan, the prince of darkness, whatever . . . there can be no devil, no fallen angel who tried to pervert the truth to his own purposes, no beautiful creature cast out of heaven because of his unwillingness to repent—it can't be if there is no God. And God *is*." She turned and smiled at Ivy, and added, "Works for me."

The office door was locked, and Ivy stood by while Shannon dug a set of keys out of her pocket and unlocked it. They went in together, and Shannon turned on the lights, then went to her desk and fired up her computer.

"Pretty cool, huh," she said over her shoulder. "We've still got the Web, we're on-line all across the country and in most places around the world where the governments have stabilized things. America was strong enough, praise God, and we've had great leadership from Clara Reese, our president since the disappearances."

"A *woman*," said Ivy.

"A *black* woman," added Shannon with a grin. Then she said, "Look here . . . this is the Prodigal Project Web site."

"That's the one Reverend Smith is always including in his sermons," said Ivy as she leaned over Shannon's shoulder to read with her.

They were quiet for a moment as Shannon scrolled through the different pages, graphics, and text. The site was professionally done, attractive and informative.

"There," said Ivy. "Go back. Yeah. Azul Dante. Not a bad-lookin' specimen, huh? Single?"

"Uh-huh," responded Shannon as she chewed her lower lip. "Had a young wife and child at one time, according to a bio I read when I first pulled up the site. Lost them both during one of the conflicts in the Balkans, some kind of terrorist bombing. The society and entertainment pages feature him more often than they used to, but he is never shown escorting anyone. Has a female assistant you see now and then. Here. Sophia Ghent."

"Attractive," said Ivy, "for a big-boned girl. Young, too." She laughed. "Well, young and tender will make up for a lot of faults with some older men."

Shannon laughed too, not as interested in Dante's love interests as Ivy. Then she said as she leaned forward, "Here. Now this is a page where they give kind of a synopsis of what they're all about."

"From what Reverend Smith tells us," interjected Ivy, "the Prodigal Project is about bringing all the faiths of the world together to kind of . . . welcome the one new faith, and Azul Dante is the *head* of the new faith. Azul Dante, the world's great white hope."

"You sound skeptical, Ivy," said Shannon.

Ivy thought about that a moment, then said, "I guess I am, but I don't know if I can put my finger on why. After the disappearances I heard Reverend Smith's voice on the radio, and I swear that was about the only thing that kept me going. I *had* to come here, even then knowing I was lost, Ronnie was lost, there would be no happy ending, or peace." She stopped, and the room was filled with the sound of their sadness. She swallowed, and continued. "Since I've been here I've accepted this place as a place to *be*, but I feel like I'm spinning my wheels. I listen to his sermons, and they're comforting and thought-provoking. But I don't know. He seems to be pushing this Prodigal thing pretty hard, and Azul Dante, too."

"Yes," agreed Shannon. "Billy's church—my husband— his church and a few others in our area had already heard of the Prodigal Project several months before the . . . disappearances. They were excited and secretive about it. Billy even wrote it in his Bible, as if he wanted to come here and listen, or as if leaving it for me to find."

"But doesn't it, and Azul Dante, seem *political* to you, Shannon? I don't understand why churches, or Christians, would find it so appealing."

"I don't know for sure, either," said Shannon as she

moved to a different site on the screen. "But my Billy lived his life in Christ, was nobody's fool, and had like a secret smile on his face every time he tried to tell me about it. He mentioned the *return*, and I think they expected . . ."

"The Second Coming?"

"Well, Ivy," said Shannon, "that's what Revelation is about, right?"

"Yes," replied Ivy thoughtfully. "But isn't there also a little something about the Antichrist, tribulations, charlatans, false prophets . . . thousand-year reigns, mark of the beast . . . the world suffers while evil triumphs?"

"Yep."

"Well," said Ivy, "is it the return of the prodigal son, or not?"

They were silent, looking at each other, their faces reflected on the screen over the Prodigal Project graphics.

"Here," said Shannon after a moment, working the keyboard. "Look at these."

Ivy leaned closer. "Financial stuff? What?"

"I don't know," said Shannon. "I'm just pulling up some of the work Reverend Smith has asked me to do. In my former life I worked for a civil law firm that was involved in church financial matters, and Reverend Smith thought I could help him and the NCC a bit."

"Yeah, baby," said Ivy with a low whistle as she looked at the numbers. "The good ol' American dollar has remained tough through this whole thing. Gold standard still good—oh look, there's Azul Dante's name again in reference to the three big global currencies. So? The New Christian Cathedral works on cash, what church doesn't? Gotta have the bucks to keep the lights on, to keep the choir in robes, to pay for the buses, the sound system, the books, the whole kit and caboodle. So? That's what the collection plate is for, that's what tithing is for." She looked at Shannon sitting beside her, and added, "Especially *now*, in these uncertain times when people don't know what tomorrow will bring, if there will *be* a tomorrow . . . they'll dig into their pockets and give to the church, hoping to be on the winning side."

Shannon, knowing she definitely would not have put it the same way, nodded. Then she pointed at the screen and said, "But look here. Reverend Smith has been pressuring me on these accounts. They are strong, and he wants them . . . liquid. You can see here that he has final say and authorization over disbursement, and he has the master access code, no one else. My code is limited."

"Basic safeguards?"

"Yes, I guess." Shannon looked at Ivy and made a face.

They were quiet a moment. Then Ivy surprised Shannon by going off on another tangent altogether. "Shannon," she asked quietly, "what's going on between you and Ted Glenn?"

Shannon shook her head, off guard, and held back the silly reply she had on the tip of her tongue when she saw the intense expression on Ivy's face. She could tell her answer would somehow be important to her.

"Oh," she said, "he's a nice guy, and I enjoy talking with him, and sharing Bible-study time with him. Why?"

Ivy shrugged, embarrassed. "I don't know," she said. "It's kind of nice to see you two. Nateesha Folks told me about it first, and I have seen you two having meals together sometimes, and sitting out on the back patio and stuff, talking."

"It's nice?"

"Well yeah," continued Ivy, "I mean . . ." she stopped, hugged herself, and her eyes went far away for a moment. They came back into focus, and she went on. "The end of the world. The end times. The devil, the saints, mankind suffers, and then is lost. It's bleak. But there's a man, and a woman talking. Looking at each other, laughing about something, sharing time, sharing moments. Perhaps their hands might touch accidentally, or their eyes meet." She shrugged again, gave Shannon a rueful grin, and said, "I don't know. It means *life*. Life, and hope."

Shannon, understanding Ivy's words *completely*, assailed by many conflicting emotions, *including* hope, could only smile, and shake her head.

Ivy reached up, touched Shannon's cheek gently with the fingers of her right hand as she brushed a tear away from her left eye with the other, and whispered, "You go, girl." Then she straightened, her eyes hardened, and she said, "But like you said about the Prodigal Project . . . I can't put my finger on it, but something is not kosher . . ."

Shannon took Ivy's hand from her cheek and

squeezed it. "And we're running out of fingers," she quietly replied.

+   +   +

The midday prayer service at the New Christian Cathedral usually drew a pretty good crowd. This day was no exception, and while not as jam-packed as a Sunday morning, the church was fairly full as the Reverend Henderson Smith prepared to speak. He liked to watch the congregants file in, looking for familiar faces, watching for new. There were new visitors all the time, hopeful, battered, hanging on his words for dear life. He saw Ivy Sloan-Underwood and Shannon Carpenter come in together and find seats near the front, on the left side. Ted Glenn came in a moment later; he lightly squeezed Shannon's hand and the two exchanged smiles. Two men were already in the pew, and stood as the ladies slid past.

"Shannon Carpenter," said Shannon as she turned to a middle-aged man with a gray beard, dressed in hiking boots, jeans, and a plaid shirt. She liked his face, which was broad and open, his intelligent eyes bright with interest and expectancy. Sitting with him was a younger, leaner version without the beard. The younger one had cowboy written all over him, not the store-bought kind, but the real thing. He was slim, with big knuckly hands, a sunburned face and neck, and short hair. He wore no hat, but had that line on his forehead where the skin went pale. He wore frayed jeans like second skin, a leather belt with a large silver buckle, and serious working cowboy boots that were so dusty and broken, they had reached a certain nobility. She offered her hand to the older one, who took it in his firm, dry grasp.

"Thomas Church," said Church. "And this is my son, Tommy."

"Ma'am," said the young man as he nodded at Shannon and Ivy. It was then Shannon noticed his wounds. Looked as if he had been in a fight, a bad accident, or both.

"This is Ivy Sloan-Underwood," added Shannon as she turned and leaned back so Ivy could reach across and shake their hands. "And Ted Glenn." Ted gave a small wave.

"First time to the cathedral?" asked Ivy, liking the looks of Thomas and Tommy Church. Then she added, "I'm from California, and Shannon and Ted are from Ohio. Where are you from?"

"Long Island, New York," said Church.

"West Texas," said Tommy.

Thomas Church was immediately aware of a subtle energy between Shannon and Ted. It reminded him of what he once shared with his ex-wife. He felt their energy was directed toward him as well. He looked at both of them carefully, trying to see if they were people he had somehow known previously, but that wasn't it. He was comfortable with the way they looked at him, and figured maybe they were kindred spirits. Well, he thought, of course we're kindred spirits. All of us who were not taken share something. He saw the sadness in the eyes of both women, and knew they had lost children. The darker one, Ivy, there was something else there, an anger or something.

Shannon gave a small laugh and said quietly, "Seems like I've known you before, Thomas Church, like I *know* you . . . but that can't be."

Ivy was aware of a connection too, couldn't identify it, and brushed it aside. "What made you come to the cathedral, Mr. Church?" she asked, trying to be polite even though still disturbed by meeting Thad Night that morning. She glanced around at the faces, disquieted.

"Thomas, please, Ivy," said Church. "I . . . uh . . . I went looking for Tommy after the, uh, disappearances, and managed to find him." He looked at Tommy, and grinned as he went on. "He was a little worse for wear when we stumbled onto each other out there in the desert."

"He means out there in God's country," said Tommy shyly.

"Then, on the trip here," continued Church, "he ran in and out of a huge explosion and fire a couple of times to pull victims out, and he got more scar tissue—"

"Dad—"

"And we had heard Reverend Smith on the radio and were talking about what has happened to our world and we're on our way to Virginia to hook up with Tommy's sister, Lynn—we call her Sissy—so we decided to stop in to get a bit of the good Word from Reverend Smith before heading north."

"You mean that terrorist bombing incident, where they blew up the gas trucks?" asked Ivy, looking at Tommy intently.

"Yes, ma'am," said the young man, then turned to look up at the huge pulpit reaching up and out over the pews.

"It was bad," said Thomas Church quietly.

"Well, welcome to our church, Churches," smiled Shannon. "After the service we gather for coffee and stuff. Reverend Smith likes to maintain a sort of ongoing welcoming thing. Why don't you join us?"

"Coffee sounds good," said Church. "We can visit a bit, right, Tommy? But then we're gonna get right back on the road toward Virginia, and Tommy's sister." He saw Ivy craning her neck as she looked at the people in the rows behind them, sensed her nervousness, and wondered if she was expecting someone. He could not shake the feeling of a connection between Ivy, Shannon, and him; he had the impression it wasn't a bad thing, the connection, but it was somewhat unsettling. The Reverend Henderson Smith climbed up into the pulpit, and they turned their attention to him.

+   +   +

An hour later, as people filed out of the church after Reverend Smith said the final prayer, which asked God for the courage to accept the new world, Ivy told Shannon and Thomas and Tommy Church she'd meet them in the Club Room in a few minutes. She knew he was there, sitting in a back pew probably, had been watching her the whole time. She had felt a vibration all through the service, felt the eyes on her. It surprised her a little that Thad Night would, or even could, enter the cathedral, being who and what he was, but she was convinced he had. She had no idea what she would say to him when she found him, other than *Get out*.

Many people remained in their seats in the pews, some reading, some lost in thought, a few weeping silently, dabbing at their eyes with crumpled tissue. She had walked closer to the back and was scanning the faces when he spoke behind her.

"Hello, Ivy."

She turned, her fists clenched, her jaw tight, and saw standing there her husband, Ron Underwood. One hand went to her mouth; the other reached out for him. "Ron?" she said quietly as she touched him on the forearm. "Ron?" The man looked like Ron when she had first met him: slat thin, bony elbows and knees, big Buddy Holly glasses, pale skin. But there was no youthfulness there, only deep lines and creases in his face, watery eyes that almost bulged with the intensity of their stare, a dusting of gray on a chin that needed a shave. Ron wore travel-worn clothing that hung on him, tan slacks and a blue work shirt, and he held a small soft-sided suitcase with one hand. She saw he had even stuck his beeper, cell phone, and Palm Pilot on his belt, even though probably none of them were functional, and in his shirt pocket were half a dozen pens.

"How did you get here, Ron?" asked Ivy, pummeled by conflicting emotions. There was a part of her that was immediately and genuinely pleased to see him there, and another part that didn't want him there at all. She did not want to be Ron Underwood's wife right then, that much she was sure of. "What? What are you doing?"

He gave her a lopsided grin, and said in a strained voice, "I was sitting there in Ronnie's wheelchair, oh, I don't know how long. Just sitting there. Had a recurring dream that if I sat in the chair long enough my body would sort of meld with it, I'd become the chair, and I'd be ready when he came back for it. He didn't, and I didn't."

She said nothing, and moved a bit as several people passed her in the aisle as they left. One or two stole a quick glance at Ron.

"But then one day, or night, I looked around and remembered you had gone," he went on. "You had gone off to Alabama after having had lunch with the devil."

"Shh, Ron," said Ivy, looking around to see if anyone had heard him. No one was paying them any attention now.

"You were going to Alabama to hear this preacher," said Ron, leaning closer to her, his breath foul, his watery eyes staring. She had never seen his face wear such an expression of manic confusion, and it frightened her. "Then I was sitting there, you were gone, and I began to hear the preacher too, his big fat condescending words oozing out of that radio. His smarmy little Bible stories, his smirking guarantees of salvation if we would only get the truth from *him*." He nodded, smiled, and added, "So I got up out of that chair, took a long cold shower, grabbed some stuff, and headed out." He paused, looked all around, then back at her. "I started out hitchhiking, but people are so mean. Then I took buses a couple of times, but I got confused trying to figure them out. Then . . . I don't know, I walked a lot. A nice policeman let me stay in his jail for two days while it rained in Oklahoma or somewhere." His eyes went out of focus, then came back. "They had really good sticky buns in that jail."

"Ron," she said, frightened for him. He was a well-respected college professor, an educated, urbane, witty, fun man with a good moral structure who had done his best through many hard years. The Ron standing in front of her now seemed so lost.

"I don't know, Ivy. I finally got here, well, to Selma, in a car. I don't know who it belonged to or how I got it, but I locked it up when I parked it and walked away."

Ivy did not know what to do next. She was sure Reverend Smith would find a place for Ron to sleep for a few days, feed him, let him rest and clean up a bit, but then what? She had no time for this. It would have been bad enough if Ron had showed up squared away and capable of participating in things, but in this state he would need care, would need watching over, would need her.

She was not ready when he reached up, touched her left cheek gently with the fingers of his right hand, and said, "Ivy. I love you. I love you and I've missed you and I've found you and I want to be with you."

"I . . . I love you too, Ron."

"Do you have a place to live here?"

"Yes. Yes I do," she answered tentatively. "I have a room that the cathedral provides for me now."

"Good," he said. "Let's go there. I need a shower. Then I need you. I've been away from you too long."

"But, Ron . . ."

"No buts, and no headaches, either. None of that stuff. I'm your husband, I've found you, and I want to be with you. Even in this screwy world a man can be in the same bed with his wife if he wants to."

She fought an onslaught of panic, and for one inexplicable moment her mind flashed to a picture of them when they were young and in love, how physical it was, how satisfying, how fun, how *good*. But that was then, and this was now, and all he was doing was frightening and angering her. She needed time to think, time to figure out what to do about Thad Night, what to do about *her*. . . . She needed time.

"Ron," she said, "it's not like that here. I can't."

"What's that supposed to mean? Can I come to your room, or not?"

"I . . . I have a roommate, Ron, another woman who lost everything. She shares my living quarters, and we can't just—"

"You didn't lose *everything*, Ivy," said Ron as he stared at her. "Just your child. You still have your husband."

"Yes, Ron, but—"

"Tell that preacher to move your roommate to *his* room. Then I can come and stay with you."

"No, Ron. We can't do that."

They were silent as they stared at each other.

"Okay," he said after a long moment. He grinned, and shrugged.

"Ron, I . . ." There were too many words, and not enough. She stopped and looked at him helplessly.

"It's okay, Ivy," he said as he brushed her cheek once more with his fingers. "You don't have to explain. I can't just show up here and expect you to . . ."

"But what will you do now? Where will you go?"

He lifted his small suitcase off the floor, looked all around slowly, and answered, "Oh, I'll find a place near here. Might want to come back and listen to the good preacher some more. I'll be close, in case you need me." He rubbed his nose, took off his glasses, polished the lenses between his thumb and forefinger, and said, "Pencil me in for a cup of coffee or something."

Ivy, relieved but still unsettled, said, "What . . . what did you think of Reverend Smith's sermon, Ron? Make any sense at all? I mean, really, we're all kind of . . . groping here."

"Oh," said Ron, "I guess he thinks he's got it goin' on, and he's dishing it out fast and hot for all the hungry and scared people who don't know what to do next. He didn't tell me a *thing*, and I don't know . . . seems like he's trying real hard to sell that Prodigal Project, and that fancy European guy that runs it."

Ivy knew she should have been surprised that he had the same misgivings about Smith's sermon, but she wasn't, and she knew she should try to defend the reverend, but she didn't.

"Anyway, Ivy," said Ron evenly, "don't you worry about the Reverend Henderson Smith. I'm here to take care of *that* problem."

"What do you mean, Ron?"

"I love you, Ivy," he said. He turned and walked out, and did not look back.

She watched him go. Her stomach cramped, she felt dizzy, and she took several deep breaths to try to calm herself. Then she headed to the Club Room to join Shannon and those two new visitors. She had heard Church tell Shannon he and his son were going to leave right away, and she felt the need to spend more time with them. It was as if she already knew them, or something.

CHAPTER EIGHT

Israeli prime minister Daniel Pearlman rubbed his left earlobe between his fingers, looked at his lifetime friend and confidant, Moishe Schimmel, and said, "So?"

"'So?' 'So?' You sit there like the Great Sphinx and say to me, 'So?'" responded Schimmel. Many observers of Israeli wars and politics had stated or written at one time or another that when God got done making Daniel Pearlman, who was a big man, tall, heavyset, powerful, with a broad, handsome face, a full head of thick silver hair, and a heroic nose, He picked up the shavings and made Moishe Schimmel. Mutt and Jeff, Frick and Frack, said the observers. If Pearlman doesn't want some combative statement to come back and haunt him, he simply puts Schimmel on his knee and keeps his lips pressed tightly together while Schimmel seems to talk. They said it with an undertone of respect, though, for Moishe Schimmel had left a few pieces of his left side and several pints of blood on the desert sand in defense of Israel.

Schimmel held up his left hand and grabbed his fore-finger with the fingers of his right. "Look at how he has risen since those crazy disappearances," he said to his friend. "All of a sudden he's leading one of the most diverse and powerful coalitions to be seen in ages. I mean, they can't sign the agreement treaties fast enough." He took the middle finger. "The Russians, if we can still call them that—they look more like the old Soviets nowadays—are kissing him but giving *us* the evil eye, and they are from the north, yes?"

"Everybody is to the north, from here," said Pearlman. They sat in his office in Tel Aviv.

"Listen, and learn," replied Schimmel. He let go of his middle finger and grabbed the last two, which had been welded together by fire. "Last, he promises peace and prosperity, if . . . *if* the world does it his way."

"So?" said Pearlman.

"So there is a worldwide drought, in case you haven't been paying attention. Millions are starving, the world's food production is plunging, and here in Israel we're growing more than we need. . . . I mean, we are exporting *tons*—countries are begging us, *us*, for food. They hate us for it, but what else is new? His 'prosperity' will come from *our* fields. So now he's got your signature on this agreement, this promise—he actually used the word 'covenant' in one of his speeches," said Schimmel, sitting up in his seat and leaning forward. "A covenant between his European Coalition—which the Americans are a part of even if they are all the way over there across the sea—

and Israel, *us*. Don't act so obtuse about this, Daniel, you know what I'm saying. Go back to your Bible studies."

Like many educated Jews, both men had studied the Bible as a theological and philosophical exercise, and were conversant with its similarities to and differences from their own Talmud. Daniel Pearlman sighed and nodded his head, but did not respond.

"The thing they are calling the disappearances," said Schimmel. "It occurred on a global scale, in an instant. Remember the series of odd earthquakes that racked the world just before? Do you not feel that gaping hole in your heart where all the children used to be, Daniel? *All the children*." Moishe Schimmel's eyes went out of focus a moment, and he added quietly, "If you know there is going to be a terrible action taking place in a certain section, a certain town, one of the things you do—you've done it yourself—is remove the children from there, *all* of the children, if possible. *You get the children out of the line of fire, out of harm's way.*"

Pearlman looked out of the window of his office toward the courtyard below. Leave it to Moishe, he thought, to go right to the place of greatest pain first.

"All right, Moishe," Pearlman said quietly. "It is the Christian prophecy we're looking at—for the sake of argument—it is the end of the world. The really bad times, the tribulations, begin when Israel signs a pact with the devil, right? The disappearances are something our Christian friends call the Rapture, an act of God, no less, and now we can go to the section called Revelation and read what will happen next, point by point, yes? Is this what you are telling me, Moishe?"

Schimmel shrugged. He had the ability to convey volumes with a shrug, and this one covered a myriad of philosophical hypotheses. "Who knows from any literal interpretation of Scripture, Daniel? The children are gone, that is fact. The European Coalition is shaping up as the next great world power, with China remaining quiet and neutral for now, and America tilting the balance any time it wants—that is fact also. The mujahideen are apparently unstoppable—"

"Ah," interrupted Pearlman.

"What?" asked Schimmel, knowing already where his friend's argument would go.

"The mujahideen," said Pearlman. "Yes, there is that one little problem right now, my good and intelligent friend Moishe Schimmel. Hundreds of thousands of absolutely crazed radical Muslims on the move, led by this Izbek Noir animal who seems to live a charmed life. They have now swept into Saudi Arabia, as you know. They opened the festivities with air strikes and missiles, then their armor came rolling in. The royal family is long gone, of course, camped out in luxury in one of their many properties scattered around the world, leaving their fellow countrymen to their fate."

Both men were silent for a moment. They had no need to verbalize their feelings about the Saudi royal family. After a moment, Schimmel said almost to himself, "Oil supply."

"Oh, it's going to make a bad situation worse, all

right," agreed Pearlman. "But my point is that Noir didn't think twice about turning against a Muslim nation. Yes, I know he expects most of the Saudi citizens and military to simply join him, rather than die defending empty palaces. What do you think he'll do to Israel? Even though we tried to help against that attack on Mecca, the world's Muslims are not ready to embrace us. Those criminal hordes he commands are already salivating over the prospect of destroying us once and for all."

Moishe Schimmel stifled a pretend yawn. "News flash: The world hates the Jews, Israel stands alone. Film at eleven." He looked at his friend until Pearlman's eyes were locked with his. "Israel stands alone, Daniel, always has, always will. That's the way it is. We're going to have to defend ourselves against the mujahideen, Russia, the Palestinian fleas, and anyone else who wants to take a turn."

"Sure," agreed Pearlman. "And we can use nukes against Noir and his troops, and probably America would back us on it."

"Maybe."

" 'Oops,' we could say."

"Then turn around and nuke Russia?" asked Schimmel.

"See?" said Pearlman gently. "You're making my point for me."

"What point?"

"Israel can fight to stay alive, yes, that's apparently our lot in this world's scheme of things," explained Pearlman. "And I believe we can defeat any enemy, using whatever weapons the situation calls for. But . . . but . . . why not have an ally now, an ally later? They don't have to be the same ally at the same time, Moishe. America is traditionally with us, our staunchest friend, good. But if you go back to that same scripture you are touting, you'll see that eventually we are given a choice . . . yes? No? And they are Christian. Yes? No?"

Schimmel nodded.

"So we'll take an ally when we can get one, and when we need one," said Daniel Pearlman. "You don't trust this Azul Dante fellow, Moishe, all right. But he's got the power right now, he's talking, the countries are listening, and I think he's the one who will stop this Izbek Noir and the mujahideen. I think now it is okay for Israel to have a covenant or whatever he wants to call it, for now. What if none of this has anything to do with the Bible, the Talmud, or any other prophecy or whatever? What if there is another explanation for the disappearances, and there are coincidences that make people want to read things into them?" He looked at his friend, and reached out and patted the small man's chest. "*It doesn't matter*. Israel must survive. Clear threat at this moment, the mujahideen. Powerful ally, Azul Dante . . . and Clara Reese will be okay with it because she's okay with *us*."

They sat together in comfortable silence for several minutes.

"You just keep one hand on your house keys when you're with this Dante guy, Daniel," said Schimmel after pursing his lips and drumming the scarred fingers of his left hand, "and your trusting eyes wide open."

"My eyes will be open, my friend," responded Pearl-man, "and I'll be watching his every move through *yours*."

+   +   +

"Oh, look," said Lynn Moss, "the prodigal son returns."

Tommy stopped at the front door of the small apart-ment just off the University of Virginia campus. He had seen how run-down the place was when his dad parked the Bronco on the street in front of the building, how the bit of front lawn was parched and neglected, and the small garden along the front wall choked with weeds. He was tired from the drive. His dad had admitted a certain reluctance to leave the New Christian Cathedral down there in Selma. He liked those two women, Tommy could tell, and there was no denying how immediately comfortable the three of them had been with each other. He liked Shannon and Ivy too, and would have stayed longer if his dad hadn't insisted they get going. The road trip had been uneventful, his wounds seemed to be heal-ing nicely, no infections, and he was cautiously rebuild-ing his relationship with a dad he had never really known. He discovered his dad wasn't so bad. It became clear to Tommy as they talked that his dad regretted not spending more time with his children, and wished he could do it all over again.

They had pulled into the college town in the late morning, and Thomas Church became quiet as they drove up and down the side streets until he saw a familiar landmark. A few minutes later Tommy had walked toward the door, but Sissy opened it and stood staring at him before he got a chance to knock.

"Why'd you say that, Sissy?" said Tommy, not prepared for the way his sister looked at him.

She shrugged as she turned toward the interior of the apartment, and said listlessly over her shoulder, "Hey, Dad. I see you found your long-lost boy."

Thomas Church, equally disquieted by her attitude, managed, "Yep." Now we are three, he said to himself. One more to go. He closed the door behind him as he walked into the living room, and hugged Sissy. He stepped back and looked at her. She looked tired, with dark circles under her eyes, pale lips, and no makeup. Her hair hung to her shoulders, not brushed, and she wore baggy shorts and an old T-shirt several sizes too large.

What used to be the letters UVA hung in tatters along the front of it. Her look caught both Tommy and his dad off guard because Sissy had always been careful about her appearance. She was a pretty girl, with a nice face, big eyes, fine skin, and a cute figure. Neither of them had ever seen her like this. The apartment was a mess, with clothing, dishes, and papers lying here and there on the furniture and floor. Sissy tried to pull away from the hug, but Church held her arms tightly, leaned back so he could see her face, and asked, "Sissy . . . what's wrong? Did something happen while I was away looking for Tommy?"

"Did something happen?" asked his daughter, stepping out of his grasp, pushing a pile of newspapers off one end of a sofa, and sitting down slowly. "Why, no, Dad. Nothing happened." She laughed, buried her face in her hands, and said in a muffled voice, "Nothing happened but the end the world, and now nothing *can* happen."

"Is it Mitch?" asked Tommy. "Did Mitch take off or something?" He went to her, knelt in front of her, and took her hands in his. He held her like that until she raised her head, and her eyes met his. "C'mon, Sissy," he said, "it's still just me, Tommy, that's all, your brother even if you don't want me to be. Don't be mad at Dad just because he took off lookin' for me. Since I've been with him all he's talked about is getting back here with *you*, so . . . so maybe we can all be like a family again." He watched as a big fat glistening tear formed in the corner of her right eye, hung a moment, then rolled down her cheek, leaving a silvery trail. "Is it Mitch?" he asked again.

"Is it your mom? Did something happen to your mother?" asked Church.

"No," she said, and snuffled. "No, it's not Mitch, Mitch is *fine*. He's fine, and it's not Mom, she's fine too. We're all fine, and Mitch will be really glad to see both of you, and it's all . . . fine." She put her face in her hands and began crying again. Tommy held her and looked across the room at his dad, who looked back and shrugged.

"Listen," said Sissy after blowing her nose, "I don't want to be rude or anything, and I know I'm not looking like Miss Hospitality here, but I've got like a killer headache, and I just took one of my boomer pills, and I need to lie down for a while." She looked up at Tommy, then over at her father. "Okay?"

"We'll be fine, honey," said Church. "You go rest a bit. We'll make ourselves comfortable."

An hour later, the door opened and Mitch Moss, Sissy's husband, walked in. He was a tall man, awkward and angular, with reddish brown hair worn long, tied in back with a piece of leather, a bushy rust-colored beard that covered most of his face, round glasses with wire frames. He wore a blue long-sleeved buttoned shirt, a gold knit tie, faded bib overalls, and construction boots. Mitch was a full-time student working toward a second doctorate, a part-time professor, was liked and respected at the university, and dressed in a manner that stated he did not take himself too seriously.

When he saw Tommy and Thomas standing in his living room, he lifted his arms toward the ceiling and said with a grin, "All *right* . . . I was *hoping* that was your road-weary Bronco sitting on the curb out front." He shook Church's hand, then grabbed Tommy's hand in his firm grip and said, "Well, well . . . the prodigal son returns." Then, seeing their expressions, he said, "What?"

"You're not the first person to call Tommy that this morning, Mitch," said Church with a small laugh.

"Well, boy," said Mitch as he clapped Tommy on the shoulder, "if the shoe fits . . . right?" He seemed to notice how the apartment looked then, and said, "Wow, this place looks great, did you guys clean it up? And what's that I smell coming from the kitchen, chili or something?"

"Sissy had a headache and went to lie down," said Church with a shrug, "so Tommy took the kitchen, I took the other rooms, and we made ourselves busy. Then Tommy got into your cupboards and threw the chili together."

"Let me check on Sissy, then," said Mitch.

A few minutes later he came out, slumped down into a big leather easy chair, and looked at Tommy and his dad. He took his glasses off, pulled a white handkerchief from a back pocket, and polished the lenses. Then he put them back on and said, "Man, Thomas, since you left to go off in search of your long-lost boy, she has gone straight downhill. She's like, listless, no energy, despondent. It's hard for me to get her even to leave the apartment. She won't do anything with her class schedule, won't go to any activities, nothing."

"Is it because of what happened? The state of the world right now?" asked Tommy.

Mitch hesitated, then said quietly, "It's related to the whole big picture." He looked toward the bedroom door. "She's hard asleep right now." He pulled at his beard for a moment, looked at Church, and said, "It's the children thing that's gotten to her. She's frightened, she doesn't understand. She's got friends on campus who are like, born again . . . you know? Bible thumpers, talking to anyone who will sit still for it about Jesus this, Jesus that."

He pointed one long finger at Church. "Thomas, you and me had our big conversation about religion and other myths back before Sissy married me. Seemed then we were on the same page. If I remember right, you didn't think the whole story amounted to a hill of beans either."

Church just nodded back, waiting. He was very worried about his daughter.

"So," continued Mitch, "I mean, I get along with everybody, you know, and I don't mind sittin' and talking about different religions, philosophy, who or what is the human race and why does the man in the moon only come out at night . . . all that stuff. I respect people for their beliefs, and now and then I've gone to the chapel with Sissy because she asked me and she liked it and all. Good. Didn't hurt me, and it was peaceful. Gives a man time to think, you know?"

Tommy and his dad knew Mitch was stalling, holding something back, and waited for him to finally get to it.

"Now, you take those disappearances," said Mitch. "Man, you both know when that first happened, why, everybody on CNN and every other news channel had an opinion as to what it was. For some reason, within all that babble, Sissy could only hear the ones who equated it with some type of Biblical event. To her, the ones holding up the Bible in explanation were the only ones who made sense. There were a lot of wackos spouting goofy theories, that's for sure, and I discounted most of them just like you did. But I knew somewhere in between what everybody was saying was the truth. It wasn't Biblical. People have always turned to myth, blind faith, some scripture, when they were too frightened or too lazy to buckle down and try to work something out on a level of reality consistent with their capabilities."

"What?" said Tommy.

"The Bible is an easy answer, Tommy," replied Mitch with a grin. "God did it, so it must be okay. God did it, He loves us, so it's okay. All we have to do is pray on it, and He will make sure we're okay." He pushed his glasses up on his nose with one finger. "Instead of using our heads, our history, our sciences, our knowledge of our world and the surrounding universes, instead of *investigating* it, or *working* at it, we can just turn to the deity of the month, blame Him, and stand there with a blank look on our face, waiting to be saved."

"But Sissy had a problem with it," said Church, "with the 'children' thing."

Mitch nodded. "Yeah. I tried to talk to her, I mean, we've always been able to have great conversations— sometimes they'll even turn into shouting matches—but we can argue, and talk. She's known my feelings about organized religion since she met me, and I know she's still searching. But we respect each other's feelings, and it works. But on this? Man, I tried to tell her it had to be something that would eventually be identified, evaluated, and explained. The universe is a *physical* thing, I told her, still growing, expanding. The whole time-space thing has so many possibilities. It's endless."

"To infinity, and beyond," said Tommy under his breath.

"Exactly, cowboy," responded Mitch with a grin. He

and Tommy had always liked each other, and he knew Tommy thought Sissy had chosen well. "Anyway," he said, "I tried to tell her the disappearances had to do with some anomaly in the system, something having to do with time, perhaps, or a flex in the expansion of universal matter . . . probably would come down to simple physics as a means of interpreting it. She didn't want to hear from simple physics, man. She kept going back to the Bible, the end times. The earthquake—tremors, really— that happened worldwide before the disappearances. She used them to back up her argument. I asked her if she had ever heard of tectonic shifts."

"And what was her answer to that, Mitch?" asked Tommy.

"Aw, she said *I* had had a tectonic shift, and it had caused my brain to trade places with my . . ." He patted his seat with one hand, and they all laughed quietly.

He grew serious again, and went on. "For Sissy, no matter how I argued against it, it kept going back to the Bible. She's been listening to that Reverend Smith on the radio . . . broadcasts out of Alabama. Heard of him?"

"We just left there," answered Church.

"No lie? Well, he's got the voice, you know, and he knows his Bible passages, and he's not only preaching to the choir now, he's preaching to everyone who wants to be *in* the choir, for crying out loud. I mean, man, people are hurting, scared, and he tells them what they want to hear . . . gives them sketchy explanations based on faith, and lots of hope, based on hope. Sissy likes him, likes what he says. Okay. It don't mean nothin' to me one way or the other. But she's still hurting, and withdrawing, and now she's begun to let herself go, and she's so listless." He stopped, and looked down at his hands.

"What's really bothering her, Mitch?" asked Church.

Still looking at his hands, Mitch coughed slightly, and said very softly, "She did not want me to tell you. Says you'll somehow equate it with failure, like she couldn't cut it or something."

He closed his eyes. "She was so excited, Thomas, so excited. She had gone and bought one of those home test kits—foolproof thing for your own privacy and all. She tested herself, and it said she was pregnant."

He stopped, took off his glasses and pinched his nose, hard. Then, still not looking at them, he said, "Man, she was so happy, so . . . her face, her eyes, I've never seen her like . . . and I . . . I was too, I mean . . . she was holding me and calling me her big hero and all, and we were like dancing around on the bed till we tripped over the bed-covers and fell in a heap, just laughin' and stuff." He looked at his curled hands in his lap, and said, "She was with child."

The room became very still, and quiet. Tommy felt a hard sadness grip his chest, and Church felt a pounding in his ears. It didn't have to be said, but Church said it anyway: "And then she wasn't."

"And then"—Mitch snapped his fingers; it sounded loud in the quiet room—"she wasn't."

"But do we know for sure we can't have any more

babies?" asked Tommy. He knew this was a topic of discussion at the New Christian Cathedral, and probably
other churches too.

"We don't know squat," replied Mitch. "It doesn't
matter anyway. Sissy lost her baby, and now she's listening to the Bible folks, and she's not sure if we'll get another shot at it." He looked at both of them, then said,
"And what if we *could* have babies? Would we want to
bring them into this world anyway? And if these are the
end times? What would be the use?"

No one in the room had the answer, so no one spoke.

+   +   +

They ate a quiet dinner, the four of them. The conversation remained light, as Tommy and his father let
Mitch tell them about his new lessons, how he was trying
to mix current world politics with his history and sociol-
ogy lectures. He told them about the doctoral thesis he
had in the works, how he had drifted for a while but now
felt focused and back on track. Sissy joined them, but remained quiet, withdrawn. She had showered, washed her
hair, and changed, so she looked more like the Sissy they
knew. They agreed Tommy's chili was pretty good, if a
tad spicy.

"Dad," said Sissy as she reached out with one hand
and took his wrist, "will you come sit with me, and talk?"

Church wiped the beads of sweat off his brow, took a
last swig of iced tea, and said with a smile, "Of course.
We'll let these two clean up the dishes while they talk
about quarter horses and the meaning of life."

+   +   +

Each apartment had a small backyard, and Sissy and her dad pulled a couple of lawn chairs together, and watched the evening sky in silence. Church knew he had to let her begin when she was ready.

"Dad," Sissy said after a few minutes, "I know Mitch told you about the baby."

"Yes, he did, Sissy," said Church. "Why didn't *you* tell me when I came through here right after the disappearances? When I was on my way out to try to find Tommy?"

"I don't know, Dad," she replied. "It was like I was in some kind of dream state, and state of denial at the same time. I couldn't make sense out of what had happened everywhere, let alone what happened to me . . . to *us*." She hung her head, her eyes closed. "I wanted it to be fun. First grandchild. I wanted you to be proud of me."

"Sissy," he said quietly, "I'm proud of you every day, always have been." He took one of her hands in his. "Look. You didn't *fail* me or your mom because you became pregnant, then lost the baby. Even without the disappearances, that same thing could have happened for many varied reasons, especially with a first baby. Sometimes they just don't *take*, you know? If that had happened, do you think your mother and I would have felt you had somehow failed? Certainly not. We would have said we love you, be strong, and grab that goofy husband of yours and try, try again."

"Oh, Dad."

"No, I mean it," continued Church. "Babies happen, or they don't. All you can do is keep yourself healthy, think good thoughts, and perhaps work at it a bit harder, if that's the right word. And you did, you did that, Sissy," he added. "You and Mitch, you got a baby started. Then something unprecedented, something unimaginable, happened to the entire world, and the life forming in you was taken." He looked up at the night sky. "Who knows why."

He looked at her. She was very still, and her tears fell freely down her cheeks.

A few yards away a squirrel came hop-running across the sparse grass, its tail twitching this way and that, sprang a couple of feet through the air, hit the bark of a large pine tree, and went vertical at a high rate of speed. Not far behind it came a clumsy black-and-brown puppy, tripping over its own floppy ears, sniffing and whoofing, and searching in vain for the squirrel. The puppy circled the tree several times, looked at Church and his daughter for guidance, received none, and loped away.

"Dad," said Sissy, wiping her cheeks with the backs of her hands, "why did you get so focused on finding Tommy after the disappearances? You and Tommy were not . . . close, and it kind of seemed like you really didn't care, you know . . . what he did, or where he went."

"Guilty," said Church with a shrug. "I took my relationship with you for granted. I knew I'd always be able to stay in contact with you. Tommy and me." He shook his head. "I just never really tried, I guess. Too busy being Thomas Church during those years."

"You took good care of us, Dad," said Sissy. "You provided for us, we never wanted for anything."

"I was a good provider, Sissy, but a lackluster hus-

band, and an invisible dad," he replied. "After the disappearances, it was like being hit in the face with a cold wet
towel or something. All of a sudden I *wanted* to have a
real relationship with my son. It's hard to explain, Sissy.
Between the two of you, he was the furthest from me, in
mind and body, furthest from me. You, I felt I could find,
could save. Tommy I feared was lost to me, and it hurt. I
became almost panicked about it, angry with myself. My
mission was to find him, bring him here, and have the
two of you together again."

"What about Mom?"

Church took a deep breath, balled his hands into fists,
shook his head again, and answered quietly, "Honey, I
don't know. I feel sort of the same way about her, like I
never really *tried*. She was a smart, vibrant, attractive
woman who wanted lots of challenges from life, and I
relegated her to a position of nonperson, sort of. Again,
it can be argued that I cared and provided for her, was always a gentleman with her, respected her and tried to be
a decent husband for her. But . . . but, I never really tried
to be with *Iris*, the person, the woman."

"She still loves you, you know."

He was silent.

"Dad?"

He looked away, not trusting himself.

"I know where you can find her, Dad," said Sissy. "She
told me not to tell you, but I know she figured I would
eventually anyway." She waited, but he did not respond.
After a moment she asked, "Dad, do you want to know
where she is?"

He turned to her, smiled, and said, "Yep."

Mitch came out the rear sliding doors then, carrying a tray with two cups of hot tea on it. He also had one of Sissy's sweaters, which he draped over her shoulders. He bent and kissed her on top of her head, and said, "If you guys get chilly out here, come in and join *our* conversation. I never knew there was so much to learn about the care, feeding, and training of horses."

After Mitch went back inside, Sissy sipped some of the tea, looked up toward the top of the pine tree across the yard, and said, "Dad. The disappearances. All the children taken. It *is* a Biblical thing, isn't it?"

"Well . . ."

"No, I know. We were not raised to be believers, not *real* believers, and that's okay. I mean, we were like a lot of people, right? Church was something we did on Sundays, more when we were younger, we went, listened to the sermon, tried to catch some glimmer of what it was all about." She pulled the sweater tighter to her. "Dad, Mitch doesn't want to hear it, but I want to learn more . . . more about the Bible, God, Jesus. I know it might literally be too late, and too bad. But I've got a *yearning*, a hunger now." She looked at him, and asked, "What did you think of that New Christian Cathedral, and the Reverend Henderson Smith?"

"Oh," answered Church, "it's a growing concern, lots of energy, lots of good people like you sincerely interested in finding some answers. Some are there, of course, because they just don't know *where* to turn, and they're trying to cover all the bases. Most are for real, they have study groups, they pray. And I mean, they pray like they're really trying to commune with God. I liked what I saw there, and Tommy was actually reluctant to leave."

"What about that preacher?"

"It's funny," said Church. "I liked his sermon, and I spoke with him briefly afterward, and came away with the impression that he was a believer, a good teacher, and a man of God trying his best to explain the unexplainable to his flock. But you know, both Tommy and I thought he—I don't know how to say it—he seemed to be trying too hard to include the Prodigal Project, and its founder, Azul Dante. For me, right now, any resolution I have with Jesus Christ, or God, will be more private, and personal. I'm not ready to join some universal movement."

"I heard him mention that during one of his radio sermons," replied Sissy. "I thought it sounded pretty exciting, and that man Dante sounded like someone we could turn to. I mean we as the world could turn to during these crazy times."

"Tommy and I had coffee with a couple of ladies who have come to the cathedral, did he tell you?"

"Yeah. Shannon and Ivy? Said you acted like you'd known them forever."

"I know. It was pleasantly weird. Anyway, they told me—sort of under their breath and mysterious and all—told me they wished Smith would ease up on the Azul Dante pitch too. The one, Ivy . . . she's got something dark boiling inside her, you can see it in her eyes. The other, Shannon, she is one of those people who is 'born again,' but it doesn't grate on you. I mean, she's found

Jesus, simple as that, and her whole life is lived in her relationship with Him, no baloney, nothing forced, just . . . real."

"I wish that could be me," said Sissy, almost to herself.

Thomas Church, beyond being surprised by any of his recent feelings or actions, said, "It can be, Sissy."

"What do you mean, Dad?"

"I mean I think . . . I've come to believe this event, what has happened to the world, is the work of God. I believe God not only exists, He is real, and He has a loving hand in what happens to us, as individuals, and as a world." Church smiled at himself as he heard his own words. He shook his head. "I know I'm like the last person you'd ever hear say something like that, but finding Tommy the way I did, where he was, in his condition, it wasn't an accident. Not only that, I think God has a Son, like me, I have a son. His is Jesus and the story of Jesus being the Son of God and the Son of man is fact. He exists too, and walked here on this very Earth, sent here to teach us if we'd only listen."

"Dad," said Sissy as she stared at her father, "does this mean, are you like, born again?"

"Well," answered Church, rubbing his nose and making a face, "I don't know. If I say I don't know, then it must mean I'm not not like that woman I met, Shannon. With her, there simply is no doubt. She says she has 'given herself over to Him' and 'put her life in His hands.' I can't look at you and say that. I'm pretty sure it comes down to commitment. I'll tell you what I *am*, though. I am hungry. You used the word 'yearning.' I understand. I too have a yearning now, and I am going to throw myself into that Bible, and I'm going to learn how to pray, *really* pray, and then I'll see what happens. If I'm going to be true to myself about this, I must be totally honest. If I don't feel it, I don't feel it; if it happens, and it's *real*, then I'll know."

"Well, let me know when it happens."

"Sissy," said Thomas Church with a smile, swept with a warm wave of gratitude, "maybe you'll find Him before I do. Then you can take my hand and introduce me."

"Maybe I will, Dad," she said softly. Her heart ached with loss and anger. Her soul ached with what might have been. I want to be like Mary, her inner voice whispered in her heart, I want to have a life form inside of me, a child, and I want to give birth to that child and hold him against my breast and feel his sweet breath against my face and watch him live, watch him *be*. Oh, dear God, I want to be a mother. If we are without child, we are without life, we are without future or potential. If we are without child, we *stop* . . . and it will truly be the end of the world. I want to feel what Mary felt, not to give birth to the Son, but to give birth to my son, or my daughter, a child of mine, a child of God. Oh, dear God, I want to be a mother. "Maybe I will, Dad."

CHAPTER NINE

They were in the killing fields, a warped and macabre desert where their dead lay sprawled across the landscape like misshapen bags of blood, mucus, hope, desire, and dreams. A hard wind blew, hot and gritty, scattering veils of dust and sand in sweeping waves. Above the wasteland hung a grim sun, illuminating the cruel acts of man on man with stark, burning clarity. The horizon was broken here and there by twisting columns of black smoke, fueled by hungry fires that chewed at the oil wells, nearby structures, and burst trucks and tanks. The choking air was filled with the mournful cries of the wounded and dying, spiked now and then with the pitiful screams of a man reduced to begging with his knees in the dirt, pleading for his insignificant life as he looked into the apathetic eyes of his deliverer.

The mujahideen were in massive movement across a broad front, crashing against the combined forces hosted by the Saudis, that formed line after line of defense in the sand. Steel and fire were met with steel and fire, the full-throated war cries and howls of anger a faint and wavering monotone beneath the tearing, almost continuous explosions. Man has always called on a higher power during battle, praying for victory, and on this killing field thousands on both sides exhorted Allah to bless them. It had become a bleak and dirty contest between men, this battle, with no quarter given or expected, no honor, no decency. Man became the beast, and as the beast he descended into a berserk brutality that sickened and seduced the soul, and became addictive.

He liked to watch their eyes. As the window to the soul, a man's eyes were the perfect place for Izbek Noir to see, feel, experience, drink in the finite moment when a prisoner faced with absolute, unyielding, unimpeachable certainty his own death. The mouth slackened, the head tilted back slightly, the eyes widened and stared that unique, all-encompassing, blind stare of forever. What do you see now, puny, defeated one? Noir wanted to ask. How far, to what imagined or hoped-for place does your stare take you?

He understood how watching the death of a man was a sensual pleasure for him; he neither denied nor refused it, but embraced it, and drank it in like the sweet nectar of the gods it was. Man, sorry vessel of life, tiny, useless carrier of petty dreams and inflated expectations, became soul-frozen at the *moment* of death. At the precipice he would realize how little he knew, how empty and shallow his knowledge and awareness, how baseless his preconceived designs. Noir liked to stand close, and lean his intense and focused eyes toward the prisoner's tortured face; he felt his own mouth open slightly and go bone dry, felt his own borrowed heart pound in the shell that was his body. More than once, during his time, he had held the back of a prisoner's head, smiled at him, and caressed his hair affectionately as the time approached. Every pore of his own skin would come alive, tingling with anticipation, as he put the barrel of a pistol against the prisoner's face, and slowly squeezed the trigger until the explosion. Then, with a spasm, a momentary awkward flailing, a burst of blood and kicking of heels, life was *taken*, and what was one second ago a living person called man became a corrupt and distorted bag of nothing. It was a sick and twisted moment of truth for Izbek Noir, a man's death, and each one he witnessed validated all he was.

"Do another," said General Izbek Noir to one of his mujahideen troops.

The body of the prisoner the soldier had just shot in the head lay back on its legs, mouth agape, skull burst open, hands balled into fists.

"You," called the soldier to a man kneeling, head down, in a tight knot of prisoners, shoeless, hatless, hopeless. The man looked up, opened his mouth to speak, and began shaking his head. He was grabbed roughly from behind by another mujahideen and flung bodily toward the general. The prisoner sprawled in the sand at the feet of the soldier, and though his hands were tied behind his back, he leaned forward and put his face against the soldier's boots, nuzzling them. He pleaded softly, "No, no . . . don't do this to me, brother, I am a son of Allah also, like you."

"You are not like me," said the mujahideen soldier, "because I am alive, while you are already dead." He stepped back, kicked the prisoner in the face, and pulled the trigger on his assault rifle.

Izbek Noir felt a pleasant warm jolt in his gut as the bullet tore into the prisoner's forehead, and the man's body was punched down and back by the impact. The dead prisoner seemed to flatten into insignificance in the sand even as Noir watched.

"Rommel," said Noir to the tall dark soldier who stood a few feet away, watching grimly. "Have your men finish this group quickly, then report to the command vehicles. I want to discuss something with you."

"Sir," asked John Jameson, "in the past haven't we assimilated many of the captured soldiers into our ranks— of course, the ones who were our Muslim brothers?" He knew Noir was especially dangerous at that moment. He had witnessed Noir's reaction to the executions before, as had they all, and knew Noir could be brutal if his reverie was interrupted.

"What?" said Noir, irritated. "What?"

"These soldiers that surrendered today, sir," continued Jameson, unafraid. "There are almost one hundred left in this group, they are Muslims, we might be able to use them."

Noir looked at Jameson, took a deep breath, let it out, and said, "Muslims." He was going to spit into the desert sand, their present hard killing field, but knew he still had to play the game, to stick to the plan. "Rommel," he added, "not today, and these are mostly Saudis. They are worthless, even to Allah. Have your men kill them as fast as you can, then you . . . you come to me, and we'll talk."

He was excited about his new idea. It would be a grand test, and add a bit of deadly spice to the plan. He saw something in the way Rommel watched his eyes, and from deep within his core came the word *seven*, as if from the mouth of a snake. "Here." He walked briskly to the huddled group of prisoners, grabbed one by the upper arm, pulled him quickly to his feet, and shoved him stumbling toward Jameson. "This is a skinny and sickly one, Rommel, but a soldier who *fought* us, a soldier who did not submit, understand. You, Rommel . . . *you* kill this one." He turned away, strode a few yards to a waiting armored personnel carrier, and walked up the rear ramp and into the dark interior. With a rumble the hatch closed, and the tracked vehicle turned in the sand and roared off toward the command vehicles.

Jameson was aware of the other mujahideen sur-rounding him. They were watching him closely, waiting. He felt heartsick, helpless to prevent what was about to happen, saddened by his inability to change the moment. He felt unworthy, diminished, a hapless and ineffective witness to cruel carnage. He looked at the enemy soldier who had been thrown at him. The prisoner was just a boy, really, young, with fine pale skin, very big brown eyes with long lashes, a small mouth with full lips. The boy had stood and fought before being captured along with the rest of his unit, and was slightly wounded in the left arm and shoulder, where his loose-fitting uniform was torn and bloodied.

Jameson looked at the mujahideen soldier who had done the killing for Noir, a squad leader. He nodded at the man. Then he grabbed his own prisoner, turned him, and began to walk away from the rest. "I want to hear mine pray, and I want to hear him beg as he scoops out his own shallow grave in these foul sands." The squad leader shrugged. They had all heard of Rommel's strange acts, like covering the dead bodies of enemy soldiers, and discouraging mutilations right after a battle. But he was an effective leader, a brave fighter, and General Noir obviously had him picked for some reason. He nodded back at Rommel, then turned to his own grim task.

Jameson led the prisoner across the sand silently, and as he walked he saw how the rope binding the man's small hands had actually cut into the skin, bringing more blood. But the soldier did not whimper, sob, or beg. When the two of them were almost fifty yards away, Jameson hit the soldier in the hip with his AK-47 and said, "Stop." Using his K-bar knife, he cut the binding rope with one swift move. Then, "Turn around." The soldier slowly turned, his big brown eyes meeting Jameson's calmly as he massaged his wrists.

They stood in an area cut with a small series of low dunes, where the wind had built shallow walls. "Kneel," commanded Jameson as he pointed his weapon at the soldier.

"I will not kneel, for you or any man," said the soldier quietly, "but will stand to meet God."

It was the voice, combined with the other characteristics of the soldier, that finally told Jameson the soldier who stood before him was a young woman. He already knew what he had to do, and this fact only reinforced his decision. "What is your name?" he asked evenly.

"I am Faseem."

"Then listen carefully, Faseem," said Jameson, his back turned to the shooting and screaming coming from where he had left the others. "You will live, if you do as I say, and do it now. We have no time."

"I don't want to live, but to die," said the young woman, her eyes bright.

"Why?" asked Jameson, unprepared for her.

She looked at him, pointed with one hand in a sweeping arc that covered the battlefield, and shook her head. "You must ask me that? Have you not seen with your own eyes what we have become? No. There are no more reasons for me to live. Kill me, mujahid."

"Your life is a gift from God, child," said Jameson, panic welling in his heart.

"Then we shall return it with one bullet from you."

"It is not yours to return, but to accept, cherish, and love," said Jameson through cracked lips.

"He has forsaken us, forsaken me, and I will tell Him to His face the moment you pull your trigger," she replied. "Why do you tease and torment me now, mujahid eunuch? You have discovered I am a woman, do you wish to use me as your vessel before sending me away from this horrible world? Do you?"

"You torment me now, child," said Jameson softly. "I don't want you to die here, today. Perhaps God has sent me to you with His message. Why else would *you* have been selected to be executed by *me*?" He lowered his voice. "God is mysterious, child, and He loves you, and now, here, you have a chance to live—to *live* in this horrible place of death. Seize this chance, child, and take it as another gift from God, respect Him for it. . . . Don't turn your back on it."

She began to cry, and the tears shone like diamonds in the hard light. She lifted her chin, looked at him, and said, "I am Faseem. Who are you to offer me a chance to keep living in this hell?"

"I am John," said Jameson. "And consider your life a gift to me."

"John," she said softly, then lowered her eyes.

He heard the firing behind him slacking off, and said tersely, "Get on your knees, child, to help *me* survive. I will leave this bag that has fallen off my shoulder. In it is a water bottle, some rations, and a small first-aid kit. Pretend to be dead until nightfall, then get out of this area, the front is shifting more to the west. Move east, and north if possible. Get on your knees now, and scream loudly, and may God bless you and keep you in His heart, forever."

The girl soldier fell to her knees, lifted her face to the uncaring sky, and screamed in anger, pain, and hope. Jameson squeezed the trigger of his assault rifle, and when the bullet cut through the collar of her shirt and grazed the tender skin of her neck, she fell away from his legs, into a cut between two low dunes.

Jameson could hear her crying softly as he hurried to rejoin the other mujahideen troops. He knew now the job he must do was a righteous mission. He was a man of Christ, a soldier of Christ, and he would kill another in cold blood because *it would be the right thing to do*. He would meet with Izbek Noir now, as ordered. He would listen to what the evil general had to say. Then he would kill him. He had given his heart to Jesus Christ, and he feared nothing.

+   +   +

Cat Early sat in the back of Simon Blake's car with her backpack on her lap. The car was taking her to the airport, and she felt anxious and excited, as she always did when heading out on an assignment. She had left a gift— a small wooden cross she had found in the ruins of a church a few months ago—and a card for Tanya, who had perhaps unknowingly provided a place to stay in Paris. Simon had given her the use of his car and driver for her trip to the airport, a gracious gesture of defeat after losing an argument with her.

Azul Dante was at The Hague, involved in many meetings, perhaps the most important of which would be the one with the Russians. Dante was close to naming the general he had picked to lead the European Coalition forces against the mujahideen, and he wanted to ensure complete cooperation from the bigger powers. The

United States was on board, quietly insisting that any military leader should come from their ranks, as was Britain. China had sent an envoy to Dante with the message that China agreed the mujahideen were a destabilizing threat to the world; they would carefully monitor the actions, but would not participate or interfere at this time. Japan and Germany still sided with the United States, although Germany dragged her feet more. All of this was big doings, and Blake, Cat's boss, thought she should capitalize on her obvious success with Dante in Paris, follow him to the Netherlands, and interview him again.

But Cat wanted to put some distance between herself and Dante. He disturbed her and intrigued her, but his story was one, for now, that could be covered by one of the veteran political reporters on Blake's staff. Cat was a combat journalist, and Noir's mujahideen were crushing their way through Saudi Arabia, leaving destruction in their wake. The stories of atrocities coming from the desert sands, in a Muslim country, were beyond belief, and if they conquered a largely leaderless Saudi Arabia it would put them in very close proximity to Israel, and *that* would ratchet the situation up several notches. The Jordanians were looking for help while at the same time attempting to form a treaty with Noir. Iraq, a fractious republic since the assassination of the last Hussein by one of his wives, was quaking in its boots, turning to Iran for help with one hand, the United States with the other.

Cat had stood firm in the face of Blake's insistence. Her bureau chief had even hinted that Dante had let it be known that Cat would have better access to him than

any other correspondent, this communicated in a terse
e-mail from his assistant, Sophia Ghent. But Cat argued
that she could return to Paris anytime it looked as if
Dante was actually going to *move* against Noir, rather
than form coalitions, meet with envoys, military plan-
ners, and other bigwigs . . . and extol the good intentions
of his Prodigal Project. War was happening out there,
and Cat needed to cover it, she told Blake. He had reluctantly given in after seeing her determination, and he
knew her stories were pure gold, so he gave her a kiss on
both cheeks, squeezed her hands in his, and wished her
"Bonne chance."

She would fly to Cairo, which had recently reopened.
The mujahideen had ravaged most of southern Egypt,
and the infrastructure had been ripped apart. But with
assistance from other countries, including Israel, Egypt
was working to re-form and regroup. From Cairo she
could make her way into Jordan, move south toward
Mecca, in Saudi Arabia, or watch things for a while from
Tel Aviv, a place she really liked anyway. She looked out
the window as Paris slipped past, hugged her backpack,
and thought about Slim.

+   +   +

Shannon Carpenter felt a soft warm breeze on her
cheek, lifted her face from the Bible in her lap, and
looked up into the forever blue sky. She took a long, deep
breath, filling her lungs tight, and let it out slowly. She
wore a pale yellow sleeveless buttoned blouse with a
small collar, white walking shorts, and white sandals. She

paused, then took another breath, savoring it. She was alive, very aware of the natural world around her, and grateful.

Sitting on a large quilt under a spare tree with Shannon was Ted Glenn. He wore jeans and a blue polo shirt, and was in his socks. His boots sat in the grass a few feet away. He had closed his Bible, and sat watching Shannon. They had been under the tree in a far corner of the church property for almost an hour, talking, reading, and studying quietly. Since coming to the New Christian Cathedral and finding Shannon, Ted cherished these moments. He was learning to quiet his inner voices of conflicting emotions—the loss of his Rhonda and their daughter was still so raw—and was learning to simply live day by day. That Shannon made each of his days worthwhile was a simple truth, and he accepted it gratefully. He had not come to the Cathedral looking for someone. He was not sure *what* he searched for when he came there, other than some answer, some *reason*. He was drawn to Shannon the first time he saw her, and the first time he stood a moment looking into her eyes he knew she was at least part of that reason.

Shannon looked at Ted, smiled, and said, "It's a beautiful day, isn't it?"

"It is," he replied.

"One of my regrets about my life before," Shannon continued, "is how I forgot to breathe deep once in a while. You know, forgot to stop and smell the roses. When my kids were real little I used to take them to a park not far from our house. It wasn't a national forest preserve or anything, just a park. But it had trees, and grass, butterflies, flowers, and the wind. Sounds so simple and obvious now, but it was a tiny bit of this incredible world God made for us, and it was good."

"It still is . . ."

"Yes, Ted. It still is." She looked at him, and added, "And *we* still are . . ."

He waited.

"By that I mean, we . . . people . . . man, and woman . . . the children of God," said Shannon, comfortable with their conversations, their friendship and trust. Having Ted as part of her day was something she had grown to look forward to. Other than her teasing conversations with Lakeesha Folks about him, she did not let herself think about him in any way but as a friend, but she had become very aware of the comfort he brought, his quiet strength, his shy and awkward but discernable attraction to her. "God made the world, this beautiful setting, and he made man and woman to live here."

Ted watched her face as she spoke, captured by her eyes, her voice, the curve of her cheek, the fullness of her lips. He felt the wind across his face, the warmth of the sun on his shoulders, and his own blood pumping through his heart. He knew he was in one of those moments you wish would never end.

"Now we believe we are in the end times," said Shannon as she took her eyes from his and looked at their surroundings. "God's plan for mankind." She brought her eyes back to his, and added, almost to herself, "And you know what? Even with the unhealable pain of losing my children, my husband, even with that I feel privileged to be here, to witness it, be part of it. Does that sound crazy?"

"No, it doesn't, Shannon," answered Ted. "It sounds true. We are alive, we are here. We don't know why, but it's a simple fact. We are the same intelligent, thoughtful, wondering creatures we were before it happened. We're still living in this world with the gift of free will and thought. It is still God's world, here where man dwells, and we *should* be grateful to be a part of it."

"Life goes on, doesn't it, Ted?"

"Yeah," he nodded, "life does go on."

"In God's plan," said Shannon, feeling her heart begin to beat harder, feeling her cheeks warm, "life goes on, life is continued, by man and woman. In His design, there must be both, and together they can create, through Him, life. And with life comes the future."

"Yes," responded Ted.

They looked at each other for a long moment, both afraid to speak. Finally Shannon said, "Simple, right?"

He nodded, then laughed, "Then why does it always seem so complicated, so *tangled*?"

She just shook her head.

"I remember the first time I slow danced with a girl," said Ted after a moment. "It was high school, out on the gym floor in our socks, you know? I could not believe she let me come in so close to her, holding our hands together, coming close and dancing slow. Me sliding my feet over that polished wood like a wooden soldier. She pulled me even closer, and I could smell the skin of her neck, and her hair was pulled behind one ear and tickled my nose, and she felt warm, and soft. And I felt like a clumsy oaf and I didn't want the song to ever end."

She smiled at him, picturing his shyness, his wonder. She was a grown woman, but what she said next frightened her. "Ted," her eyes fell away from his, "my husband was the first and only man I ever really kissed."

He watched her face until, after a long pause, she slowly lifted her eyes to his again. They sat in the sunshine and soft breeze, dappled by bits of shadow from the tree, and allowed themselves to bask in the moment of trust and chance. He reached out, took her right hand in his left, and pulled her gently toward him. They kept their eyes open until their lips met, then they both closed them, and were suspended there in soft nearness. Neither took a breath, and when they finally pulled apart they were both changed.

+   +   +

"Not a bad pickup truck," said Tommy Church with a grin. "For the price."

Thomas Church, disquieted, his heart heavy, nodded. The pickup truck had been free, given to them by one of Mitch and Sissy's neighbors when Tommy had approached them about buying it. It wasn't new, but had been cared for. It was white, with red trim. The truck had belonged to the couple's teenage daughter, who had been taken in the disappearances, they explained, and they hoped he got good use out of it.

"C'mon, Dad," said Tommy, not wanting his father to worry.

"Well, Tommy," replied Church, "I find you, we're here with Sissy, and she has told me where I can find your mother, out there in Idaho, where else? I've almost got us back together again, can't you see? Now you're going to go back down there to Selma, to the cathedral, and then maybe from there to Paris, or—or—some other crazy place."

"Israel."

"Israel," sighed Church.

"Dad," said Tommy, "I can't just sit here with Mitch and Sissy. She's doin' a lot better since you talked with her, and the last couple of days have been good, but it would drive me nuts to hang around while the world is goin' through whatever the world is goin' through." He punched his father on one arm. "And you know why I'm not goin' with you to find Mom. We talked about it, right?"

They had agreed that Church needed to find and confront Iris on his own. He understood having Tommy, Sissy, or both of them with him would change the energy of it.

"Okay," said Thomas Church. "But this time we stay in contact. I don't care if it's e-mail, telephone, jungle drums, or carrier pigeon, Tommy, you let Sissy know where you are and what you are planning next, right?"

"Right, Dad," answered Tommy. "And you do the same."

"When you get down to Selma, hook up with those two gals, Ivy and Shannon. They'll make sure Smith finds a place for you to bunk out, okay?"

"Okay, Dad."

Church didn't want it to end, but he was torn. He had found Tommy, and wanted him close, but now he knew where Iris was, and he felt drawn to her. He couldn't wait to see how she lived, the people, their beliefs. Some New Age cult, Sissy had said, although she seemed to think it was harmless enough. Iris was happy there, Sissy had told him, growing spiritually, finding peace. New Age cult, thought Church. Coven would be more likely. He was excited, though, about seeing her, telling her about their kids, telling her about his own spiritual awakening. *That* ought to blow her mind.

"Tommy," he said.

"Dad?"

"You . . . you take care of yourself." He stepped to his son and hugged him tightly, not wanting to ever let go of the man his boy had become. "Godspeed."

"I'll say my prayers like a good boy, Dad," said Tommy quietly while they still embraced, "and I'll ask Him to watch over you, too."

"Let's go in and say good-bye to Sissy and Mitch, then."

An hour later Thomas Church was in his Bronco, headed west toward the midwestern states, and Idaho beyond. He had a new Bible with him, a new energy and determination to find Iris, and a certain desire to learn all he could about Jesus along the way.

Tommy Church headed south toward the New Christian Cathedral in his newly acquired pickup truck. It was in good shape, he had discovered, and came with a couple of accessories that pleased him. One was a well-read Bible, with a white leather cover embossed with a gold cross, he found in the glove compartment.

+   +   +

Sissy Moss looked at her husband, Mitch, sitting at the small desk in the corner of their living room. He was working on some paper for school, dressed in shorts and a raggedy T-shirt, the skin of his muscular legs pale like most of him. He leaned forward, pushed his glasses up on the bridge of his nose, very intent on what he was reading. She liked the way he looked.

He looked over his shoulder, saw her standing there with her arms folded across her chest, and said, "Sissy? Do you think when Auberon Waugh—English guy— when he said, 'Equality is an absolute of morals by which all men have a value invariable and indestructible and a dignity as intangible as death,' do you think he meant our value and dignity are indestructible in the eyes of God, or in our eyes?"

She walked to him, took one hand, and pulled him to his feet, and they embraced. She held him tightly, her face against his chest. She liked the way he smelled, the warmth, the strength of him. "I think he was saying you should hold tightly to your wife any time you get the opportunity."

Mitch leaned his head back slightly so he could look into her eyes, studied them a moment, and said, "He couldn't have had time for a wife if he was busy thinking all those great thoughts."

"Here's a great thought, Mitch Moss," she responded quietly. "Come hold me tight." She began to pull him toward the bedroom.

"But, Sissy." He pulled her to a stop. "Sissy, I . . . I don't want you to be, uh, disappointed. I mean, not in me, or us, you know. But I mean, we don't know, there might be no real reason? Purpose? I don't know. I just don't want you to get hurt anymore."

"We live," she said, a tear hanging at the corner of her right eye. "We are. And we are still God's children in this world. Man and woman. I am your wife, I love you, I want you to hold me tight. Need any more reason, or purpose, Mitch Moss?"

He looked at her, and was hit with the same feeling he had almost every time he did: Without her, his world would be a vast, empty, cold, unlivable place. He squeezed her hand, bent and lifted her off the floor in both arms, and kissed her. "You *are* my reason, girl," he said softly.

CHAPTER TEN

Ron Underwood sat under a tree across the street front the huge front steps and doors to the New Christian Cathedral. He had his right hand buried in a deep pocket of an old fatigue jacket. He admitted to himself that he did not know too much about guns, but he had his hand around the solid wooden grips of one just as sure as he sat there. He knew it was a revolver, and it held six bullets. He had even figured out how to open it, check it to see that there were indeed six bullets nestled in it, then close it again.

He liked the feel of it, the weight of it. He found it amusing, from a scholarly self-awareness point of view, to learn that secretly carrying the gun while he talked to people gave him some sort of primal sense of power. It was as if he could . . . control things. He had never been a combative man, certainly, never even had a schoolyard fight as he grew up. As an adult he entered into intellectual combat within the academic realm, but really was that anything more than the combustible combination of ego and hot air?

He remembered how he came to possess the weapon. It was after the nice policeman had released him from the jail. He had headed east out of Oklahoma, then into Arkansas, and that's where it had happened. He hid from a rain shower, in a large culvert beside the highway. He did not see the other man lurking there at first, but then the man attacked him for no reason, screaming at him to get out of there. He remembered trying to reason with the crazy man, but it had no effect, and the man kept trying to hit him. He picked up a board, swung it wildly, and felt it go *chunk* against the crazy man's head. The man fell in a heap, coughed a couple of times, and became very still. He turned his back on the man, sat and watched the rain, and after a while he became cold. He turned and looked at the crazy man, who had not moved. He looked at the man's fatigue jacket. An hour or so later the rain had stopped, and he headed out on the highway again, now wearing the fatigue jacket and gripping the warm weight of the gun in its pocket.

He stood beside the tree, saw some activity around the front of the church, and began walking slowly toward it, and the Reverend Henderson Smith.

"Do we have a choir, or do we not have a choir, that is all I want to know, sister," said the Reverend Henderson Smith to Nateesha Folks.

The imposing black woman smiled at him, pinched his cheek, and said, "Good heavens, Reverend Smith, why of *course* we have a choir, and you know it. What's got you so tightened up today? Even if you *are* a man of God, you ought to know better than to butt heads with thirty women all tryin' to get to your rehearsal on time."

"Time, time, Sister Folks, that's my point. We set a time for each rehearsal, and I don't think it's too much to ask—"

"Shush, now, Reverend Smith," said Nateesha, her eyes twinkling. "I'll get the ladies into rehearsal, don't you worry. You go collect your thoughts, so you'll be ready for your next sermon." She looked at him, and shook her head. "You been stomping around here all morning, chewin' on this and chewin' on that. What's wrong with you? You act like a man who slept with his boots on and his spurs got tangled in his pj's."

No, he thought, I slept like a man who found the devil under his pillow. He took a deep breath, patted Sister Folks lightly on her forearm, and said, "You are right, as usual, sister. I am not behaving like a man in a state of grace. I'll go get some coffee, eat something with lots of sugar, and try to reform before it is too late." He walked off, troubled.

It had been a dream, of course, but there was so much to it that was real that it had substance, somehow. He had gone to bed last night, restless after spending several hours reading his Bible, immersed in thought. He had argued with himself about his own salvation. Was he truly lost? He wanted to think there was still hope, and his heart ached for it. He had found solace in his Bible, as he always did. The words of Scripture comforted him, and gave him strength.

Scripture told him, over and over, to admit his failings, expose his shortcomings, repent, ask for forgiveness, and He will forgive. Even the most wretched, the hopeless ones seemingly beyond redemption, all they have to do is call out to Him in His Son's name, call out and ask for forgiveness. Even in these times, he had reflected, as long as man walks on Earth and takes a breath, his merciful God will take him back, will welcome him back to His heart. He had lain against his pillow, his Bible a comforting weight on his chest, and fallen off to sleep knowing he had failed God, but knowing God would not fail him.

That's when the trouble started, he reflected now as he sat alone in the dining room, his mug of coffee untouched at his elbow. Oh, yeah. Andrew Nuit . . . rhymes with sweet. Large, rotund man, porcine, sweaty, wore a linen suit. Andrew Nuit was the one who had visited him at his old church, back before the day of the disappearances. Andrew Nuit, his small bulging eyes staring right through him as they sat in his small run-down office in that tiny wooden church that had his name hand-painted on the sign out front. That little church where a preacher could be trapped in smallness for his entire life. Andrew Nuit rhymes with sweet knew all about it, knew what was in his *soul*, and just by looking into the man's bottomless eyes, he knew it. Nuit had arrived with an offer, of course. He brought the offer of a great new church where a preacher could *be* somebody, a church of power and respect, a church where the words of the preacher in his high pulpit would resound with power and certainty, resound with such thunderous clarity that people would *hear*, and after hearing, they would respect him.

He didn't remember saying yes to Nuit, but something in his heart must have given the man his answer. Nuit had left smiling, after twisting the words of Scripture around to bolster his arguments and validate his seduction. Not long after that visit came the day of the disappearances. Smith went to his small church, only to find it had burned to the ground. Witnesses said a heavyset white man wearing a linen suit had carried two gasoline cans into the church, soaked it and himself, and burned the whole thing down around him, laughing maniacally. A short time after that Smith had been chosen to head the New Christian Cathedral, his head filled with information about a new interpretation of Scripture, about a new prophet. He had lost everything in the disappearances, and then had been given all he had ever dreamed of, and stood upon that reaching pulpit drinking it all in like a rich and heady wine.

Someone dropped some silverware in the kitchen, and it startled him. He sipped the lukewarm coffee, rubbed his face with both hands, and went back to his dream. It had begun when he felt his Bible slip off his chest. He had reached for it, not been able to find it, and sat up in bed. He was assailed by a terrible stench, and it confused him. Then a familiar voice said quietly, "Hello, Henderson Smith. Are you enjoying your exalted and respected position here with your expanded flock?"

There was a large man standing beside the bed, and Smith rubbed his eyes as he tried to see who it was. "What? Who are you? Get out of my bedroom," he stammered. He thought he was going to vomit from the smell that filled his nostrils.

"But, Henderson," said the man, "it's me, your old pal Andrew Nuit rhymes with sweet. Surely you remember me?"

"But you . . . died!" Smith replied, staring up at the shadowy figure. "You died when you burned my church."

"But here I am," the man said. "Let me turn on the light so you can recognize me."

Smith knew it would be bad, and managed to say, "No." But in his dream the light filled the room in an instant, and there beside his bed stood Andrew Nuit. The porcine man still wore the linen suit, but it was blackened and welded to his immense, fleshy girth. The fingers of the man's hands had melted and become claws, and his shoes were like puddles of black tar. It was his face and head that gripped Smith, of course. It was a face made featureless by the flames' killing caress. It had dark holes where had been lips and a nose. It had no hair, and no ears, only two obsidian eyes, bulging black orbs that glistened like marbles. Such a face could not speak, but the condescending voice of Andrew Nuit came from it.

"Henderson," he said, "my boss is worried about you."

"I've . . . I've done what I said I'd do," answered Smith defensively. He didn't know why he felt the need to defend himself, and he knew having a discussion would prolong this macabre and odorous visit.

"And admirably, I agree," said Nuit. "And I said that very thing to my boss. But he thinks you could try harder."

"I . . . am doing what I said—"

"Here's the thing, Henderson," continued Nuit. "You seem to be waffling on us. In your heart, I mean. It's like you're having second thoughts, reading your Bible, mooning over your lot in life, wondering about your soul." At that moment, Nuit leaned closer to the bed, his foul stench wafting over Smith. There was a short flare-up of flame around his puddled shoes, and Nuit looked down, and said, "You know, that still hurts my feet." His black eyes locked on Smith's again, and he said, "Forget it, Henderson, okay? Forget the mooning, the wondering. You made a deal, and a deal is a deal. Don't begin to wimp out on us now, boy, and wobble back to your little book of Scripture."

In his dream, Smith was afraid to try to speak, afraid he would vomit. Nuit didn't care about a response anyway.

"One more thing, Henderson," the big burned figure asked, "what's all this about the number *seven*, do you know? It's like ringing in my ears, boy, and it's really beginning to bother me. Seven . . . seven . . . seven . . ."

The room went dark, and Smith knew he was awake, and alone. Even the smell was gone, thank goodness. He had left the lights out, and reached down to the floor and found his Bible. He had lifted it gently to his chest, hugged it, and spent the rest of the night in fitful attempts at sleep.

He had awakened with the sun, relieved the night was over. He was dispirited and concerned about the dream, but relieved it *was* a dream. Until he swung his feet out of bed and stood on the soft, pale carpet. There, a few inches from his left foot, were two blackened areas, burn marks that cut parallel curves in the pile, like six-inch quotation marks. He had even bent down and run the tips of his shaking fingers across them. They felt rough, and rigid, and when he brought his fingers to his face he was hit once again with the smell, and it rocked him.

The rest of the morning he had operated on automatic, grumpy, defensive, and scared.

He left the dining room and walked down a long hallway toward the church offices. He saw Ivy Sloan-Underwood approaching, and put a tentative smile on his face. "Good morning, Ivy," he said, "how are you?" He thought she looked a little more subdued than usual. She was a looker, no doubt, and most days she dressed and did her hair and makeup in a way that accentuated her natural gifts. She looked pretty today, but her look was less aggressive somehow.

"Oh, I'm doing okay, I guess, Reverend," Ivy answered. "You?"

"I'm okay, too."

She looked at him. He looked tired, and had a gray

pallor to his dark skin. His eyes had a bit of desperation in their focus, and he seemed to be licking his lips a lot. "You coming down with something, Reverend?"

"No, no," he answered irritably. "I'm okay. . . . I wish people would stop asking me if I'm okay. I'm *okay*."

She just looked at him.

"I'm sorry, Ivy," he said. He let out a breath, rubbed one hand across the top of his head, and loosened the crookedly knotted tie at his throat. "I had a bad night . . . couldn't get settled down, no real good sleep," he said. Then he straightened his crooked smile and added, "Bad dreams, and stuff."

Ivy smiled too, patted him on the arm, and said, "Well, you'd better get some rest. We need you around here."

He took her by the arm then, looked up and down the hallway, and pulled her toward a nearby door. She followed him, until they were standing outside on the walk that led to the dormitories and other outbuildings around the church. They both seemed to notice the odd cold wind that gusted around them, and Smith glanced up at the tumbling clouds overhead and said, "Must be a rapidly moving front or something. Well, the rain won't hurt us, but it might turn some of our flock away from worshiping today." Then he stared at her. "Ivy. Don't take this wrong, please. I've wanted to talk to you since you first arrived here. You spend a lot of time with Shannon, and we both know she has found Jesus and is living her life in commitment to Him."

"Yes?"

"But I know you are still struggling a bit, searching." He stopped, then took a chance and charged ahead. "I see something in your eyes, Ivy, something I think I recognize. Like we are kindred spirits, or have a shared experience or something."

She waited, not sure where this was going. Perhaps he was just being a man, she mused, and this was his clumsy way of coming on to her. What he said next ended that speculation.

"Is there anything special about the number seven to you, Ivy? Something that makes seven important to you, or in your life?"

She felt as if someone had punched her in the stomach, felt the air burst from her lungs, felt her legs and arms go rigid. Yes, she thought, someone recently asked me about that very number . . . Thad Night. And we *know* what Thad Night is all about, don't we?

He saw her reaction, how her face had paled, how her eyes had widened, and he knew.

"Yes, Reverend Smith," she managed to answer through lips cold and tight. "I mean, I have never considered seven a special number. It's supposedly a Biblical number and all, but it was not special to me at all, until recently."

"What happened, Ivy?"

"Oh," she answered, "a man asked me about the number seven, asked me if it meant anything to me."

"This man," asked Smith, his heart pounding, "did he come to you in a dream?"

"Once," she replied, frightened by this conversation,

but grateful for it at the same time. "I think I saw him in a dream. Then . . . then I met him for real." She hesitated, then added, "And then a couple of days ago, I saw him, here. That's when he asked me."

"A fat man, smelled really bad?"

She actually managed a small laugh, and said, "Hardly. This guy I'm talking about is a hunk, a hunk of burnin' love like he just stepped off one of those calendars." Her eyes went out of focus, then cleared again. "He's a good-looking man, but he's beyond poison."

They stood looking at each other, each one wondering, frightened.

"Maybe," tried Ivy. She chewed her lower lip before adding, "maybe there are seven of us who experienced something, well, somebody like Thad or like whoever it was in your dream. Maybe we are somehow *connected*, or there is some purpose for us, or . . ." She shrugged, her eyes searching his. She could see the pain there, the fear, and her heart went out to him. "Oh, Henderson I don't know."

At that moment Shannon Carpenter came out of the church offices, saw them, the way they stood, their expressions, and called out, "Hey, you guys. What's up?" She began to walk toward them, a concerned smile on her face.

Both of them were glad to see her, but before they could answer her they heard another shout, distant.

"Ivy! Ivy!"

They looked across a corner of the parking lot, toward the street that fronted the cathedral, and saw Ron

Underwood hurrying toward them, wearing a jacket that Ivy did not remember seeing on him before. Shannon stood beside Ivy and Henderson Smith as they watched Ron approach. There were a few people milling around the front of the cathedral, early for the next sermon, and they could hear voices behind them in the hallway. A white pickup truck with red trim came down the street and pulled slowly into the lot behind the figure of Ron.

"What's up with the weather?" asked Shannon as she seemed to notice the darkening sky for the first time.

+   +   +

John Jameson waited. One of Izbek Noir's staff officers saw him approach the command vehicle, asked him to state his business even though he recognized him as a squad leader with the security unit, and told him to stand by after he heard Jameson's explanation. It was late in the day, hot and gusty, with a sky rapidly changing above them. The front was temporarily quiet after both armies had attempted assaults on different positions. The Saudi resistance was stiffening, and Jameson, among others, guessed the Saudis were beginning to get help from other countries. Jameson felt coiled tight; he had gone through the day waiting for the summons, and had become more intense and focused with each passing minute. He recognized the pounding of his heart and distant roaring in his ears from other moments in his life when he had stood poised on the brink of a dangerous and deadly action. All of his senses were tuned to their highest frequency, his awareness heightened to a knife-edged state. It was time now, today, within a few moments . . . time for him to act. He felt a cold wind brush his right cheek, looked up at the low, roiling clouds, and thought, That is one angry sky. . . .

"Rommel," said General Izbek Noir. He stood a few feet away from Jameson, in full combat uniform, his eyes bright in the late-afternoon haze. He glanced up, and asked, "What do you make of that sky, soldier of Allah?"

"It would appear Allah is in an angry mood, sir," answered Jameson. "Or perhaps it's just a battlefield sky." He referred to the phenomenon caused by the concentration of explosive chemicals that often accumulate over an area of battle, like a miniature nuclear winter.

"So it will be death in the rain, then, yes?"

"Oh, most certainly, General Noir."

"Come, Rommel," said Noir. "Walk with me."

Jameson followed Noir away from the command vehicles, in the direction of the reserve units that lay huddled behind the front, which was less than a kilometer away. They walked side by side across the interior of the headquarters perimeter, and Jameson felt himself tightening even more. His plan was simple. He would hear what the general had to say, then bring up the stock of his assault weapon and smash it against Noir's head. As Noir fell, he would pull the pin on a hand grenade, drop it on his stunned target, then jump back and fire his AK-47 into him before the grenade cooked off. General Noir went through the motions of having elite security troops close around him, but he had the bad habit of never restricting anyone in his presence from being armed the whole time. A foolish and fatal flaw, as Jameson saw it.

"You do not enjoy executing the prisoners, isn't that right, Rommel?" stated Noir easily.

"I try not to think about it too much, sir, as a simple soldier of Allah," Jameson replied.

"But I was told you did in fact shoot the one I ordered you to kill yesterday," continued Noir. "And you will kill again, yes?"

"I serve Allah, General."

"It has been reported to me that you have a current Belgian passport, is that accurate?"

"Yes, sir."

"In what name, please?"

"Johann Rommel, sir."

Noir stepped back slightly and examined him. "You are not Arab. You are a faithful soldier of Allah, but you are a Westerner, and look non-Arabic."

"There are others in your vast army that—"

"No, Rommel," said Noir as he held up his hand, "I mean nothing negative by my observation. I'm simply stating fact, and your looks and your passport are an important part of my plan."

"How can I serve you, General?"

"Azul Dante is in the Netherlands, for a day or so, then he will return to Paris for more meetings. He will remain there for as long as a week."

Jameson did not doubt the accuracy of Noir's intelligence.

"I want you to travel toward Paris," said Noir as he kicked a few stones away from his left boot. They both felt the sand blown against their necks by the strangely cool gusty winds. "I will give you some contact names that will assist you. The front is fluid and confused, so you'll be able to slip through at some point. You can make your way to Jordan, Iraq, Afghanistan perhaps. . . . I have agents in any of these places. You will need to shed the combat gear along the way and take on the garb of a simple merchant, or a traveler attempting to locate members of his scattered family . . . something innocent and nonthreatening. A Belgian passport, your age, your Western features and languages, these will serve you well." He paused, cocked his head as if listening for the sound of distant thunder, and continued, "Make your way to Paris, have some champagne, look at the women, and somehow get in close to Azul Dante."

"Do you wish for me to make this journey so I can deliver a message for Azul Dante, General Noir?"

Noir took a couple of steps from Jameson, shook his head, laughed, and said, "No, soldier." He looked toward the front. They both heard the sudden increase in artillery and rocket fire. He turned back to face Jameson, and said, "No, Johann Rommel, I want you to get close to Azul Dante, and become an assassin for Allah. Find Azul Dante, soldier . . . and kill him."

He watched Jameson's face, then began to laugh. He

had his hands on his hips, his legs spread, and he put his head back as his laughter grew.

Jameson stepped closer to him and brought his slung assault rifle off his right shoulder. It was time.

At that moment their world was ripped apart by an incoming barrage of rocket and machine-gun fire. Punching bursts of shrapnel-filled explosions erupted like orange-and-black flowers carpeting the whole area. The screams of men warning others, and the screams of men torn apart by hot steel echoed throughout the perimeter, and the numbing roar of battle howled toward a crescendo as all manner of weapons began to return fire. It was an air assault by flocks of attack helicopters and tank-buster fixed-wing aircraft, terrain hugging under the low-hanging blanket of thunderclouds. It was devastating in its volume and accuracy. Many mujahideen soldiers died as they took their first steps toward their weapons or vehicles, and many tanks became places of writhing pain as they burst into flames. It was chaos, swift and deadly.

Jameson reacted instinctively, falling back toward a small ravine where he had seen a few foxholes dug in the loose sand and buttressed with sandbags. He gripped his AK tightly, his jaw clenched, and as he rolled he watched General Izbek Noir. The general stood amid the crashing and tearing fire, still laughing, firing a .45 automatic pistol at the sky and screaming obscenities through his evil laugh. His countenance seemed to be surrounded by a halo of fire, an almost blue flame that shone weirdly in the gloom. Several times as Jameson watched, incoming rockets exploded close enough to rock the general where he walked, hot pieces of shrapnel appeared to cut into his body, tearing at his limbs, his face, but still Noir remained.

Several times men and tanks a few yards from him were blown apart, but he stood whole. Jameson found himself filled with a cold resolve as he watched what could not be. The man cannot be killed, he told himself, but I *am* going to kill him. He jumped out of the foxhole, ducked and flinched as another explosion ripped the rocks a few feet away, and stumbled toward another shelter he had seen nearby. He wanted to get close, really close, to the general.

It was at that moment that the dark and angry skies finally let loose with a rain like none seen in the time of man.

+   +   +

A cold and hard wind hit the Reverend Henderson Smith as he stared at the man approaching him across the parking lot. He could see the man's mouth moving, but heard no words. From close beside him he heard Ivy Sloan-Underwood call out, "Ron? Ron! What . . ." The man had one arm outstretched, one finger pointed at him. The man's other hand was jammed down into the old fatigue jacket he wore. The figure of the man approached before a far backdrop of conflicting masses of silver, black, and gray thunderclouds, impossibly rolling, twisting, and boiling in various directions, tree branches, leaves, and dust blown first this way, then that by the confused gusts. More people filled the background too . . . pointing at the sky, or huddled together looking toward Smith. He heard shouts of alarm, and a woman screamed briefly, very near.

Then the man seemed very close, only a few feet away. Smith realized it must be Ron Underwood, the odd character with the fifties-style black-rimmed glasses, disheveled clothes, and sneering manner Ivy had told him about, her husband, who had recently arrived at the cathedral, upsetting her somewhat. He tried to understand what the man was saying. The angry sky was twice reflected in the man's eyeglass lenses, and behind them his eyes were angry too, wide and staring, crazed. Smith saw that the man had begun to pull the hand out of the jacket pocket. The hand held something black and sinister. Behind him, small eruptions of mist or dust began to speckle the parking lot.

Shannon Carpenter watched the sky, and thought the clouds heralded more than a violent rainstorm. She felt a chill trip down her spine, and for a tilting moment felt fear in her soul. Then, as quickly as the fear washed against her, it was washed away as she told herself she had Jesus Christ in her heart, and He held her in his hands. She reminded herself right there and then that she had given herself over to Him. She found herself instantly cloaked in peace—calm, watchful, unafraid, but aware of everything taking place around her. A change in the tone of Ivy's voice close by made her turn.

There came a spattering of heavy moisture, fat drops, in arrhythmic sequence.

Ivy was frozen by the expression on Ron's face, the hard focus of his eyes. She heard him yelling at Reverend Smith, watched as he leaned forward, saw his hand come out of the jacket holding a gun. "Ron!" she yelled at him as she took a step in his direction. "Ron . . . *no*!" Ron does not have a gun, she thought, he can't have a gun so that can't be a gun but it is a gun. Oh, Ron, oh, Ron . . . no. She was aware of the storm that surrounded them, aware of Shannon beside her, of Reverend Smith shouting something. Her eyes saw the people in the lot behind Ron, and among them, smiling, was Thad Night. He seemed riveted to the pavement, his hands loose by his sides, his obsidian eyes gleaming like lasers in the cold and windy gloom.

It began to rain.

Henderson Smith understood in his heart and immediately that his entire life was now distilled down to this micromoment in time. He saw with certainty that Ron's hand held a revolver in its tight white-knuckled grasp, that his lips were pulled back from his stretched mouth in a screaming grimace, that his nostrils were flared, his eyes twisting into the flat eyes of an animal, cold, unmerciful. He felt his legs turn to lead, his bowels loosen, his mouth go bone dry and slack as his eyes ballooned so quickly he thought they would burst, leaving him blind and rooted to the mocking grounds of the cathedral that had never been his. His eyes were not shown the mercy of darkness, however, but saw all too clearly as death approached, hungry grin widening in anticipation. He watched, spellbound, as the evil black revolver came up in an inexorable, perfect arc, passing his groin, his stomach, his sternum, stopping with unwavering accuracy at the point of his Adam's apple.

It began to rain, a hard rain, cold.

Ron Underwood felt the warm weight of the revolver in his fist, caressed the smooth wooden grips in his palm like a lover, and felt complete. He felt so calm inside, so sure, so good about what he was about to do. He tightened his grip, tightened his finger on the trigger, and began to pull back. The steel tension teased him momentarily, but he squeezed in response, and the trigger gave slightly to his knowing touch. His eyes followed the barrel of the gun as it tracked up the reverend's body, and he noted how perfectly motionless his target was, captured and held spellbound by his, Ron Underwood's, power. He saw the man's face, saw it become a convulsed mask of immobilizing panic and dread, and this pleased him.

He stopped the barrel of the gun as it pointed into Henderson Smith's throat, then wavered, momentarily undecided. Should he send his perfect bullet crashing into the reverend's throat, or face? Perhaps into his heart would be best. He became aware that he did not want the moment to end. It was his defining moment, this moment when he stood in front of God, God's people, and Ivy, his wife and the mother of their child and had the selfless guts to blow this charlatan liar into his grave.

The rain swept across them in waves, a hard rain, heavy and sulfurous.

It was the foul, black, obscene hole at the end of the

barrel that Henderson Smith became fixated on. It stared back, expressionless and unblinking, sure purveyor of truth, absolute ruler over the *now*. His eyes became riveted, transfixed, and his mind saw the hole grow and widen enough to suck his soul into its unending and forever downward spiral, leaving his body a rubbery empty bag of guilt, shame, and unfulfilled promise. He realized at that fixed and precise moment in the time of man and God that he was going to die, there, today . . . now, and he felt a howling fear come welling up from behind his soul, from within the sobbing walls of his heart. The fear geysered up through the marrow of his bones, a shrieking and wailing ghoul-witch of fear with long twisted tresses of lost dreams and innocent lies, cackling at his helpless impotence.

A passage from Scripture came to him then, echoing in his resisting mind, whispering to him, "For he is the minister of God to thee for good. But if thou do that which is evil, be afraid; for he beareth not the sword in vain: for he is the minister of God, a revenger to execute wrath upon him that doeth evil."

Oh, Lord, he heard his own voice cry from a far chamber of remorse, I need help I need help I don't want to die, I can't die like this I can't die like this. His eyes darted out in wild search for a savior, for a reaching hand, for something, or someone, to cling to. His eyes found Andrew Nuit, standing charred and repulsive in the parking lot, pelted by a hard rain that seemed to turn to blood as it burned into Nuit's already burned flesh.

Without wonder or question Henderson Smith saw

that Nuit stood beside a tall, dark, cruelly handsome younger man dressed in a fine suit, his full thick hair brushed back, his sensual lips parted in pleasure. Without wonder or question he knew this was Ivy's Thad Night, come to witness his befouling. He didn't care. *Andrew,* his soul called out, *Andrew help me as you have done before.* But Nuit ignored his plea, more concerned with the bloodred drops of hard rain that pelted him with enough force to make him flinch. *"Jesus!"* cried Henderson Smith then. "Jesus don't forsake me now! I don't want to die, I don't want to!" *I am a Christian man,* his terrified mind shrieked, *a Christian man and therefore aware of but* unafraid *of Satan or his minions, God, give me the strength of a real Christian.* He felt his knees hit the pavement, and saw his hands in front of him, palms flattened, fingers laced together in a childlike posture of prayer. "Oh, Jesus God," he heard his own lost and hollow voice implore, "I don't want to die like this. . . ."

His voice was answered with the roar of the weapon as Ron Underwood pulled the trigger, which sent the hammer into its rotation until it slammed its rigid firing pin into the shell casing. The powder in the shell exploded, and forced the lead bullet through the barrel, into the tumult of air surrounding them all for an instant, then on a ripping line toward Henderson Smith's heart. Like all of its uncountable brothers, the bullet had no conscience, no prejudices, and no second thoughts, only an insatiable and unstoppable hunger.

Ivy Sloan-Underwood saw the death of Henderson Smith as it unfolded in front of her, and acted. She was

aware of the hot and hard rain, saw the bloody runoff as
it pounded all around, but ignored it as she shouted at
Ron, then lunged forward toward him and the Reverend
Smith. She did not know whether to try to knock the
gun away, tackle Ron and push him over, or slam into
Smith to shove him out of the line of fire.

She managed to do none of these things, but the
force of her lunge threw her into the unwavering path
of the bullet. In total and instant comprehension she realized exactly that, and was pleased. Her body was between that of her husband, Ron, and Henderson Smith,
between the wicked barrel of the gun and Smith's
pounding heart. She heard him calling out, but did not
know to whom and did not care. She felt Shannon Carpenter's hand on her arm, trying to pull her back, but it
was too late.

She was punched back and down as the hot slug
slammed through the skin and muscle of her chest like a
powerful fist. Yes, oh God let it be, she thought as she
collapsed against Smith. Yes . . . now it will finally happen, the choice will be made. Now in this moment of
God's time I will be Thad Night's willing lover or I will
walk beside the loving and graceful light of my Lord
Jesus Christ, keeper of my soul and keeper of my only
child. She found herself lying against Henderson
Smith's legs, on her side, her left cheek flattened to the
concrete sidewalk.

Her chest felt loose and splintered, it became hard to
breathe, and warm liquid seemed to be flooding her
lungs. She coughed, and her spit was crimson. Her ears

were filled with a sweet roar that began to block out all other sounds, but her eyes remained open for a few seconds. They struggled to comprehend the raindrops falling all around her and the others, spattering her, stinging her face. It wasn't rain, really, but *hail . . . burning hail that fell bloodred, hot and wet.* It couldn't be, and she knew she was dying. It all faded to gauze, then gray, then black, and her last thought came, *Oh, God . . . let it be Jesus that comes for me.*

+   +   +

In that moment of time, all of the world's skies were as one sky, angry black, silver, and gray, and they unleashed a torrent of hail upon the fields around the globe. The crops longed for rain, of course, as drought had ravaged much of the earth's crust for too long. Not this rain, though. It came as hailstones, millions of tiny frozen fists raining down, blown as gusty scattershot by impossibly hot winds, remaining as ice as they hit field, pavement, brick, glass, or flesh. But the hail fell as burning ice, blue-red, scorching all that it hit, bouncing and ricocheting across the land like a great handful of burning, irregular marbles. Where they hit they left a lick of flame, and a smear of blood.

Whether the farmer is in the fields of Japan, Indonesia, Australia, France, South Africa, Venezuela, Mexico, Canada, or the United States, he stands with his feet in the soil, and his eyes cast to the skies above. He puts his weight between the furrowed rows, bringing up the rich earth so the seeds of plenty might be sown, and then he prays for enough nurturing sun, enough sweet rain. Too much of either, he does not want, but trusts in the season, the goodness and the benevolence of God above to cast down the perfect mixture required to bring his sustaining crops to fruition. He labors with his hands, his back, his experience, and does all that man can do. Then he stands back, head bowed in hopeful supplication, and prays.

Now came this frozen, burning, forged and tempered rain of fire, ice, and blood. It swept across the fields that embraced the shivering crust of the earth, and in a moment parched and ruined fully a third of all that might grow, down to soft expanses of green grass that gave not to the belly, but only to the comfort of man's bare feet. Where it fell, the farmer fell also, fell to his knees in despair, fear, and wonder. It mattered not whether he scratched at the soil in Russia, England, India, Germany, Barbados, Cuba, the Dominican Republic, or South Dakota, his helplessness and frustration were the same. He flinched as the stinging hail left burn marks on his flesh, but he knelt there in the rows, and dug his fingers into the hot soil already weeping blood and charred stalks of soot and salt.

In the many varied languages of man, the noble farmers of the world cried out as one, beseeching the heavens for respite, begging for the terrible scourge of impossible rain to stop. Many died as they tried to keep inviolate their soil and crops with the perfectly inadequate protection of their own bodies, which they laid down upon the rows as cover. Fully a third were consumed, and left rusted and bloodied, barren, wasted, dead. Fully a third of the earth's crops and grasses, gone.

+   +   +

Thomas Church stared out through the windshield of his truck and thought, This isn't right, this can't be right. This is burning hail. He was on the outskirts of a place called Crowheart, Wyoming, headed west on I-20 toward Idaho. When the rain first began he hit his windshield wipers and kept driving. Then the moisture on the glass turned to syrupy mud, pushed back and forth by the wipers, making it hard to see. Then the rain turned brittle-hard, pinging and ringing off the hood of the Bronco, reaching a metallic crescendo within moments. Church stared in wonder at the small waves of blue flame that coursed over the hood in front of him, and managed to pull over under a highway overpass. It was hail, he could see it, hail as frozen rain, but it burned, it burned blood-red and wet, and left fingers of fire as it scratched at all it pummeled. He grabbed his Bible and thumbed through it wildly, finally settling down and going to Revelation, the scariest and most difficult section of Scripture for him to comprehend. Yeah, he thought, Here it is, Revelation 8:6, The Trumpets . . . hail and fire mixed with blood, one-third of the crops . . . okay, okay. He stared out the wind-shield, saw the ripples of icy fire ripping across the highway median, and said out loud to take some comfort in the sound of his own voice, "This must be what it's talk-ing about, the burning hail. But it's not time, is it? It's out of sequence, right? What about the Seals, the hundred and forty-four thousand?" There was no answer. He felt a moment's confusion and panic, then steadied himself. All things will be revealed, all things explained. He took a deep breath. He thought of Sissy and Mitch, and he thought of Tommy. He had no doubt they were seeing the same thing he was, and said a silent prayer for their safety. He thought of his wife, Iris, out there in Idaho someplace. She would be looking into those angry skies now too, thinking . . . what? He was impatient to find her, impatient to share with her what had happened in his heart. He watched the hail fall, and said softly, "The Lord is my shepherd, I shall lack nothing. . . ."

+   +   +

Cat Early huddled with a terrified old woman in the ruins of a brick house a few miles from Medina, on the west coast of Saudi Arabia, north of Mecca. She and several others had hastily abandoned the open jeep they rode in when the burning hail began to fall, and she had become separated from them. It was impossible, what she was witnessing, and she knew it. But there it was. It came with a strange hissing sound, this burning ice that pelted the earth, hungry for what little vegetation there was in that region. Many of the fields were irrigated, and where there was green, came fire, where there were any crops, came ice . . . and blood.

She saw more than one person running wildly through the narrow streets in blind panic, their robes aflame, their skin searing even as they tried to escape what could not be, but was. She did not know Thomas

Church, but shared the same initial thoughts: Wait. This is in Revelation, yes, but is it supposed to happen now?

That it was Biblical she had no doubt, and as she huddled with the old woman, who wept uncontrollably, her eyes cast to the broken rafters above, she pulled her sister's well-thumbed Bible from her backpack. She heard the old woman mumble "Allah" several times, rocking back and forth, her thumbs between her teeth. But there came no comfort for the woman, and Cat felt her tremble in her arms. She managed to open the Bible on her lap, flinched as a monstrous clap of thunder reverberated across the land. She thought of Slim, hoped he was safe, and resolved at that moment to find him again, and somehow get him away from Izbek Noir and the mujahideen. She wanted to be with him. She watched the skies, listened to the fury of the storm, and began to read in a soothing voice, ". . . He makes me lie down in green pastures, he leads me beside quiet waters, he restores my soul . . ."

+　　+　　+

"I believe this is what the man meant when he sang, 'It's a hard, hard, hard . . . a hard rain is gonna fall,'" shouted Slim as he crouched next to John Jameson in a foxhole reinforced with sandbags and covered with a sheet of corrugated iron. The noise levels surrounding them made a normal volume of speech impossible, but Slim saw Jameson nod in agreement. Outside of their refuge was a world gone wild. The storm's fury overrode the roar of the attack on the mujahideen's positions, scattering soldiers with impunity, ripping aircraft from the sky and adding their burning steel skeletons to the hailstorm of fire and ice. Men died from rocket fire, and men died as they ran from the burning cold hornets that pelted them from the heavens. Tanks crashed into trucks, friend fired on friend, and destruction and chaos were everywhere.

Mujahideen soldiers, draped in ammunition, flares, and hand grenades, became pyrotechnic punctuation as the burning hail ignited them throughout the front lines. Many soldiers who witnessed these horrible deaths tried to strip away their gear as they ran here and there seeking shelter, climbing on tanks and pounding on turrets, chasing trucks that would not stop. They burned too, maddened by the stinging impact of the millions of tiny laser missiles, succumbing as they writhed and screamed for mercy that did not come.

Jameson pointed at something and yelled to Slim, "Look at that!" It was the lone figure of Izbek Noir, strolling through the destruction like a man enjoying the sudden onslaught of nothing more than a cool spring shower. Clearly, as evidenced by the rapt expression on his face and the glowing of his eyes, he appreciated and reveled in the horrors occurring around him, the screams of pain-maddened, dying men, the roar of exploding ammunition, the scorching flash of ragged lightning and timpani of bone-rattling thunder. They could not hear him, but he seemed to be laughing, his head thrown back, his arms outstretched as if welcoming the on-slaught. He turned and surveyed the scene with a de-monic intensity, his grin one of sensual evil, his eyes delirious with greedy pleasure. Slim shivered, and said to himself, "What a freak of nature that animal is."

John Jameson tightened his grip on his assault rifle, and contemplated emptying a full magazine at Noir as the man moved past their position. He held back, how-ever, because he wanted to be *sure*. What was happening around them held his attention anyway, and he observed with awe what he knew to be the work of God as prophe-sied and promised. He did not worry about sequence. It was in Scripture, he had read it, and he understood that all he had to do was recognize it, accept it, and be a lov-ing, obedient, and respectful witness to the work of the Father. It was in Scripture, he had read it, and he be-lieved it. He closed his eyes for a moment, sought a deep inner calm, and said in his heart, Thy will be done, Lord. Then he reached out, took Slim's right hand in his left, and said, ". . . He guides me in paths of righteousness for his name's sake. . . ."

Slim looked at his hand in Jameson's, and left it there. He wondered about Cat, listened to Jameson's words, and prayed for her safety. Jameson looked out at the howling fire falling from the skies, and said, ". . . Even though I walk through the valley of the shadow of death, I will fear no evil, for you are with me; your rod and your staff, they comfort me. . . ."

+   +   +

Azul Dante stood looking out through the tall glass window in an office in The Hague. Sophia Ghent stood behind him. They both stared out at the burning hailstorm sweeping the city, the buildings, the parks, the people. Sophia felt a questioning terror in the bosom of her soul, and bit her lip to stop herself from crying out. She could not stop the tears from forming in her eyes, and they fell heavy and wet, salt and water.

Azul Dante looked through the thin membrane of glass with a small smile on his face. His cold heart told him what he witnessed, and he was filled with a twisted and adversarial admiration for the *comprehensiveness* of the act. He watched the fire and ice, saw the fury in the skies, heard his own heart beating in his chest, and said softly, "I'll be damned."

+   +   +

Against the backdrop of the storm, the New Christian Cathedral seemed to glow with a weird, bright light. The Reverend Henderson Smith, stung and harassed by the hail, morally eviscerated by the vision of his own death, frightened to the point of insanity, saw the almost liquid smoke coming from the black hole that was the barrel of the gun pointed at him by Ron Underwood. He realized the weapon had been fired. He remembered the roar, remembered the shouting, the tingle of his skin as his body waited for the intrusion of the hot lead slug that would surely rip him from this life, from this world. But . . . but, no. There came no piercing pain, no ripped or burst heart. There was the blast, the smoke, the falling backward, but no wound. I am not shot, exalted his mind, I am not killed, I am not slaughtered on the street like some worthless cowardly dog.

He saw the form of Ivy Sloan-Underwood draped across his legs, saw her pale face in repose on the concrete, saw the blood. Then he looked up, and saw Ron Underwood standing over them both, the gun still clenched in his fist, his eyes terrible in the black light of lightning flashes. The gun, that evil, black, unforgiving engine of death still pointed toward him. It still owned his soul. He knew he had to get away, away from the storm, from the hail, from Ron Underwood and the gun, away from the blood washing over Ivy Sloan-Underwood away from the sweet hands of Shannon Carpenter, away from the calls of sorrow and fear of the people milling around the cathedral. Most of all, though, he had to get away from the laughing personage of Andrew Nuit, obscene seducer, soul stealer, monster. Death and humiliation surrounded him, and he knew what he must do. Get away.

He pulled his legs free of Ivy's weight, pushed himself back from her body, and stood shakily. He knew Shannon was speaking to him, but he heard no words.

His wild eyes looked beyond the gun, and saw Andrew Nuit, who had his face and arms raised to the clouds, letting the burning hail wash over him. With that image seared into his heart, he turned and ran. He slammed through the double doors leading to the hallway, across the carpeted expanse, and into the cathedral itself. He ran up the carpeted steps leading to the main stage of the church, and scattered a pile of hymnals as he skidded across the parquet floor that bordered the choir loft. He reached the pulpit, grabbed the rail, and hurled himself upward into it. His Bible rested on the top rail, and he pulled it down to him as he fell against the inner curve. There on the floor, he curled into the fetal position, hugged his Bible to him, and wept uncontrollably as he shivered in a terror that took from him all control. "Jesus, oh my sweet Lord Jesus, oh, God . . . help me. Help me, Jesus, I swear I'm just a man whose soul is worthless, a coward of a man who loves you in spite of himself. Oh, Jesus . . . help this poor sinner. Oh, God . . . I don't want to die. . . ."

Ron Underwood watched the preacher run off, but his eyes were drawn to Ivy. His wife, the mother of his son, Ronnie . . . his Ivy. He had seen her out of the corner of his eye even as his finger pulled the trigger on the gun. His senses were rebelling even as the shot rang out, sending the bullet toward Smith, and at that moment he knew it would not reach its target. Ivy's leaning and lunging upper body filled his vision then, and he watched helpless and horrified as the bullet burned its path right into her chest. He saw how her head snapped back, how her shoulders and arms jerked forward spasmodically, how she collapsed to the ground even as the gush of blood mushroomed from her blouse, soaked her chest, and bubbled from her lips.

It was too much. Her body was crumpled at his feet; her eyes searched his, then went to the woman who crouched beside her and pulled her onto her own legs as she sat on the ground. The pelting fire stung him, cold, but it was the image of Ivy on the lap of Shannon that held him captivated. Shannon's expression of sadness, love, and acceptance cast down on the unresisting body of Ivy was the embodiment of all that had come to pass.

He could hear the Carpenter woman saying something to Ivy softly, but Ivy's eyes were closed, and she made no response. *I've killed her,* he screamed at himself, *I've killed her with my rage, my anger, my foolish act of madness. I've killed Ivy . . . and so, myself.* He took several steps backward, stumbled, turned, and ran, unable to bear what he had done. As he fled from the two women he passed several people running and ducking as they tried to escape the hailstones. Two figures stood still, watching him. One was heavyset, horribly burned. The other was handsome and well dressed. They stood with an otherworldly calm, and it infuriated him. "Be gone!" he shouted at them, and in an instant, they were.

Tommy Church had parked his truck, jumped out, and looked up at the crazy skies as the first burning hail began to fall. He wished his dad were with him, then knew immediately that wherever his dad was, he too was witnessing the event. Oh yeah, he thought, *this* is Biblical. Then he heard the shot. He looked across the parking lot, saw four people, recognized the black preacher and the two women immediately, and began to head toward them. Then he saw the gun in the man's hand, the man with the glasses and fatigue jacket, and Tommy paused. When he saw one of the women fall, saw the stain of crimson on her chest, the armed man turn toward him and begin running in his direction, he acted.

His cowboy hat rattled as it was struck with hailstones, and he felt several burning stings on his hands and arms, but remained focused on the man with the gun, who shouted something and waved his arms as he ran. Tommy timed it, then hurled himself at Ron Underwood, tackling him with enough force to send them both tumbling to the hard pavement. The force of the fall ripped the gun from Underwood's hand, but he leaned to reach for it even as Tommy came to his feet above him. Tommy saw the gun, saw the man reach for it, and kicked it hard with his boot. He watched it skid under a nearby car as the man on the ground yelled, "No! I *need* that!" Underwood rolled and began to struggle to his feet, but Tommy had seen enough. As Underwood straightened, Tommy punched him, hard, against the side of his head. Underwood staggered, his knees buckled, and Tommy punched him again. Underwood collapsed in a heap in the fiery rain, out cold. Tommy quickly grabbed him by his shoulders and pulled him a few yards to a low overhang that covered the entranceway to the dormitory. There were others huddled beneath it, sheltering from the hard rain. A couple of the men had seen the shooting also, and Tommy's action with Underwood. "My wife has already called the police from inside," said one older man, his eyes wide, "and an ambulance. We'll take care of this guy until the cops get here." He pointed down at the unconscious Ron Under-wood. "Why don't you go try to help those ladies?" Tommy took off across the lot at a dead run, flinching from the rain.

Ted Glenn, who had been on a stepladder outside behind the main building of the cathedral repairing a spot-light fixture, heard what sounded like a shot. He couldn't be sure in the noise of the building storm, and hurried to finish before the storm broke. Then he felt the burning rain, dropped his tools, jumped down from the ladder, and ran to find Shannon. He rounded a corner a short distance from the parking lot, and saw the young cowboy he had met once running toward a small huddle on the ground. His heart stopped when he saw Shannon, and the blood. "Shannon," he managed, "are you okay?" He only realized it was Ivy's blood when he knelt next to them.

"Ivy's been shot," cried Shannon softly. "Oh, Ted . . . stay with us, with me . . ."

He brushed the fingers of one hand against her cheek, and said, "I'm not going anywhere without you."

Ted saw the look in Shannon's eyes as she looked up at him, and despaired. He hugged them both, and used his shoulder to move them the few feet needed to get them under the cover of the outside walkway. He fell to his knees beside them, heard the faint call of sirens beneath the fury of the storm, and said, "Hold on, don't let go . . . hold on. . . ."

Shannon Carpenter held on. She hugged Ivy Sloan-Underwood tight to her, watched the rain fall, felt the warmth and strength of Ted Glenn beside her, and said softly into Ivy's ear, ". . . You prepare a table before me in the presence of my enemies. You anoint my head with oil; my cup overflows. Surely goodness and love will follow me all the days of my life, and I will dwell in the house of the Lord forever."

ABOUT THE AUTHORS

Ken Abraham is the author of the #1 *New York Times* bestselling *Let's Roll!* with Lisa Beamer, as well as the author of *Payne Stewart* with Tracey Stewart.

Daniel Hart had a distinguished career in the U.S. Army and as a law enforcement officer. He now writes full time and lives with his wife and children in Florida.

ALSO AVAILABLE
BOOK 1

FOR SOME, THE END TIMES ARE JUST THE BEGINNING...

THE PRODIGAL PROJECT

BOOK 1

GENESIS

A NOVEL BY

KEN ABRAHAM
& DANIEL HART

AVAILABLE WHEREVER PAPERBACKS ARE SOLD

www.prodigalproject.net

Plume
A member of Penguin Group (USA) Inc.

www.penguin.com

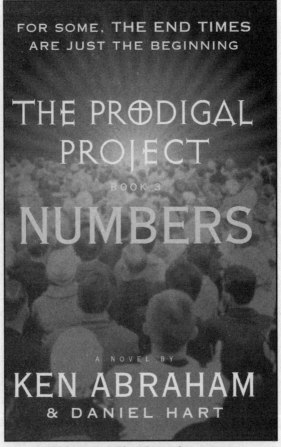
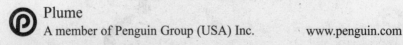